SWING

ADRIANA LOCKE

LANDRY FAMILY SERIES, #2

Cover Art:
Kari March, Kari March Designs

Cover Photos:
Adobe Stock

Editing:
Lisa Christman, Adept Edits

BOOKS BY ADRIANA LOCKE

The Exception Series

The Exception

The Connection

The Perception

The Landry Family Series

Sway

Swing

Switch

Swear

Swink

Sweet—coming soon

The Gibson Boys Series

Crank

Craft

Cross

Crave

Crazy

Dogwood Lane Series

Tumble

Tangle

Trouble

Restraint- Coming Soon

Standalone Novels

Sacrifice

Wherever It Leads

Written in the Scars

Lucky Number Eleven

Battle of Sexes

For an email every time Adriana has a new release, sign up for an alert here: http://bit.ly/AmazonAlertAddy or text the word adriana to 21000

For everyone that loves someone that's not always easy to love.

And for Danielle Monroe. You never cease to amaze me with your kindness... and love for baseball. This one is for you!

SWING

ONE

LINCOLN

"I'M AWARE THIS ISN'T WHAT you wanted to hear."

Pulling my cap down a little farther over my forehead, I try to squeeze the voice of the Arrows' team doctor out of my mind. He can't help what the test results say. Hell, his life would be easier if he could've slapped some salve on my shoulder and called it a day. Unfortunately for both of us, no such luck.

The elevator dings as the doors extend and I step inside. Hitting the button for the therapy floor, I smile, tossing the blonde chick leaning against the back wall a bone. Not my bone, of course. I can't think about that right now. It doesn't mean I don't enjoy how her tongue darts to her bottom lip and drags slowly across.

"Where're you headed?" she asks in her best Marilyn Monroe impersonation.

"Therapy," I say.

"Really? So am I."

Following her gaze as it dips from my face, across my sternum, down my abs, and hovers over my bulge, I grin. For her amusement, and maybe for mine, I grab my junk and give it a little shake. She whimpers.

Every. Time.

We stop our ascent just as Blondie starts to find her voice, the doors swinging open to what is, by all accounts, complete and utter chaos.

Kids, probably fifteen of them and all under the age of ten, are clamoring for one person's attention.

I find the button to close the doors when I see *her*: shiny, raven hair pulled away from a round face accentuated with full, pink lips. Her body is the shape of an hourglass, apparent even under the pale pink dress that just skims her voluptuous curves.

"Fuck me," I mutter as my hand lurches forward to stop the doors from shutting.

"Excuse me?" Blondie chirps. "If that's an offer, I'm willing."

I ignore her. My eyes are trained on the woman crouching in front of me so she's eye level with a little red-haired boy. I find myself taking a step off the elevator.

"Hey! This isn't the therapy floor!" Blondie yelps.

"I know." *But it might be the best kind of therapy if things go right.* The bell chimes behind me as the elevator whisks her away.

The little boy joins the others in a makeshift line before they exit the room. She stands, grabbing a cup of coffee off of a ledge next to her before turning and catching me watching her. "Oh!" she says, startled, wobbling slightly on her heels. Heels that make her legs look lean and toned with a high probability of looking fantastic around my neck.

"I didn't mean to scare you," I smile.

"I, um." She clears her throat like she's trying to compose herself. "I'm sorry. Can I help you?"

Oh, I'm sure you can.

My smirk betrays the neutrality I'm attempting to convey. As her hand reaches for the small, golden charm at the hollow of her throat, all I can do is imagine pressing my lips against it. Touching her skin. Smelling her, what I'm sure is a sweet, sexy aphrodisiac. Skimming my hands down those curves, committing them to memory.

Slipping my hand into the pocket of my sweatpants, I adjust myself. If she notices, she pretends not to.

Classy too? Fuck me. Literally. Please.

"I was looking for Therapy," I tell her, hoping to spur some conversation I can work into something more. Of course I know damn good and well where I'm headed. It's become my new home away from home.

"You need to go up three levels," she replies. "This is Child Life. There's no therapy happening here, although you might need some if you stay too long."

Her words are punctuated with a hint of sarcasm in the prettiest way. No malice. No attitude. Just a dose of playfulness that makes me want to keep her talking. Even as she turns down a hallway, effectively ending the start of a conversation, I effectively restart it by following her.

Does she think she can just walk away from me? If so, she underestimates the power of her ass.

Her dress dips at the small of her back, just above the arch of her behind. I ram both of my hands into my pockets to remind myself not to touch. I'm not that kind of guy, but it's *that* perfect. Just as I wonder whether it jiggles as she's getting slammed from behind and what noises would escape her little mouth, she glances at me over her shoulder.

"Three floors up," she reiterates. "What?"

A giggle floats through the air, my abs clenching at the thought of hearing that same sound charged with my name. While I'm inside her. Or her lips are coating my cock. Or—

"Are you listening to me?" she laughs.

Her voice pulls me from my daydream. We're standing at a doorway. She's flipping on the lights to a little office and stepping inside. I follow her, like a puppy looking for someone to play with. At least I'm not drooling . . . I don't think . . . but I probably am panting. I need to be played with. What can I say?

The room is painted an off-white color with dozens of finger paintings and macaroni art like we used to make in elementary school tacked to the walls. Glancing around, I wonder if she's some sort of art teacher.

I search for something with her name on it, a photograph to give me a clue as to who she is and what she does. Nothing. Just construction paper chains hanging off of a fake tree in the corner.

The notepad in her hand hits her desk with a smack. Fighting a smile, she gives me a quick once-over. "Do you need an escort?"

"Thanks, but escorts aren't my thing," I grin.

She leans on her desk, her cleavage just peeking out of the top of the fucking dress I want to rip off her body. She's doing this on purpose, the little minx.

She drags her gaze down my body, letting it linger on my lower half, but returns her baby blues to my eyes, smirking. "So you just prefer to wander around and see what turns . . . *up*?"

My head angles to the side as I watch her assess my reaction to her innuendo. Before I can respond, the phone on her desks comes to life. She places a hand on the receiver. "I need to get this," she says. "Three floors."

"Up," I wink. "Got it. What's your name?" "Danielle Ashley, director of Child Services." "I'm Lincoln Landry."

"I know."

She seems to think she has an upper hand because she knows who I am. Truth is, she obviously doesn't really know who she's up against because I always stay ahead of the count.

"See you later, Dani." I'm out the door, leaving her standing there with her jaw open.

"It's Danielle!" she shouts behind me, but I don't look back.

TWO

DANIELLE

"HELLO?" MY GAZE FALLS ON the spot he just occupied on the other side of my desk.

He's so tall, so wide, so broad, so . . . big. My cheeks burn, a grin splitting my cheeks as I remember the definite outline of just how big he probably is. If the old wives' tales are true and penis size and shoe size are related, he must wear at least a thirteen.

"G'day," Macie responds through the line. "G'day? Are you Australian now?"

She laughs. "I have a patient that's Australian. I'm in love with the accent. Will says he's going to kill me if I don't bloody stop."

"I can see why," I joke. "What's happening in Boston?"

"On lunch break. Called to see what my best friend is doing."

Falling into my chair and squeezing my thighs together to try to quell the ache throbbing between my legs, I look once again at the doorway. His cologne, a musky, rich fragrance, still permeates the air. It's like he's still taunting me without having to even be here. So unfair. "Thank God you called," I mutter. "I'd probably be on my back on my desk right now if you hadn't." "What?"

"I mean, I can't help it. I'm just a woman. A badass one with the restraint of a saint, if the last ten minutes prove anything, but I was cracking. I'm only human."

"Slow down there, Saint Danielle. What are you talking about?" she laughs.

"You'll never guess who was just in my office."

"Probably not. So tell me."

"Lincoln Landry." The line goes quiet. After a few long seconds, I realize she has no idea who I'm talking about. "Star centerfielder for the Tennessee Arrows?" I offer.

"Ohhhh . . ."

"Yeah, ohhhh."

"Sorry. If it's not a fighter or a player for Boston, I don't know them. I'm fairly certain Will would break up with me if he suspected I liked anyone other than his Red Sox."

"Google Lincoln. It's worth the possible break up," I say, fanning my still-red cheeks. "He's literally the best looking guy I've ever seen, Macie."

"That's saying a lot coming from you, Miss Hottie Magnet."

My mind goes through the photo album of men I've met or known in my life. It's a pretty spectacular list, thanks to being the child of Bryan and Tracey Ashley Kipling. Athletes, movie stars, models? I've seen them all. And none of them hold a candle to Lincoln Landry in person.

The confidence he carries is such a turn on. Borderline cocky. Halfway arrogant, yet he pulls it off because he has every right to be those things. He's delicious. Hot. Talented. Wealthy. From what the media says, he's also funny and kind and sweet.

Screw him and his perfect resume. And flawless face.

And delicious body.

And probably game winning stamina. I'm going to be a mess today just thinking about it.

"Why was he in your office?" Macie asks, right as I was ready to mentally remove his clothes. "*Oh my God*, Danielle! I just pulled him up. Why can't I be you? Just for a day?"

"I'm quite happy I'm me today," I laugh. "He just walked off the elevator on the wrong floor and followed me to my office."

"Why?"

"Does it matter? Now I'm sitting here with wet panties, his 'Fuck me' cologne filling my office, and all sorts of ideas as to what his body looks like under those sweatpants and t-shirt."

"He wore sweatpants?" she gulps.

"Yup."

"Shit," she breathes, a squeak in her voice. "Those are the sexiest things *ever*. Shouldn't be, but they are. Don't even tell me they sat low on his hips."

"I won't," I sigh dreamily. My eyes flutter closed as the broadness of his shoulders fill my memory, the way his chest tapered down on the sides to one trim, hard waist. My fingers sing as I imagine running my hands down what I'm sure is an etched V. "He swaggered in here like a rock star. He wore sweatpants like most men wear a tailored suit, Mace. Like . . . he must really be good if he's that confident."

"Oh, I bet he's good. Check out that arm porn in his pictures. And those hands—dear Lord! Think of what they could do to you." A camera shutter sounds through the phone. "Here, I'm texting you a screenshot of this one."

"That's precisely what I'm trying not to think about," I laugh. "I have to work for the next five hours!"

Macie sighs right along with me. "On that note, I need to get back to work too. No hot baseball players here, but one can hope, right?"

"Two words: Will Gentry."

"I need to call you later and tell you about last night. I'm being invaded by families right now, so I can't get into details. I'll just say that boy had me panting for hours, Danielle. *Hours*."

"Call me later," I laugh. "Cheerio!"

I replace the handset and settle back into my seat. A shiver tears through my body, an aftershock from being in the center of the Landry storm. I consider locking the door and getting myself off. I need the release. My body needs to return to normal working order, having been thrusted up the—

Thrusted? I'm never going to get through this day. The worst part is that the good-looking asshole knew exactly what he was doing to me.

They always do.

Which is why they're in my no-fly zone.

THREE

LINCOLN

IT'S FUNNY WHAT YOU LEARN at two in the morning when you're bored, sober, and a little uneasy. It's a trifecta I'm just getting acquainted with. I might be sober a lot during the season, but boredom and anxiety aren't familiar. Or fun.

Around. Around. Around.

I've tried to watch one blade of the ceiling fan, focusing on it and trying to block out the other four as they whiz above me. Over the last thirty minutes, I've learned it's impossible to count the number of rotations in a minute when it's set at medium speed. I've also learned that Skittles make violent projectiles when launched into the blades of the fan, regardless of the setting.

I already knew that though. That was a painful lesson learned at a party a few years back.

Rubbing my shoulder, I see the slight purple indent of the candy against the white paint of my bedroom. It will be gone tomorrow. Rita, the housekeeper, is thorough like that.

I snatch the remote off the bedside table and flip the fan off. It slows, shuddering just a bit before the spinning comes to a halt. Immediately, I remember why I turned it on in the first place: it's the silence that kills me. It's the quiet that allows all of the worries to wage a sneak attack against me. It slams into me from every direction since my meeting with the Arrows' General Manager after my therapy appointment today.

"*It's still too early to know anything, Lincoln. All I can tell you is that we want you back in an Arrows uniform next season,*" Billy Marshall, *the GM, says.*

"*I want that too. This is my city,*" I gulp, *purposefully not looking at the report on the table between us.*

"*Let's work through the rehab and see how it goes. You know it's not up to me. It's up to the owners. I'll have a say, and you know I'm pulling for you. Hell, we all are. You're a franchise player, Landry. But you know, at the end of the day, this is business.*"

"Ugh." I lift myself off the bed. My back muscles strain from the stress of the day, little sleep, and more than a little pain. Glancing in the mirror, my voice cackles across the room at my reflection. "You're a mess, Linc. But your abs look awesome."

Inch by inch, a smile slides across my face as I envision other awesome-looking things. Namely, Danielle Ashley in her pale pink dress.

"Fuck me," I mutter, thinking back to the sweet bow of her hip. It's amazing that I have it memorized without touching her. Just like that, I'm hard. Again.

I can't with this girl. She's gorgeous with her olive skin and dark, exotic eyes. Full lips that nearly reach her high cheekbones when she kills me with that smile. Her black hair was piled on top of her head with curls falling out of the haphazard mass. Sexy. As. Fuck.

Then she goes and banters with me . . . and doesn't offer her number. I mean, she wants me. Of course she does. She saw me *and* she knows who I am—let's be real. It's nagged at me all day that she didn't slip me her business card or offer the availability of when she'll be in the office so I can "accidentally" stop by again. All I can figure is that the call coming in was important. Super important. Earth-shatteringly important.

Scratching my head, my own hair sticking up in every direction, I try to remember if this has ever happened to me. I go through the list of women I've encountered recently: the redhead that gave me the coffee in the drive-thru, the chick that keeps sending me naked selfies that I met in a bar on South Padre Island the week after our season ended, and Blondie today. I could've had her number. Hell, I could've had her in the fucking elevator. So why not Dani?

Why do I care?

Moseying down the hallway towards the kitchen, I take in the pictures hanging on the walls of the hallway. Pictures of me in different stadiums, with my brothers, my parents, pictures with friends that I can't even remember the last time I talked to. By all indications, I should feel at home here. This is my house, after all. But . . . I don't.

I have no idea who hung those pictures. I don't know what happened to the guys in the pictures I'm with from Savannah. As I peek into a bedroom as I exit the hallway, I sure as hell don't know what's in all the boxes stacked against the wall.

Flicking on the kitchen light, the marble countertops sparkle, the bowl of fruit on the island looks perfect. It's all so . . . odd, like it's some kind of photoshoot and I'm just wandering around on stage, waiting for someone to whip out a camera and ask me to smile. It's been this way since I threw the ball to home plate in the last game of the season and heard the rip in my shoulder. The thing is, I don't know what it is I'm feeling, exactly.

A general unease sits atop me now and I can't relax. Not like I used to. There's a dread, maybe a fog, that sort of lingers in the back of my mind. I guess that part of me used to be filled with activity. Usually I'd be on someone's boat right now, partying and living up the offseason. Now I'm home, for lack of a better word, watching home remodeling shows because my shoulder is fucked. There are no getaways, no quick trips to Mexico, no social events to speak of. Just me and the quiet.

The worst part of it is that I don't really have a desire to be with the guys. For the first time, it's unappealing. So unappealing, in fact, that I turned off my work phone, as I call it, and am unreachable to anyone but team management, doctors, and my family. Why take calls from my friends when I know what they want: booze. Boobs. Banal conversation. I've been there and done it. Hell, I wrote a few damn chapters in the book on how to do it. But it just feels like those chapters need nothing added to them, and that's scary as fuck.

Maybe I'm just depressed.

Pulling a box of pizza out of the refrigerator from a couple of days ago, I remove a piece and bring it to my lips. As soon as it hits, my stomach rolls and I toss the slice back in, making the box bounce on the counter. I glance at the clock. It's late. Really late. There's only one person awake at this hour that's acceptable to call. I head into the living room, grab my phone, and listen to it ring.

"Hey, Linc," Graham answers, his voice as clear as it would've been if it was two in the afternoon.

"Do you ever sleep?"

"Good thing I don't or your ass would've just woken me up."

"Good point," I chuckle, flopping back on the sofa. "What's happening in Savannah?"

He blows out a long, deep breath. "Behind at work, actually. My secretary decided that now's the time to go find love or whatever she's calling it and now I'm suffering the consequences of her lack of overtime."

"So she's getting laid and that pisses you off?"

"No. She's getting laid and not doing her work and that pisses me off."

"Fire her," I offer, putting my feet on the coffee table.

"Yeah, easier said than done," he mumbles. "She's worked for me for ten years, and I'm happy she's . . . happy. No, you know what, I really don't fucking care," he laughs. "I just need her to show up and be productive."

Laughing, I run a hand through my hair. "Tell me how you really feel."

"I will," he chuckles. "So, what's keeping you up? A girl just take off ?"

"Do you think that's all I do? Fuck girls and then fuck off ?"

"No," he says, a hint of hesitancy in his tone. "But I was trying to avoid asking you how the meeting went today. You didn't call me, and Mom wasn't completely sold on your story . . ."

His voice trails off and a lump sits at the base of my throat. Even though this is why I called him, to try to work through some of this shit on my mind, it still pokes a hole in that little fucking bubble containing my nerves.

I don't even know what to tell him without sounding like a pussy. I can go through what the management said, but that's not the problem. Not the real problem of why I can't sleep or eat or get myself off the fucking couch unless I have therapy. The real problem is that I feel like I did when I was fifteen years old and broke my leg in the biggest game of the summer league tournament. While my friends played on, then celebrated, I sat in my room and wondered if I'd ever play again.

That's how I feel. Like a fucking kid. And I'm not about to admit that to Graham.

"What happened, Linc?"

Massaging my temple with my eyes squeezed shut, I feel the muscle in my jaw flex again. "I don't have a lot of time to pull some magic out of the air before we start discussing my contract. They're waiting to see how therapy goes, but it's so fucking unnerving, G."

"You expected that. You told me while you were here for Barrett's election."

"Speaking of Barrett, what's he been up to?" I say, happy to change the subject.

"What's he been up to? Up Alison's ass," Graham chuckles.

"Just saying—I'd be up every part of her if she'd let me."

Graham snorts, amused by my statement but too politically correct to admit it. He's uptight and serious most of the time, but hidden back in the depths of his cold, calculated, black heart is a funny, easygoing guy that is a lot like me, although he'd probably fight you before he'd agree.

"Just saying," he repeats back to me, "that's probably going to be your sister-in-law. You should practice choosing your words wisely."

"That takes the fun out of it."

A long pause extends between us before Graham breaks it with one of his dumbass questions. "Have you given any thought to what you might do if this doesn't go your way?"

I look at the ceiling and bite my tongue. I know what he's thinking: baseball is all I have. It's true. I don't have some inherent trait that makes me valuable to anyone or anything besides the game. I'm not Barrett, with his political bravado. I'm not Graham and his business skills or Ford and his hero military shit. I'm the youngest brother, trying to follow along. One with no skill but throwing a ball, if I still have that.

"Do you have a plan, Lincoln?"

"I just want to plan on not being out of a fucking job," I mutter. Graham chuckles. "Whatever. Even if the Arrows let you go, someone will pick you up."

"You don't know how this works."

"I know business, Lincoln. And I know you bring in millions of dollars with your talent, your looks, and because little kids buy your jerseys in the Pro Shop. They aren't letting you go as long as you're making them bank. Business 101, little brother."

Smirking, I say, "My looks do sell a lot of tickets, huh?"

"Shut up," he laughs.

Even though he offered me no assurances and said nothing that I didn't know ten minutes ago, my stomach settles just a bit and that fucking bubble scabs over for the meantime.

"I'll tell you what I want to plan for," I breathe. "Oh, I can't wait to hear this."

"I met this girl today."

"And that's different from any other day how?" he jokes.

"Dude," I say, hopping up on the counter and getting comfortable. "You should see her."

"Let me guess: big tits. Great ass. At least one nipple pierced, probably the right one, if I'm guessing."

"Fuck off."

"So it was the left one?"

The kitchen is filled with my laughter. "No, asshole. I haven't even seen them. Yet."

He whistles through his teeth. "Okay. Color me intrigued. How did you manage to remember a girl that hasn't bared her chest for you?"

"She's . . ." I think back to her sexy smile, her confident retorts to what I said. Her coolness about whether she sees me again, not offering her name up first. "She's different."

"So maybe both are pierced?"

"You're an asshole."

He chuckles, the sound giving way to a yawn. "I do think this injury thing has started to affect your head. Better watch that, little brother."

It's a joke, but one that hits a little too close to home. "I'll let you go. I'm sure you need to get back to whatever the fuck it is you do, and I need to get my beauty sleep," I yawn, stretching my good arm overhead.

"Yeah. I'm going to go work so your inheritance grows while you sleep. You're welcome."

"Go make us some money."

"Night."

I end the call and drop my phone on the couch, heading down the hallway, past two rooms that sit completely empty, and into my bedroom.

"I'm gonna be fine," I mutter, climbing back into bed and pulling the grey sheets over me. "It's all gonna be fine."

FOUR

DANIELLE

THE BELLS RING AS I push open the door of the Smitten Kitten. Scents of freshly baked bread, cinnamon, and hints of mint greet me in a fashion equivalent to a puppy licking your face. It's warm and welcoming, and some of the day's stress melts away.

"Hey," Pepper chirps from behind the counter. "Your usual?"

"Please." I settle into my spot, a little booth tucked in the corner.

The bench seat against the wall is lined with pink and white pillows to nestle against. A light fixture dripping with fake crystals hangs just above the table.

Tossing my bag on the bench, I shrug off my yellow pea coat and collapse into the seat.

Massaging my temples, I try to release the work day and welcome in the evening with deep breathing. It's a trick I learned when I was younger from the music teacher at my private school—not because I was some kind of vocalist. I can't carry a tune. Mrs. Stevenson picked up on the anxiety I carried around like a weight around my neck, something no one else ever noticed or cared enough to help me with, and taught me the steadiness of controlling the air in my body.

Within a few breaths, a steaming mug of cappuccino is in front of me, a bowl of soup next to it, and Pepper across from me. She removes her blue and white checkered apron and tosses it on the booth beside her.

"How was your day?"

"Good," I say, sprinkling some salt in my soup.

"You didn't even taste it."

"I like salt."

"It's a knock on the cook to season your food without tasting it first."

Shaker in hand, paused midair, I look at her through the steam.

"Go ahead and salt the shit out of it," she sighs, flipping her long, dark locks behind her. "I just spent two hours concocting that dish to perfection. Go on and fuck it up."

"Pepper!" I laugh, sitting the shaker down. "Geez, settle down. What has you all fired up today?"

Her dark eyes roll around in one of the most dramatic displays I've seen from her since I started coming to this little bakery near the hospital.

"My husband, if you must know," she snorts. "He wants me to take on an extra pair of hands so I can spend more time with him at home. I mean, I love the man. I do. I'd love to see him more. But I can't afford another person on payroll! We'd be in the red within two months."

"Yikes," I say, lifting a spoonful of the creamy soup to my lips. "Sounds like trouble."

"It is." She watches me like a hawk as I sample the latest Smitten Kitten creation. "So?"

"So what?"

"Is it good?" she laughs. "Damn it. I need feedback, you know that. Don't hold out on me. You're the first person to try it."

"What are we calling it?" I ask, dabbing my mouth with a napkin.

"Kitten Cup."

"Sounds like cat food," I giggle.

"But is it good?'

"No," I say, keeping my face as blank as possible. She holds her breath and it's all I can do not to burst out laughing. "It's probably, um," I say, tilting my head back and forth, prolonging her anguish, "probably my favorite soup yet."

"Score!" she says, standing and pumping a fist. "I knew it! I knew this would be the one! I'm going to enter it in the city cook-off next month. It's a winner, right? I mean, if it's not, tell me. I have time to tweak it."

"It's an absolute winner," I grin, knowing she'll create something else in a few days and will forget all about the Kitten Cup. This is a process that's never ending, and it certainly won't end with this dish.

She starts to reply, but stops. Narrowing her eyes, she wags a finger in my face. "What are you not telling me?"

"What are you talking about?"

"You. You're hiding something from me."

Rolling my eyes, I start to lie to her, but know it's useless. "I had a visitor today." I proceed to give her all the details about my afternoon and find myself getting wrapped up in the dropping of her jaw, the way she hangs on every word. When I finish, she falls back like she's run a mile.

"Did you at least give him your number?" she asks.

"No." I shrug, like it's a silly question, but my shoulders don't fall before she's squawking at me.

"Why? Why would you not give him your card or something? Danielle, sometimes I feel like I don't even know you. You refused Weston Brinkmann—"

My hand flies up, silencing her. "Stop. You know why I turned Weston down."

"I do. You're right. Because you're ignorant!"

I can't help but laugh. "I'm in my late twenties, Pepper," I remind her. "I need to start thinking long-term."

"Yeah," she nods enthusiastically. "I bet Lincoln has excellent long term power. I bet that guy can get you off—"

"Stop!" I giggle. "That's not what I mean."

Pepper doesn't bother to respond. She just looks at me, totally unconvinced. "Weston was gorgeous," she says finally.

I nod. "And he loved baseball far more than he'll ever love a human being."

This sobers my friend. She knows where I'm coming from. "I get what you're saying."

"Yeah." Swirling my cappuccino around, I watch the foam twist and turn. "Besides," I say, "Lincoln is way better looking than Weston. And funny and charming and . . ."

The door chimes and she fastens her apron. "Hold that thought," she says before jogging to the counter.

Watching Pepper and her customer, an old friend of hers that comes in here a lot. I can't help the pang of jealousy in my stomach. I don't know what it's like to have that kind of friendship with someone, a deep connection to another person that spans time and locations. The closest thing I have is Macie. We met during Freshman Orientation in college and hit it off over our mutual love for kids, although our reasons for it are completely different. Macie does it because she feels like she's giving back to the world. I find that working with them helps heal a part of my soul.

"I don't know what I did to be cursed with a daughter. For the love of God, Ryan Danielle, do not embarrass me."

I shiver as my father's voice booms through my memory, the coolness of his eyes only adding to the pain in my heart. I used to think the hurt would ease, that the longer I was out of his house, away from the mother that could have loved me but loved his wealth more, it would alleviate. Years on my own and the sting is still there.

My father always wanted a son. It's no secret that he feels cheated by the universe for getting a daughter, so much so that he named me Ryan Danielle. A boy's name. A constant reminder of the failure I was from birth. Since I failed him, I also failed my mother, a woman that's probably capable of love, but is so poisoned by her obsession with my father that her capacity has diminished. There's no room for me in her life in any measurable quantity—just for the occasional photo or to make sure I'm not doing something that would blow back on my father and taint his prestigious image somehow.

Wrapping my hands around the mug so they're pressed against the clay, I feel the warmth radiate into my skin and focus on that. The here. The now.

~My gaze lands on my bag, a file from work poking out. Instantly, I'm out of the here and now and am mentally in my office. With the door closed. With the centerfielder.

A warmth erupts in the pit of my stomach and starts to fan out until it begins to toast my cheeks.

Why does God have to love athletes most?

He does. There are no two ways about it. They're the hottest, most fit, most calculating and passionate people. They're delicious . . . and dangerous if you aren't careful.

Despite the heat roaring through my blood, I shiver. I can only imagine what it's like to be on the receiving end of Lincoln's passion. Feeling his eyes on me today was enough to make me crazy. Feeling his breath hot against my cheek? His fingers caressing my body? The weight of his cock as it sits on top of my ass, waiting to glide into me?

Because I'm cursed, both with loving athletes and having them love me, reality douses the fire as quickly as it starts. The passion, while white-hot and intoxicating, turns steel-cold and suffocating.

It's why I'll continue to remind myself just how bad it hurts when they prove, as they always do, that their first passion is, and always will be, the game.

FIVE

LINCOLN

"MOTHERFUC . . ." I STOP SHORT OF saying the rest, wincing as my injured arm is raised up and back as far as it will go. No, farther than it will go. It most definitely doesn't go this far back.

This guy is a fucking sadist.

"There you go," Houston says, guiding my screaming arm to my side. "You're going to be sore tonight and really sore tomorrow. Ice it and be back here in two days for another session."

I look at him. "Two days?"

"Yes," he says, turning his stocky body away from me and heading to a big purple ball.

"You do realize I need this thing completely healed in about six weeks, right? And our progress is negligible."

He nods, eyeing me like I'm the crazy one. No, I'm sane. I'm clear about what has to be done. His blasé attitude about this entire thing is the problem.

"Okay, let's start over," I gulp, irritation racing across my forehead. "I have exactly two months to have this one hundred percent. I have less than that to prove to the Arrows owners that I am worth a contract."

"I understand that."

Waiting for him to continue his thought, I stand and roll my shoulder back and forth. By the time I'm on my tenth rotation, gritting my teeth through the fire, he still hasn't responded, and I'm about ready to lose my shit.

"So . . . I'm hoping we can be at one hundred percent by, say, Christmas? End of January at the latest. I need substantial rehab by Thanksgiving, Houston. We need to make that happen," I insist.

A wide, cheeky grin stretches over his face, his head shaking side-to-side. I'm not sure what he finds funny about this, but if I could raise my arm far enough, I'd be tempted to throw punches.

"Lincoln, listen. Your shoulder needs stretching to regain your range of motion. Once we have that we can build up your strength in several ways. But right now it also needs rest."

"I don't have time for rest."

"Spoken like a true athlete," he snickers. "You do have time for rest. Give your body time to heal itself. We'll do the work in here, but when you're not, you have to let it do its thing." He walks in front of me, looking me right in the eye. "So tomorrow, no lifting. No stretching. No throwing a ball. Don't even jack off too hard. Nothing. Do you hear me, Landry?"

I start to fire back, but his gaze steadies.

"I know you're used to pushing through the pain and making shit go on your schedule, but that's what got you here. To me. The expert." He gives that a second to sink deep into my psyche. "Are you following along?"

I grab my hat off the floor and slam it on my head. "I hear you," I grumble.

"Good. See you in two days." With a little wave, he and his attitude problem head to his office.

I turn towards the elevator. I need out of here before I explode and damage this thing further. I doubt it would help my shoulder or my relationship with Houston if I picked up a dumbbell and sent it soaring out of the tenth floor window.

The door dings and I enter, taking a spot next to a woman in a grey skirt and white shirt. She's cute with her curly hair and golden lips, and she clearly likes what she sees, but I'm so pissed off by this two-day bullshit, I can't even find it in myself to flirt. That might be the most shocking thing to happen to me all day.

Since when do I not flirt?

That's it. Graham was right. This injury has affected my brain.

I'm dying.

"Ground floor," I say with a hint of a smile, trying to find the philanderer I know is lurking somewhere inside me.

She uses a red fingernail to punch in the number. "You're Lincoln Landry, aren't you?" She pulls the clipboard she's carrying towards her body, her lips stretching into a dazzling smile.

"That's me." I watch the floor numbers drop, feeling her watch me. The air like the dugout before a game in July—stale and hot with the promise of more if you're willing to make it happen.

I'm not. Strangely.

Yup. Dying.

The door stops and chimes as it opens. "See you later," she breathes.

The doors make the grinding sound that happens right before they start to swing closed. And then, just like that, everything changes. I see her. Danielle Ashley, the fiery little raven haired beauty that gives as good as she gets.

Oh, how I would like to know how true that is.

She's holding the hand of the little boy she was with the last time I saw her. He threatens to touch her with a very blue, drippy hand and she tries to look at him sternly, but it doesn't pass as anything more than adorable. They both look up just as the doors begin to close.

Her steps falter, her eyes go wide, as the little boy's light up with recognition.

"Lincoln Landry!" he squeals, tugging the hand she's holding until he's free.

The doors inch closer and closer, the window of visibility narrowing as they prepare to shut me in and whisk me away. Not happening. Not after I've thought of her every hour since I left here yesterday. Not after I had to jack off three times to visions of her bent over, her riding me, and me caging her into my mattress while I bust it deep inside her tight little body.

My hand shoots in front of me. This is fate. A pitch offered from the heavens. My cheeks start to ache, right along with my forgotten shoulder, as I smile at the look of pure amusement on her face.

The room is vacant besides Danielle and the little boy as I step onto the tile. He runs to me and jumps straight into my arms with no warning, his blue painted hand stamping a perfect little print on the front of my The Resistance t-shirt. Danielle's face bunches in horror.

"Rocky!" she shouts.

The little boy giggles, positioning his face directly in front of mine. Bright blue eyes look back at me above a spattering of freckles. "You're Lincoln Landry," he breathes like he's just seen Santa Claus.

"I am?" I ask, my eyes going wide.

"You are," he breathes in awe. "I know who you are. My big brother has a poster of you in his room."

"And you don't?" I ask, frowning.

"My mom won't buy me one. She says I'm too little."

I lean forward until our noses are touching and whisper, "She can't say no if I give you one as a gift, right?"

He giggles. "No." Rocky presses his paint free hand against my shoulder, making me grimace in pain. Danielle is to our side just as I stifle the string of profanities threatening to spill out.

"Rocky," she says, reaching us. "You can't go jumping on strangers. Look at Mr. Landry's shirt." He doesn't look at her. He's still watching me. I'm still watching him, too, even though the entire universe seems to be pulling me to the woman at my left.

"Did that hurt?" he asks.

"A little," I say with as little evidence of just how bad as I can manage.

"Lincoln, I'm so sorry," Danielle apologizes, taking Rocky out of my arms. "Give me a minute, please."

She bends her fine ass down until she's eye level with the boy. I'll give her all the minutes she needs if I can stand here and watch her about to burst out of that dress.

"I need you to go back to your room and wash your hands," she tells him. "Can you do that for me?"

He nods, but looks at me over his shoulder. "Lincoln?"

"Yeah?" I ask.

"Will you come paint with me tomorrow?"

"Rocky . . ." Danielle scoffs.

"Sure I will," I say, grinning at her. "What time, Rockster?"

"I don't know how to tell time," he says, his brows coming together. "After lunch I watch the Muggies on TV. After that, you can come."

"Okay. I'll be here after lunch and Muggies."

He darts down the hall, his hospital gown blowing in the air behind him like a superhero's cape.

"I'm so sorry about your shirt. Let me put something on it so the paint comes off easier." She turns away and pads over to a little closet. She rummages around, and when she faces me again, nearly drops the bottle in her hands.

"What?" I ask, extending my hand in front of me. My t-shirt is balled up, a smirk deepening as I watch her gaze sear my abs. "Didn't you ask for my shirt?"

She starts to speak but gets stuck on the lump in her throat.

"I think," I say, running a hand down my front, "it'll be a ten pack soon."

"If I came closer, I'm pretty sure I could count ten."

"What's holding you back?"

Her cheeks heat, but she turns away from me and puts the bottle back in the cabinet. "Put your shirt on," she orders. She looks at me and then pulls her gaze away instantly. "Now. Please. For both of our sakes."

"Fine, fine," I say, trying to pretend to huff. "Now my shirt will be ruined."

"I'll buy you another."

"Johnny Outlaw signed this one. You're not going to *just* buy me another one."

"Johnny touched that? Well, in that case, give it to me!" she nearly sighs.

"I also touched it," I say, a little snarkier than I care to admit. "You know, the best centerfielder in baseball? The guy with these abs?"

She rolls her eyes. "What are you doing here anyway?"

"I believe a little boy ran at me like a bullet. I had to catch him. Catching things midair is what I do best, if you didn't know." I slide my arms through the shirt and drop it over my torso. Her eyes don't leave mine.

"Interesting," she smirks. Her chin lifts a touch, enough to elicit an automatic shift in power from me to her. "I figured your best attribute was something . . . else."

Her lips twist in amusement as she flips a strand of hair off her narrow shoulders, tosses me a wink, and heads down the hall. I'm not sure what she's expecting, but I follow. Of course I do.

Left. Right. Left. Right. Her ass sways side to side in front of me, like a hypnotist erasing my mind from any thought other than the one she's driving home.

God, how I'd like to drive her home.

Glancing over her shoulder, she flips me a look that makes me wonder if I growled out loud. I might've.

Stepping inside her office, I shut the door behind me. When I turn around, she's sitting at her desk.

"Would you like to know what I'm doing here?" My chest is rising and falling to the beat of the sway of her hips from before.

"What makes you think I want to know anything?"

"Because you asked earlier, sweet pea."

This time, it's me leaning across the desk. It's my eyes digging into hers, my energy rolling across the faux wood desk. She feels it. The uptick in her breathing gives it away. Her lips are slightly parted, as she waits for me to speak.

"You can play this game, Dani—"

"It's Danielle."

"—but I can see right through you."

"You think?"

"I *know*. But I do like your confidence. It works for me."

"That's so good to know," she retorts. It's almost a mock, a little edge of haughtiness cut stealthily along the ridges of the words. "You wanna know something?"

"What's that?"

"I can also see right through you."

"Is that so?"

"Sure is."

The air is charged with our quick exchange, our bodies nearly buzzing with the excitement of the moment. We're so close, near enough to reach out and touch the other, and that's precisely what we both want. Our bodies, our gazes, our words are dripping with so much sexual frustration it's palpable.

"Tell me," I say, breaking the ragged breathing filled silence. "What do you see when you see through me?"

"I don't think this is the place for that conversation."

"Would you rather move this to a locked conference room? I'm so, so game for that."

She laughs, her melodious chirp ringing through the room. It cuts through the tension and I find myself heaving in a fresh breath of air. Picking up a pencil as if she's about to work, she smiles easily. "This was fun, but I really need to get to work."

"What?" I don't mean for it to sound as brusque as it does, but fuck it. What is she doing? She has me worked up to beat all hell and she's going back to work?

A few seconds later, I'm still standing, trying to grasp what the hell just happened. She looks up from a notepad on her desk, seemingly surprised to see me still here.

"I guess I'll see you tomorrow," I say, shoving off her desk. "And why is that?"

"I'm painting with Rocky."

"We only paint one day a week. There won't be supplies here tomorrow."

I just grin. She sighs.

"You aren't cleared to come by. There is protocol to follow, Landry, even for you."

"Good thing I'm me then," I wink, knowing I'm pissing her off. "I'll have my people call your people, and I'll see you in the morning."

"I don't have people," she says through gritted teeth. "I am people."

"Sounds good. You'll like them. My people are good people."

We stand off, each of us as determined to get our way as the other. She narrows her eyes. I widen my smirk. She throws her shoulders back, I shrug mine. This little game incenses her, riles her up. If I were the true gentleman my mother raised, I'd warn her that seeing her pissed off only makes me want her worse.

Good thing I'm not.

SIX

DANIELLE

THE WATER SPLASHES DOWN THE sides of my favorite teacup. I hold it under the faucet, letting my dirty chai tea wash down the drain. Sitting it in the strainer, I pad through the simple little kitchen adorned with sunflowers and into the tidy living room. As much as I try to make it feel like home, it doesn't. It lacks a flourish of warmth or coziness that I can't fill with all the throw pillows and candles in the world.

I glance at the handful of framed pictures on the mantle. There are two of me and Macie in college. One is of me and Pepper that was taken by a newspaper doing a feature on the Smitten Kitten. The other is of me and my parents, taken on the day I graduated high school. It's one of the only pictures I have of the three of us. I've stared at it for hours over the years, dissecting how we look to the world. We are all smiling, my father's arms stretched around my mother and I. We look normal. If only.

The rumble starts in my chest, and I watch my hand reach for the phone. My brain tells my hand to stop. It warns my heart not to have too much hope that my mother will answer, and if she does, that we'll have a nice conversation.

Warning in hand, I dial the numbers and wait as it rings, once, twice, three times before she answers.

"Hello?" she breathes into the receiver.

"Hi, Mom. It's me."

My heart leaps in my throat and I can feel my pulse in my temples.

My mouth goes dry as I wait to see what she has to say.

She takes in a sharp breath and blows it out in one long, drawn out action. "Hello, Ryan."

"How are you?"

"I'm fine. Ryan, I'll have to call you back shortly. Your father will be in soon, and I need to be ready. You know how he hates to wait."

Forcing the words to come out of my mouth, my hand not to drop the phone, I tell her it's fine and even manage a laugh. And before I know it, I'm sitting on the sofa watching the shadows move across the wall with the setting sun. She won't call me back. Not tonight, not tomorrow. This is a fact, the way it is, but it doesn't mean it still doesn't sting. I wish it didn't, I tell myself it doesn't. I lie.

Grabbing the remote, I flip on the television and wander through the channels until it lands on some reality drivel. The noise helps fill the house and keeps me company as I go into the kitchen and pour a large glass of red wine.

Taking a sip, I consider heading downtown and grabbing a drink in a public place. Getting out. Fresh air and all that. Even as I'm thinking about it, I slide under a blanket on the sofa and take another drink.

The show on the screen is about a dysfunctional family. I've seen it before. They fight and carry on but at the end of every episode, they reunite. Make amends. Reconvene as a family. And, as I do every time I tune in, I wonder what that feels like. Even the arguments are appetizing to me because they have each other. Looking at the picture of my parents and then at my phone again, it hits me again that I only have me. I could die tonight and it would be days before anyone finds me. Pepper would probably send the police because she needed feedback for her soup.

"In, out," I breathe, filling my lungs with oxygen and closing my eyes. As soon as they do, I see Lincoln Landry. His rugged jawline, the way those blazing eyes light up when he's toying with me. The way his hand, large and calloused, cups his chin as he waits on me to process an innuendo, makes me shiver despite the flannel pajamas covering my body.

"I deserve a cupcake for that," I say out loud, mentally patting my back for holding my ground against him. "Maybe two."

There's something about him, about the way he looks at me, that makes it absolutely clear he would be a force to be reckoned with if he had an opening and wanted in. Not that I need to, because I'll probably never see him again, but I must keep that door closed.

As if on cue, his smirk pops in my mind. I throw the blanket off and sit my wine on the table in front of me.

"Why, God?" I say into the air. "Why couldn't he have tormented someone else today?"

Stomping towards my bedroom, I'm going to have to take matters into my own hands. That or risk pouncing on his delectable body if I ever see him again.

***

Lincoln

"HEY," I DRAWL AS UNASSUMINGLY as I can. My hand adjusts around the plastic handles of the craft store bag. It was my first and last visit there. Besides the thirty-four million paints and brushes, there are nearly as many mommy types that apparently know who I am.

I mean, of course they do, and I'm not averse to some MILF action. But all of them at once with no security? It got a little hairy for a minute.

Danielle looks up from her planner and removes a pair of black glasses. My brain is racing, picturing her lying on my bed, her hair up just like it is now in a messy pile on the top of her head and dressed in nothing but those fucking glasses.

"Can I come in?" I ask, my throat a little parched. I set the bag on the chair in front of me and just take her in. She's this mixture of sophistication and sex appeal, something that's hard to pull off but she does perfectly. She could've stepped out of a charity meeting with one of my sisters or off a swimsuit cover, one I'd buy the fuck out of. "I'm early."

"You aren't early," she smiles, standing. "You aren't on today's schedule."

"Maybe not yours." I flash her a grin that always gets me what I want. "I have an appointment with Rocky."

"I believe I told you there are no paint supplies here today."

"You did. That's why I brought some." I dip a hand into the bag and pull out three finger paint kits. "See? One of my best traits is that I'm always prepared."

"Maybe I was wrong about you."

"Why is that?"

"You keep alluding to these best traits of yours, and they're things like *preparation*. Maybe I overestimated you."

It takes a full three seconds for me to find my voice. I'm not used to being on this side of the conversation. "Preparation is half the battle, Ms. Ashley."

"And the other half is follow through."

"Trust me, babe. I follow through. There's nothing I like better than executing so well it knocks everyone else out of the game. Driving home the win. Being so fucking good that my name is the only one they remember." I pause a second to watch her react. "If you would like to see my best attribute, I'd be more than happy to demonstrate."

"I'm sure you would," she says breathily. "But you know, I also have strengths."

"I bet you do," I breathe.

"One of them is the same as yours."

"I have little doubt," I nearly growl, the bag crunching under my fist as I squeeze it in anticipation.

"I'm prepared . . . to have you escorted out of here." My face falls.

Hers lights up as she laughs at my reaction. "I'm just kidding," she says, scooting her chair back and standing. "You can stay. But only because I said so."

"Oh, is that how it is?" I laugh.

"Uh-huh. I call the shots. This is my domain."

"Hey," I say, holding my hands in the air, "I'm fine being dominated. I think it's sexy. However you want it."

"You're ridiculous," she laughs, but the ripple in her breathing betrays her. The candy apple red silk shirt stretched over her breasts nearly pops the buttons on the uprise. It's hot as hell. "I have to say, I'm impressed you came."

My brows pull together as I try to make sense out of that comment. "Why is that?"

She smiles softly, her features relaxing. Gone is the little vixen that gives me shit. This is another side of her, one that will probably be harder to forget. Vixens are a dime a dozen. This side of her? It's not.

"We have celebrities in here often, making promises to the kids," she tells me. "Most don't follow through. I didn't expect to see you here today."

Her words are full of a pain I can't identify. But it's there. That I'm sure of.

"I'm not sure what most people do," I tell her, "but I honor my word. Thank you for letting me come by today."

"You didn't give me a choice."

"True," I grin. "But you could send me away, and you aren't."

She starts to speak but catches herself. After reassessing her words, she smiles. "You're right. I'm not. But can you answer something for me?"

"Sure."

"Why are you here, Lincoln? You just come by and tell a child you'll be here the next day like you have nothing else to do. I know what your schedule must look like, and I just can't wrap my head around the fact that you showed up."

Shrugging, I laugh. "Maybe I don't have anything better to do."

"I doubt that."

"Maybe I like kids."

That makes her smile, which makes me smile. "Maybe I wanted to see you too," I offer cautiously.

Instead of responding, she walks by me, indicating with the crook of her finger for me to follow. A few minutes later, I find myself sitting at a table across from the one and only Rocky. He starts jabbering away about the Muggies, and before I know it, I'm wearing a streak of white paint and Danielle is nowhere to be found.

We paint for almost an hour, joined off and on by other little people. The kids are a riot, but I keep looking for Danielle. She never appears. Finally, after painting every farm animal I can think of, I'm relieved to see Rocky's eyes get heavy.

I hold up his last picture, a blob of red and yellow. If I had a few beers in me, the thing in the center might be a baseball. Maybe. But probably not. Looking at my new buddy out of the corner of my eye, I grin. "You think I could have this? It would look awesome in my house."

"I don't know," he says, yawning. "My mom really likes my paintings. I don't want to make her sad."

"You know what?" I stand and place the paper in front of him. "Always take care of your girl. And your mama is always your girl."

His big eyes peer up at me. "Do you have a mama?"

"You bet. And even though I'm a grownup myself now, technically, anyway, my mama still takes care of me."

Rocky stands too, his face smoothing out in an attempt to stay composed. It's a look I could identify anywhere, a guise I put on often to keep everyone from reading what I'm thinking. Once I was drafted into the league, I learned real quick you have to keep up your guard. Keep shit, like feelings, to yourself or be exploited.

"You're a baseball player. Your mom still does stuff for you?"

"Man, you better learn this now," I say, chuckling. "You will always need your mom. Even when you're a grownup and have your own house, sometimes your mom is the only one you can count on when you don't know how to make microwave macaroni and cheese. She's the only girl you can count on, so make sure you take care of her."

His yellow sock clad feet shuffle against the linoleum. "The doctor said I might not get to be a grownup. The stuff inside me is fighting the medicines."

The wind knocks right out of me, the same way it does when my brother, Ford, is being an ass and tackles me when we're playing touch football at family barbecues. Only this time, there's no hand to pull me up. Just a little boy looking at me, wanting me to say something. To be the adult.

"Rockster, I . . ." I crouch to his level, certain he can spy the lump in my throat. He reminds me of Huxley, my brother Barrett's soon-to-be stepson, with the way he looks at me like I can fix the universe. If only I could. "Doctors don't know everything."

He puts his hand on my shoulder. "I had fun painting with you today."

"And I had fun painting with you too." The words leave my mouth automatically, but as they ring through the room, I realize how true they are.

"Hey, guys." Danielle's voice fills the small room off the main corridor, and Rocky looks at her over my shoulder.

"Hi, Danielle," he says.

I turn sideways, still crouched, and look up at her. Even from this vantage point, she's something to look at. An understated beauty, fine features, with a magnetism I can't quite put my finger on, she has my full attention. As I stand, a full blown smile drifts across her face.

"Looks like the two of you had a good afternoon," Danielle says, one heel crossed in front of the other. "What did you think, Lincoln?"

Grabbing Rocky's boney shoulders in front of me with one hand, I muss up his hair with the other. "I think this kid is the next Van Gogh."

Her laugh dances into my ears. "Good to know. You ready to go get some lunch, Rocky?"

"Yes! It's pizza!" He tosses me a wave and races through the door, nearly knocking a laughing Danielle over.

"He's a cool kid," I say when she finally looks at me. Her cheeks match the color of her shirt as she smooths her skirt like my sister, Sienna, does when she's nervous before a fashion show.

"He is."

"I think he thinks I'm pretty cool." I try not to laugh while she decides if I'm serious or not.

"That's subjective," she says finally, backing out of the doorway. "I need you to sign a release, if you don't mind. Even though you're here for the day only, I should've had you do it before you started."

I let the "day only" thing slide and follow her down the hallway. As we approach the elevator, it dings and a man in hospital scrubs exits.

"Danielle," he says happily, *too happily*, extending a hand.

An easy grin touches her lips as she places her palm in his. "How are you, Dr. Manning?" she asks, clearly comfortable with this guy I'm absolutely sure I don't like. I might even hate him.

"Great. Just dropping by your boss's office. Gretchen is down this hallway, right?"

"Yes," Dani confirms. "I'm not sure that she's in though. Our department is in the middle of budget hearings."

"I was thinking of grabbing a coffee in a little while. Can I get you something?" he asks, taking a step towards her. So do I.

"No, thank you," she responds politely. "The place across the street has great espresso if you need something quick and hard."

I gulp. The asshole nods, a sparkle in his eye that makes me want to stake a claim to Danielle. As my brain races to come up with some-thing, he turns to me, his brow cocked. "You look familiar," he says.

"It's the face," I say, starting after Dani down the hall. "Are you Lincoln Landry, by any chance?"

Danielle pauses mid-step, her head turning to me. Her teeth tug at her bottom lip. I search her eyes, a swirling blue that could sink me if I let it. And I would really fucking like to let it, but I'm sure it's going to be as hard as hitting a fastball from our starting pitcher.

"Me?" I laugh. "Hell, no. I hear he's way bigger and better looking than me."

I feel Danielle release a breath right before her heels start down the hall again. With a little salute to the doctor, I follow her.

"You lied to him," she says under her breath as she enters her office ahead of me.

"Would you rather me tell him I'm me and have him coming back to shoot the shit?"

"No," she says quickly.

I ignore the idea that maybe she might be inclined to chat with the good doctor and press on. "Me either." She laughs. "Why is that, Landry?"

"I think he's an asshole."

"He is not!" she exclaims. "He's here for training from Phoenix. He leaves next week."

It's obvious I just relaxed, but whatever. "Good."

"Lincoln Landry, are you a little jealous?"

"Of that? Please," I scoff.

Her head shakes, a chuckle escaping much to her chagrin. Instead of answering me, she fishes through a drawer and pulls out a file. A piece of paper is slipped across the desk with a bright red circle scrawled in the middle and an X denoted on the bottom.

She holds my gaze and doesn't say a word for a long time. The air between us crackles, and at the same time, I remove my hat and she tugs at the collar of her shirt. We both notice, but don't bring it up, and instead, exchange a knowing grin.

"Can you just fill this out?" she asks breathlessly.

"Sure." I give it a quick review before reaching across her desk and picking up a pen right by her arm. My forearm skims the inside of her wrist. Her gasp at the contact ripples through the room and heads straight for my cock.

I don't look at her. I don't want to embarrass her. I also don't want to let her know how badly I want her, and if I look at her right now, she'll know. It's written all over my damn face.

And the crotch of my shorts. In an attempt to adjust the package, I reach inside the pocket and try to discreetly get comfortable. As I pull my hand out, I grab my wallet and sit it on her desk like it was the intent of my movement. With a still raging hard on, I fill out the circled information, sign the document and scoot it back to her again.

"Landry" she breathes, just as her desk phone rings. Her lips are pressed together, obviously torn about what to say next.

"Take it," I say, smirking. "I was just leaving anyway."

"I . . ." she says as I turn my back and head out, leaving her hanging.

Let's see what you do at the plate, Dani.

SEVEN

DANIELLE

TURNING THE CORNER AND IGNORING a passing car with a driver laying on the horn, I make my way down the cobbled sidewalk and into the Smitten Kitten. Pepper looks up as the chimes alert her of my arrival.

"I hope you want soup," she says, sitting a paper bag on the counter. "I had this dream last night about clam chowder. Weird, I know, but I woke up and had to try it, and it is delish. I can't even lie."

Plopping my bag on the floor in front of the counter, I fork over my credit card. "I bet it is."

"No, this one is it, Danielle. The flavors married so well. I hope you love it."

"I've never met a Pepper soup I didn't like."

She runs my card through the machine then zooms off to refill a customer's coffee cup. Sorting through my bag, I find my wallet . . . right next to Lincoln Landry's. My hand stills over them side-by-side beneath my car keys.

His luxe brown leather lies next to my pink and yellow floral print. They touch barely on one corner and I can't help but think of all the metaphors that could be made out of that.

I slide my card into mine, feeling the buttery texture of Lincoln's as I do. It's smooth against my skin, the rich material oozing opulence. It's the best leather. My father had one similar.

"See you tomorrow," I tell Pepper as I pull the front door open, my mind still on the baseball player.

I tried to run him down as soon as I saw his wallet perched discreetly behind a picture frame on my desk, but he was gone. Considerations were made about leaving it with security, but all it would take would be for someone to realize exactly who it belongs to and who knows what would happen. I also couldn't leave it in my desk for fear of it getting stolen. So into my purse it went. Now it feels both like a responsibility and an opportunity as I lug it through the parking lot and into the back seat of my car.

Pulling out onto the road, a call rings through the car. I press the button on the steering wheel to answer.

"Hello?" I ask.

"Hey, you!" Macie's voice sings. "How are you?"

"Good. Just grabbed dinner and heading home."

"Smitten Kitten?"

"Yeah," I laugh.

Macie scoffs through the line. "Seriously, Danielle. Expand your horizons a little bit."

"I like it," I pout. "It fits into my routine. I know Pepper. I like her food."

"You're comfortable there," Macie cuts in.

"That too."

"Well, I have something to break you out of your comfort zone." The tone of her voice pulls at a knot in my stomach. "My friend, Jules, is starting a nonprofit here in Boston. I told her about you and your experience with management and kids and scheduling and stuff."

Piloting my car into my driveway, I pull into the garage and cut the engine. "How is she?" I think back to the stories Macie has relayed about Julia Gentry and her family. It's crazy what they've been through, yet she seems to march on. I wish I had half her strength.

"She's good. She's always good. Strongest woman ever. I told her you might be interested in working for her."

"Maybe. We have a budget hearing coming up, so that might work out great," I wince. "I think we're going to lose some funding and no one is safe when that happens."

"I'll let her know I asked."

"So," I say, moving the conversation along, "I had something interesting happen to me today, and I need your advice."

"Go on."

Envisioning her getting comfy in her chair, waiting to spill her thoughts on my life, I laugh. The kitchen lights are bright as I drop my bag on the counter.

"Okay, so Lincoln came back in today."

"See this face? Well, you can't, obviously, but if you could, you'd see I'm so freaking green with envy! I'd never tell Will this because he'd go all alpha-crazy if I brought up a thing such as a Hall Pass, but Lincoln would be mine. I can't help it. I've spent the last twenty-four hours looking at his pics online."

The chair squeaks against the floor as I pull it out from the table and collapse into it. I picture her boyfriend, Will Gentry, a man I've met once before, being told that Macie wanted a Hall Pass. I laugh before I can stop myself.

"What?" Macie asks.

"I'm imagining Will's face if he overheard this conversation."

"I'd be bent over this chair. Come to think of it, maybe I should let him hear . . ."

"Anyway, so Lincoln was back today to paint with a boy named Rocky."

If a pin dropped on the other side, I could've heard it. "Macie? Are you there?"

"Yeah," she draws out. "I'm trying to figure out why a man like him was painting with a kid today. On a day's notice."

"I questioned it too," I sigh. "But seriously . . . Macie, he was so fantastic with him. With all the kids, really."

My heart swells as I remember seeing him sitting his tall frame in those little kid's chairs. I peeked in from across the hall a couple of times and nearly melted into a puddle on the floor.

"There's nothing like a man with a kid," Macie sings.

"It wasn't just that," I say, trying to find the words to say what I mean. "Yes, seeing him with these little boys was super cute. But it was more than that. It was the way he was with them. With me, he's funny and sexy and kind of full of himself. But when he's sitting at this little table, covered in paint, flanked by two kids talking his ear off, you'd have no idea he was a big deal. None at all."

I'm grinning and I can't stop it. It was one of the most endearing things I've seen in my career. Usually celebrities come in and go through the motions, but Lincoln was more than that. He stayed a long time. He didn't ask for help. He didn't look bored or get mad when they had accidents. He seemed to actually enjoy it.

"Is he coming back?" she asks.

I gulp. "Maybe. He left his wallet on my desk."

"And his wallet was out why?"

"Your guess is as good as mine. Maybe he thought he was going to need his ID for the paperwork he was filling out? I don't know."

Her tongue clicks against the roof of her mouth. "Where was it?"

"Behind a picture frame."

"Huh." She's quiet again, which is fine by me because the more I think about it, the harder I find it to breathe. "So he left it for you to find."

"You think?"

"Of course. A man like him with an unlimited credit card isn't going to whip it out and leave it sit. I don't care who he is, Danielle. It's not going to happen."

A long sigh escapes my lips.

"What are you sighing about?" she laughs. "You're going to have to meet Mr. Sexy and give him his wallet back. Poor you."

"I think I'll just leave it at the front desk."

An exasperated breath rumbles through the phone and I brace for the onslaught that's coming. "Ryan Danielle," she starts, using my given name for emphasis, "the one thing I don't like about you, besides your ability to eat shit and not gain a pound, is the way you lump people together. It's not fair."

"It may not be fair, but it's logic."

"So every guy I dated before Will with green eyes was a monster. What would've happened had I not dated him?"

"You would've found someone else?" I offer just to irritate her. She groans.

"Look, Macie. No one knows athletes, baseball players specifically, better than me. They're a unique bunch full of superstitions and a love of—"

"Baseball before everything else," she says, finishing my sentence for me. "I've heard."

"This would be so easy if he weren't so fucking hot," I groan, picking at a napkin on the table. "It's like the devil sends me these men just to torture me. What do you think I did in a past life to deserve this?"

"Whatever it was, let's hope I figure it out and do it in this one."

***

Lincoln

IS THIS HOW THE REST of the world lives?

Sitting on the counter in my kitchen, an apple in my hand, I toss it into the air and catch it. Once, twice, three times. On the fourth catch, I whip it around and throw it at the trash can. Instead of landing in the liner, it hits the wall above. A spray of juice and pulp splatter everywhere.

"And that's why I don't play basketball."

I listen to the clock over the sink tick. How have I just noticed how annoying this is? Hopping off the grey marble, I leap onto the counter and pull it down. The batteries come out with a loud pop.

Silence. It's a relief for about fifty seconds.

"Fuck," I say, getting back to the floor again. "Fuck, fuck, fuck." Humming a tune from the radio just so it doesn't seem so empty in here, I pad into the living room. I'm not sure why. There's nothing to do in there, either. I gave up video games a long time ago. There's no one I want to hang out with, no party I want to attend. I'd just go to Savannah if I didn't have therapy.

Testing the rotation in my shoulder, I feel it pull deep inside. The cringe that usually accompanies the movement doesn't come, but still, it doesn't feel good.

"Is this what I have to look forward to? Being lame?" There's no one to answer my questions but me, and I sure as shit don't have answers. I don't know anything—what the future holds, what my friends are doing, who in the fuck decided an almost orange colored blanket was my style, or what Danielle Ashley is wearing under that red shirt. I know nothing anymore.

My phone starts to ring. I consider not answering it, but I'm too bored not to. "Hello?"

"Hi, Lincoln. It's Danielle Ashley."

Her voice is sweeter on the phone than in person, and it catches me off guard. Even though I'd hoped she'd call, I really hadn't expected her to, even though I bolded my phone number on the form she had me fill out. She's too unpredictable. The fact that I'm listening to her faint breathing on the other end of the line is, to put it mildly, a nice surprise.

"Well, look who it is," I kid. "How are you?"

"Good," she replies. "I had to hear about how awesome you are all afternoon from Rocky."

"Glad to know I made a good impression," I laugh. "It was a lot of fun. Thank you for letting me stay."

She waits a moment before responding. "Thanks for coming by. It was really nice of you."

"Maybe you'll let me come by again," I suggest. "I have a lot of time on my hands these days."

"We'll see."

I take that for what it's worth and dig in. "So, did you call to thank me for coming today?"

"I'll humor you and tell you that you left your wallet on my desk."

"Did I? How irresponsible of me."

"Uh-huh," she laughs. "I love how your phone number had a big black box around it. Super subtle."

"Hey, it got you to call, didn't it?"

She laughs, but doesn't answer. I know she knows I did it on purpose and find a little gratification that she isn't pissed about it.

"I guess now we need to negotiate how to get it back," I suggest.

"It will be at the front desk for you tomorrow."

Walking over to the large window in the living room, I look out across Memphis. It's beautiful this time of the evening, the buildings lit up by the early evening sun behind them. Something about the scene makes me want to watch it, breathe it in. Maybe that's what I need.

"I was afraid to leave it there overnight," she continues, "so I just brought it home with me. I'll drop it off on the first floor when I go in tomorrow."

Ding! Ding!

"Ah, that's nice of you, Dani—"

"It's Danielle."

"—but I have plans tonight so I really need my wallet."

There's no response, no witty comeback or snort that I'm crazy. I take it as a good sign.

"Should I just come over and get it?" I prod.

"No," she says hurriedly. "I'm sorry you have plans. I guess you'll have to cancel them."

Wincing at her taking my comment the wrong way, I try to backtrack. "Maybe I can change them."

"Do what you want. I'll have it at the front desk tomorrow."

"Do you mean that?" I grin.

"What?"

"For me to do what I want?"

She laughs, knowing where I'm headed with this. "No, no, I don't. I get in at eight thirty. You can pick it up any time after that."

"I'll see you around eight thirty then. I'll bring you coffee. How do you like it?"

"I don't."

"Oh, I promise you will."

The little intake of breath brushes through the phone, and every cell in my body feels it. I can see her face, the pink of her cheeks matching the shirt she wore yesterday. Her long lashes widening as she unmistakably reads the innuendo I threw in there. Before I know it, my breath is as ragged as hers. "Lincoln . . ."

"Meet me tonight. If you don't want me going to your house, that's fine. But meet me somewhere."

"Where?" she nearly whispers.

"Riffle Steakhouse."

"We aren't having dinner. It's me giving you the wallet back."

"It's me thanking you."

"If you want it tonight, no dinner."

"Oh, I want it tonight," I smirk, choosing to just lay it out there. "I've wanted it since I saw you, and I'm fairly certain you do too. I will say, I like the way you negotiate," I crack.

"What do you mean?"

"They always want dinner first."

She scoffs. "You are too much, Landry."

"Have you heard of Freeman Park? It's on 57th," I ask.

"Yes."

"Be there in an hour."

"Okay."

I start to click off my phone, my body on high alert, when I hear her try to speak.

"Hey—" she starts to say, but I hang up before she can change her mind.

EIGHT

DANIELLE

MY CAR SLIDES BENEATH A large oak tree with a placard about feeding the Freeman Park wildlife. From this angle, I can see most of the greenery tucked away behind a row of oversized evergreens. The park is almost nestled inside the trees, fields of green expanding for acres. There are little tables and sheds and play equipment sprinkled throughout.

I climb out of the car and look for him. After a few long minutes, my gaze falls on a picnic table near a little pond in the back corner. A man sits on the top, his back to me. It isn't just a man though. With a grey sweatshirt stretched across a broad, thick back, a few strands of sandy brown hair peeking out from below a purple baseball cap, it's Lincoln. It has to be. No one else can look that delectable, that unintentionally sexy.

Damn him.

I force my feet to keep going forward. This is dangerous. *He* is dangerous. My willpower is skirted, chipped away with every interaction, and I'm feeling very bare these days.

You must stay strong. Don't give in to temptation. Don't . . .

He reaches over his head, his shirt pulling up so I can see the skin on his side. The thick muscle that wraps from his front to back bulges, rolling as he moves.

I'm so screwed. No, I'm not. I'll hand him his wallet and go home. No sex.

Well, maybe. No! No sex, Danielle.

I'm not screwed. I'm about to be fucked.

Like he has all the time in the world, he glances over his shoulder. Bit by bit his face is revealed to me. His sculpted cheekbones are followed by his sharp jawline peppered with a five o'clock shadow. His full lips are displayed, then his brooding eyes that light up as they meet mine somewhere over the gravel between us.

"Hey," he says. His voice is balmy, welcoming, but he doesn't move.

"Hey." I try to suck in a breath to regain my composure but am hit with the essence of Landry and blow it out instead. It's not helping. "I have your wallet."

My words stumble out of my mouth. Something about seeing him in a place that I don't hold the advantage has me flailing a bit, my typical confidence floating somewhere on the little ripples in Lake Freeman. I have to get it back. It's the only weapon I have against this force sitting in front of me.

I glance around the park, only to find it deserted. Royal purples and lively pinks spatter the blue sky as the sun hovers over the top of the evergreens as it descends.

Turning to face him, I extend the leather in my hand. I wait for him to take it. He doesn't. After a few moments, my hand falls back to my side, and he scoots across the table, making room for me.

"I love it here," he says, taking in the ducks bobbing on the water. "It reminds me of a lake at home. My brothers and I all learned to swim there."

"How many brothers do you have?"

"Three. Assholes, all of them," he says before glancing down at the picnic table. "You going to sit or what?"

My brows tug together, and I want to say no, that he should take his wallet and I should go. Instead, I find myself climbing on the bench and resting beside him. Out of the corner of my eye, I see a look of satisfaction splashed on his face.

"I was kidding about my brothers being assholes. They're all good guys. My dad would still whip the shit out of us if we weren't."

"Yeah, well, my dad is an asshole," I huff before I can think about it. I fidget with his wallet in my hands. "I think my father was so disappointed that I was a girl that he was afraid to try again. Try growing up knowing that."

"Maybe he thought he hit the jackpot and was afraid of being disappointed the next go-round."

Trying to return his smile, my attempt lacks any genuineness. There's nothing to smile about when it comes to my parents. Lincoln picks up on it, watching me curiously.

"I'll save you the trouble of trying to figure it out," I offer. "My father wanted a boy more than he's ever wanted anything in his life. He named me Ryan Danielle. That's how bad he wanted a son."

"Ryan is kind of sexy," Lincoln whispers.

My shoulders rise and fall as I try not to focus on the fact that it does sound sexy coming out of his lips. I also heave away the little fact that I'm sitting next to him, talking about our families. "It doesn't matter. I hate it," I spill. "I grew up knowing I would never be good enough for my parents, and my name is just another reminder of that."

"Is that why you always correct me when I call you Dani? Because you think it's a boy's name?"

When I don't respond with words, just the sobering of my features, the playfulness vanishes from his. "That's bullshit," he gruffs. "Your name is who you are. You shouldn't get a bad vibe every time someone says it."

"Well, I do. I can't help it."

His lips twist together, his foot tapping on the bench. We sit in silence for a while, the autumnal wind making me pull my knit jacket tighter. I do it out of knowledge that it's probably cold and that's what

I should probably do. I don't feel anything other than the warmth from sitting next to Lincoln though.

This is unexpected. The flirting, the joking—that I was prepared for. But this side of him? This serious part, this section of his personality that's almost like I've known him forever rips the guard right down from around my heart. It's as easy to talk to him about these painful things as it is to joke about his body. That's both amazing and nerve-wracking.

"I'm going to keep calling you Dani. You need to embrace who you are. And," he says, leaning so close to me that I can feel the warmth of his breath on my cheek, "you are seriously hot."

The smile stretches across my cheeks before I can stop it. He delights in my reaction, his own cheeks splitting with a wide grin. I thrust his wallet in his hands and laugh, not able to look at him.

"Fuck your dad," he says like he's joking, although I'm not one hundred percent sure he is. He tucks his wallet in his pocket.

My spirits dip as Lincoln's words land on my ears and heart. "You probably wouldn't think that if you knew him."

"Any man that makes his daughter feel that way, yeah, I don't care if he's the fuckin' Pope, I'll guarantee you I wouldn't like him."

"He's not the Pope," I laugh, "but he's kind of a big deal. People love my parents."

"I don't. I love . . ." He leans forward, his eyes wide, watching for my reaction. As I pull slightly away, whispers, "I love ice cream. Wanna go get some?"

My laughter mixes with his, but when his shoulder bumps mine, I can barely breathe. Lincoln moves closer to me in one easy, graceful move.

"Is that a yes?" he asks.

"No. I should be heading home," I say, tucking a strand of hair behind my ear. "I hope you get done whatever you need to with the wallet you just *had to have* back tonight."

He shrugs, pressing his lips together in a mischievous look. "I was hoping for dinner with a slightly irritating lady I met on the wrong floor."

"Slightly irritating? That's how you would describe her?" I ask, raising a brow.

"All right," he sighs, rolling his eyes. "She was actually more of a moderate irritator." He flashes me a soft smile, one that is without any of the teasing or jokes. "I'd really like to have dinner with you sometime."

The water laps the shore in front of us. I close my eyes and breathe in the clean air mixed with Lincoln's cologne and feel my shoulders give up some of the stress they've been holding.

"You were great with the kids today," I tell him. When I look over my shoulder, he's watching me closely. "Rocky loved hanging out with you today. You were so patient with him."

He shrugs like it's no big deal. "Yeah, well, it's not the worst way to spend an afternoon." It's him now that's looking across the water, his thoughts going somewhere else. "Kids are so genuine. He wanted some of my time and reminded me to get him a poster," he laughs. "But that's it. They don't want the rest of the shit people usually do."

"I can't imagine."

My heart hurts a little for him, but I don't know why. The look on his face is somber, thoughtful, and I'm sure whatever he's thinking isn't the happiest of thoughts. It's my first reaction to reach for him and hug him like I would one of the kids or Macie or Pepper, but I don't.

"It's a part of the life," he sighs. "I'm lucky to play baseball. I know that. But there are parts of it that sometimes feel . . ."

"Insincere?" I offer.

He looks at me, his head bent to the side. "Yeah," he says, narrowing his eyes.

Before he can start asking questions, I throw it back to him. "You were going to the therapy floor the other day. Are you okay?"

"Maybe. My shoulder is pretty fucked up. I'm doing everything I can to get it healed up so I can be back out there this spring."

"I hope that works out for you."

"Me too." He laces his fingers together and rests them on his knees. "What about you, Dani? What are you working towards?"

"In what way?" I ask, gulping.

"In any way. What are your goals? What do you want to accomplish in your life?"

Leaning away from him, I try to wrap my head around that question. I want to accomplish so much. I want to do so many things, but I don't know how to verbalize them.

When I'm sure he's not going to talk until I answer, I take a deep breath. "Really, Lincoln? I just want to be happy."

"You aren't happy now?"

"Yes and no, I guess," I say, laughing nervously. "I'm doing what I love. I love working with kids and making a difference somehow. But I want more, you know? I want a family someday. I want stability I've never really had. That's important to me."

His lips press together as he takes that in. His gaze pulls away from mine and lands over the water somewhere again.

We sit in silence for a long time, the birds calling to each other and an occasional fish jumping out of the water. I get so lost in the peacefulness of it that I don't notice Lincoln nudge closer to me.

"You chilly?" he asks.

Looking at my arms across my chest, I realize I'm shivering. "I guess so," I laugh.

With a cautious movement, he wraps an arm around my shoulders. At the contact, my breath catches in my throat. He's so warm, so hard, that I've never felt so wrapped up and safe in my entire life.

"Have you always wanted those things?" he asks finally, the gravel in his tone singing through me. "Or did they change?"

"I think I've always wanted them. I've wanted to do different things with my life, not always the job I have, but I think that's a normal part of life. Wanting new things, evolving."

He nods. "Maybe so."

The sun starts to drop behind the trees and a chilly blast of air drifts across the water. "I better get going," I tell him. "I hate driving in the dark."

"Do you have to go far?"

"Not really."

His fingers press lightly into my arm before he unwinds his arm from around me. Taking my hand, he helps me off the picnic table. I expect him to let go as we walk to the car, but he doesn't. My palm fits so snugly inside his, the coarseness of his skin rough against mine. We don't speak until we get to the parking lot.

"Thank you for coming out here," he says, opening the door for me.

"It's really no big deal."

"Will you have dinner with me tomorrow?"

I shouldn't. I could get sucked into this vacuum faster than I ever imagined if I don't watch it.

"I don't know about dinner," I tell him.

"Okay," he gulps. "What about . . . let's play catch."

"What?" I laugh.

He grins. "Meet me back here tomorrow. We'll play catch. You can't even consider that a date," he points out as I start to object. "I'll bring two gloves and a ball and you just have to show up."

I want to say no. Sort of. But there's no saying no to the look on his face.

"What time?" I ask.

"Four-thirty?"

"See you then," I say, sliding into the driver's seat before I agree to anything else. As I drive off, I see him in the rearview mirror looking like the smug Lincoln Landry I know.

NINE

DANIELLE

"I CAN'T BELIEVE I'M DOING this." Climbing out of the car, I try to suppress the excitement that's whirled in my belly all day. I've thought about him since I left here last night—the way he touched me, smiled at me, seemed honestly interested in what I had to say. He's trouble. Deep, deep trouble.

Spying him near the picnic table from last night, I can't help the smile on my face as I approach. He has a glove on one hand and is tossing a ball in the air with the other. When he senses me coming, he smiles wide.

"I was starting to think you backed out on me," he laughs.

"You wish," I tease, tugging at my hoodie. "Did someone tip you off about my skills?"

"I don't need someone to tell me you're skilled," he jokes, leaning in and kissing my cheek. "Now put on this glove and let's get started before I start thinking about all your sundry talents."

He stands a few feet away from me and tosses me a ball. The leather cracks as I catch it and whizz it back to him. His eyes light up. "You weren't kidding. You have played before."

"Yeah," I laugh, rolling my eyes. "I played four years of varsity in high school."

"Impressive." He sends one back to me and I toss it back to him. "What else did you do in high school? I had you pegged for a cheerleader."

"God, no," I laugh. "I played softball and volleyball. I didn't love either one, to be honest, but my parents insisted I do something with my time."

"How can you not love baseball? Or softball, I guess."

I shrug, catching one a little harder. He seems surprised. "I think I would've liked it if there hadn't been pressure on me to be good at them," I say. "I had private coaches and camps and seminars. It was just too much."

"What would you rather have been doing?"

"Painting, maybe," I offer. "I always wanted to try swimming. I loved watching their competitions. I would've sucked though. My boobs are too big."

"Nice problem to have," he teases, making me laugh again.

"What about you? Did you love just baseball?"

He considers this, his features darkening for a long moment. "I do love it. I always have. I liked football too but it was so physical and I didn't want to tear my body up like that."

"That would've been a shame," I smirk.

He catches my toss and winces just a little. "I was better at baseball anyway. It was my thing. In our family, you have to have something you're known for, and baseball was all I really had."

"So if you're a nerd and aren't good at anything, what happens in your family?"

"You're Graham."

This must be a joke of some sort because he bursts out laughing. Although I have no idea why, I'm laughing too. Our voices meld together in the air, his Southern twang and my girly giggle, and I love the way it sounds.

Once we settle down, our game of toss continues. Back and forth the ball goes, a comfortable silence between us. After the fifth or sixth throw, I notice a slight cringe around his eyes.

"Hey," I say, holding the ball. "Does your shoulder hurt?"

"It always hurts some."

"Let's stop. This can't be good for you."

A shy smile touches his lips. He looks at me in a way he hasn't before, like something has shifted between us. "This is the best therapy I've had yet."

"If you mean practicing, it's not," I insist. "Not if it hurts."

I'm not sure what I said, but he laughs. "Gotta push through the pain sometimes, Dani."

"And you have to rest sometimes too, Landry," I sigh.

He holds his glove up and I throw it back to him, gently this time. The thought of him going through the motions pushing through pain hurts my heart. I wonder how many times he's tried to push through injuries and discomfort for another play or another win.

As if he reads my mind, he shakes his head. "I know my limits. I push as hard as I can and stop when I have to. It's a balance because you know you have physical limitations, yet there are all these expectations," he gulps. "It's just a part of the job." He reads my face and his features lighten. "Besides, I've prepared for this my whole life."

"I get what you're saying," I tell him, thinking back to the demands my father put on me growing up to be the best. Years of my life spent pitching two hundred strikes every day without fail. Hours upon hours of time with coaches, dieticians, physical trainers, all to achieve something he wanted. Not me. "I know the pressure to be good at something. I hated it."

"I didn't hate it," he comments. "I just have three older brothers that are all badass in their own way. It's tough living up to that."

"I can't imagine."

"Do you have siblings?"

I catch his toss and hold it in my glove in front of me. "It's just me."

"That must be lonely."

"It is. That's why I want like ten kids."

"Ten kids?" he repeats, his eyes bulging out of his head.

"Maybe not ten," I laugh. "But a bunch. I don't really have a family, so I'm going to make my own someday."

His features twist together, and I don't know what to make of that. Before I can think about it too long, he's closing the distance between us. Standing a few feet in front of me, he brushes a lock of my hair out of my face.

"You look so beautiful," he whispers. "I don't know how a woman can look more beautiful in a hoodie and sweatpants than she does in a dress and heels, but you do."

"So you don't like my dresses?" I tease.

"Oh, I do. Trust me, I do. But I love the way you are so natural right now. So . . ."

"Boring?"

"Interesting."

"Whatever," I laugh. "You're such a charmer."

He takes my hand and pulls me to the picnic table from last night, and we sit in the same spots as before. "I like you better like this," he notes.

"Like what?"

"Out of your domain, as you called it. When we both know we are on equal footing."

"Screw you, Landry," I laugh.

"Yes, please do."

That's all it takes for everything to switch between us. Unlike at the hospital, we are alone. In the course of six words, the lighthearted game changes. Our breathing is as heavy as if we'd just run a mile. Using every bit of self control I have, which is way more than I ever knew I possessed, I tug my gaze away from his. My head is angled so he can't see my face. My eyes squeeze shut in anticipation of his next move because, if I know anything, it's that there will be a next move.

The weight of his touch, forceful yet respectful, rests on the small of my back. I'm aware that I suck in a hasty breath at the contact, but there's no chuckle or tease from him. Watching a bird land on the water, I give myself a few seconds to decide how this goes. Do I want to pursue this moment or do I not?

Tucking my chin against my shoulder, I look up at him through my lashes. "Whatcha doin', Landry?"

"I'm not sure."

My blood pounds through my body, like it's a race to course through my veins. It's dizzying. Then I look into his eyes, those deep, intense swirls of green, and it's all I can do not to tip backwards.

The lights flicker on around the park as the sun continues to creep beyond the horizon. The chatter that rustled out through the trees earlier from other patrons is gone. Everything is quiet, like the world is waiting on the next move as much as I am.

"Can I kiss you?" It's the simplicity of his question, the sweetness of the proposal, that does me in. I'm a goner, putty in his large, calloused, surely capable hands.

"You better."

The corner of his mouth twitches as he leans in and touches his lips to mine. My bones turn to mush, my body temperature melting me from the inside out. The taste of his mouth as his tongue separates my lips and works against mine is hot and sweet, full of everything I feel. He breathes into my mouth, filling me with such a carnal need to feel him in so many ways.

His hands find my waist and he jerks me closer to him, the tips of his fingers digging possessively into my hips. As I moan into his mouth, he clenches harder around my sides, his lips working harder, more urgently against mine. He winds his fist into my hair, creating a knot, and holds it at the base of my neck. Using it to position my face where he wants it, which at the moment is cocked to the side, he slides his kisses off my lips, down my cheekbone, and behind my ear.

They're soft against my skin as they demand a reaction. Like I have a choice. When the stubble of his five o'clock shadow scratches against my neck, I moan much louder than I realize.

He chuckles, his breath scalding against my skin. "Shhh."

"You started this," I say, a giggle in my tone. "You picked the park."

"Because it's the only place I can get you to meet me."

"Because I didn't want this to happen."

He laughs out loud, pulling away from me. "Don't kid yourself, babe. The only reason you came here was for this."

"Liar!" I giggle.

"Oh, you came here because you really wanted to play catch, right?"

"Maybe."

His hands go behind him as he stretches his torso out. "I wanted to take you to dinner and then to my place for dessert. You didn't want that, so I switched to the backup plan."

"Which was?"

"Getting to see you somewhere without a bed instead."

I smirk. "Are you really going to let that stop you?"

He growls as he moves closer. My breath catches at the predatory look in his eye. The playfulness is gone, replaced with a look so intense, so starved, that I actually shiver.

I think he's going to kiss me, but he doesn't. Instead, his hands are wrapped around my waist and he's moving me so I'm standing in front of him. My body obeys, like it's turned over all control.

Maybe it has.

I'm turned and sat in front of him on the ledge of the picnic table. His legs are on either side of mine, my back against his chest. His lips are against my ear, whispering something I can't hear over the anticipation of what he's about to do.

He reclines back just a touch and I lean along with him. His hands find the sides of my thighs, squeezing them. I shiver mercilessly, every synapse firing all at once as he broaches the waistband of my sweatpants. His hands are flat against my skin, not missing an inch of contact on their way down my stomach.

I feel his cock harden against my back. I want to reach behind me and cup it in my hand, massage it through the fabric of his pants, but that would require more coordination than I'm capable of right now. His right hand finds the lace of my panties. One long finger runs from the underside of the wet panel to the top near my belly button.

"God," I gasp, prepared to beg for more. Mentally berating myself for not just letting him come to my house, I try to keep my breathing even. "Landry?"

"Yeah, babe?"

"Make me come."

"Fuck," he groans, the reverberation of his torso just making me wetter. His fingers slide beneath the edge of my panties, this time dipping into the seam and sliding from my clit down to my ass. "I was right."

"About what?" I grimace, raising my hips to try to initiate more contact.

"You want me as bad as I want you."

"You think?" I try not to get exasperated, but it's so hard with his finger slipping up and down my slit, his cock pressing against me. When he chuckles at my response, the urge to get annoyed gets heavier. "If you can't do the job, I can do it myself."

I almost don't get the words out before his finger sinks into my body, making me cry out. "Ah!" I moan, bucking against his hand.

"Shh," he whispers, pressing kisses along the side of my face. "Be quiet."

"I don't care," I cry.

"I can tell," he chuckles again, adding another finger into the mix.

His free hand presses against my belly, holding me firmly against him. My head falls back. My eyes flutter closed as he works his fingers in and out of my opening.

I spread my legs as far as I can, needing, craving, beseeching all the connection he will possibly give me. "Landry," I moan as the pads of his fingers find my clit. "Fuck."

"You would be getting fucked if you weren't so hardheaded," he whispers in my ear. His fingers roll over and over the swollen bud. "That's what you really want, isn't it? You're imagining my cock, the same one that's hard as fuck right behind your ass, sliding inside you. You're thinking about what it would feel like as it swells while buried in your pussy."

"Fuck you," I moan, rocking my hips to meet his hand.

"Next time. Next time, I promise."

My vision is blurred, the buildup quickening, ready to boil over. I suck in a breath.

"You feel so good on my fingers," he says against my ear. "So fucking wet. I can't imagine what you would feel like riding my cock."

"Oh, hell," I moan again as he gives my clit a final flick and sinks his fingers into my opening once again. He wastes no time stroking in and out of me, his pace in beat with my stuttered breaths. My hands grip the sides of his muscled thighs. They flex as my fingers drill through the cotton and into the muscled flesh beneath. "Landry!"

"Come for me, baby," he growls in my ear.

"Just like that? Do it just like that . . . Ah!" My head jerks to the side as my body clenches around his fingers. A dozen lights explode in my vision. He maintains his pace as I come apart. "I can't! Lincoln! I can't! My Godddddd. . . ."

His chest rumbles and I figure he's chuckling at my outburst, but I can't hear him over the roar of blood in my ears. Slowly, I begin my descent back to earth. As if he understands my body, he eases his tempo, and as I still against him, stops.

My hair is a wild mess, my head buried beneath his chin. I'm so content, so beautifully tired, that I want to curl up on his lap and go to sleep. He brushes my hair off my face and kisses my forehead.

After everything that just happened, that's what wakes me back up to reality: the kiss on the forehead. The sweet, delicate kiss on the forehead sends off warning shots in my brain. Even so, I have to literally count to three in my head to make myself sit up, stand, straighten out my clothes, and step off the picnic table.

When I turn back around, he's still sitting there. His elbows on his knees, bent forward. "You good?"

"If you're asking if I enjoyed that, I did," I smile.

He laughs. "I already knew that. I'm asking if you're okay now."

"Why wouldn't I be?"

"Call it a guess."

Sighing, I stick a hand on my hip, hoping it makes me look nonchalant. "I'm fine. Deliciously tired after that little workout." Glancing between his legs, I pull my gaze back to him. "Are you okay?"

He leaps off the table so he's standing beside me. "I'm great."

"But you're still hard," I say, pointing to the protrusion sticking from his pants. "I kind of feel like I should apologize. Or, you know, return the favor."

My mouth waters at the thought of taking him in, showing him the attention he just showed me. That's dashed as he shakes his head.

"Nope. That was perfect."

"But . . ."

"That happens to be the best thing I've ever watched."

"Oh, come on," I laugh, heading towards my car. Why I'm blushing now, after what he just did to me, I don't know. But I am.

"Can I see you again?"

I glance over my shoulder. His cheeks are pink, his hat sitting off-balance on his head.

"Did I tell you Dr. Manning came by my office to see if I knew who you were?" I ask.

"Who in the hell is Dr. Manning?"

"The guy that got off the elevator. In the scrubs. Remember? He asked if you were Lincoln Landry?"

He smirks. "The asshole. Got it."

"Yeah, and he was pretty excited about meeting you, although you denied you were you."

"Ah, he's a fanboy."

"I don't think so," I laugh. "He's a very prominent physician."

"Doctors are fanboys. Trust me," he winks. "Now, I asked if I could see you again."

I look at anything but him. I don't know what to say. Yes, he's fun. And playful. And hot. And considerate and makes me get off like no one I've ever been with. But it won't work. It can't. I don't want it to. "I need to think about it."

His brows pull together. "And why is that?"

"A lot of reasons."

"What do you want?" he asks, slipping his hands in the front pouch of his hoodie. "You want romanced? I'll romance the shit out of you."

I can't help but laugh. "It's not about that."

"Then what is it about?" He sounds genuinely concerned. Or curious. Maybe a mixture of both. "Someone really stuck it to you, didn't they? Who was it?"

"No one. I just know how guys like you tick, and I'm not sure if I can handle it, if you want to know the truth."

He strokes his chin, watching me with a narrowed gaze. All I can do is think about what that scruff would feel like between my legs. "Did he play baseball? Football? Oh, God, don't tell me you were in love with a basketball player!"

"Landry!" I laugh.

"He did play basketball, didn't he? Geez, Dani, I had you figured to be smarter than that."

Opening the door to my car, I stick my keys in the ignition. "He didn't play basketball. I don't even like basketball."

"Thank fuck," he sighs. "But there was someone."

"I didn't say that exactly."

"He's not an Arrow, is he?"

"Why?"

"It's a yes or no kind of question, Dani."

I laugh, unable to stop from smiling at this ridiculously handsome man questioning me. I should be annoyed, but I'm not. I just want to kiss him again, which is exactly why I can't. "No. He isn't an Arrow."

He blows out a breath. "Good. That would've been awkward."

"How do you figure?" I ask.

"It's like dating your best friend's girl. You don't do it."

"Um, we aren't dating."

"What a terrible thing to point out." He leans forward, one hand on my car. "We should fix that, don't you think?"

"No," I reply adamantly, hoping to convince the both of us.

"Come on," he coaxes. "You aren't even mean to me anymore. I'm wearing you down. I can tell."

Rolling my eyes, I grip the gear shifter. I need to get away from this conversation while I can, while I still have some sense about me. "I need to get going."

A look flickers through his eyes as he pushes away from my car. It's not going to be that easy. "Have it your way," he says, a huge smile on his face.

"See you, Landry. And thanks for the orgasm."

He laughs. "The pleasure was all mine. Well, not really, but it was worth it."

With a shake of my head, I pull my door closed and put the car in reverse. I back out and drive away, sneaking one final glance at the sexy man standing in the parking lot, watching me leave.

TEN

LINCOLN

MY PHONE BUZZES THROUGH THE Bluetooth as I take a right onto the freeway. It interrupts the hip-hop station with its shrill ring that tells me it's Graham.

I press the button on the steering wheel. "Hey, G!"

"Why do you sound so chipper?"

"Chipper? I'm not sure that's the right word," I laugh.

"What's up?"

"Just calling to check on your shoulder. Dad said he tried to call you earlier today and you didn't answer."

"I sent him to voicemail," I crack.

"Ballsy," he laughs.

I shrug. "Yeah, well, I have to be in the right frame of mind to talk to him. You know how we are."

"Oil and water?"

"Nah, not that bad. Maybe more like Cardinals and Cubs."

He laughs. "Always the baseball reference."

"Hey, you reference what you know. Baseball is what I know."

"Speaking of which, how's the shoulder?"

"I'll put it to you like this," I say, weaving in and out of traffic before hitting my exit, "my shoulder feels fanfuckingtastic right now."

Graham sighs into the phone. I can hear the dread in it, and I know he's rolling through a million scenarios as to why I'm not giving him a play-by-play of my pain this evening. He probably thinks I've resorted to drugs. Fucker.

"Care to elaborate?" he asks.

"She was so fucking wet," I say, strumming my fingertips on the wheel. "And when she came, her pussy clamped down on my fingers like it was a vice grip. I can only imagine what that would feel like on my cock.

"I should've known . . ."

"Tell the truth—you were sure I was on dope or something, huh?"

"With you, Linc, I'm never sure about anything."

"Which is why you love me. Barrett and Ford are boring. I keep you entertained."

"Hey, speaking of Barrett, he's headed to Tennessee in a few days. There's some convention . . . I can't remember the day, and I'm driving so I can't pull up the calendar. He'll be in Tennessee just overnight. He was mentioning that he wanted to try to see you while he was in the area."

"Is he bringing Alison?" I joke.

Graham snorts and then strings a slew of profanities about someone not using a turn signal. He takes a few seconds to gather himself before he comes back on the line.

"You get so worked up over nothing," I remark. "You're gonna have a heart attack before you're forty. And I'll tell you what, as the second smartest sibling, I'm not about to take over your job. So figure that shit out, will ya?"

"You couldn't do my job, asshole."

"The hell I couldn't." I think about it for a moment. "Yeah, I probably couldn't. You're right. Plus, I'd have to see Dad every day, and that makes me want to shoot myself in the face."

He chuckles. "You know, there's a good chance I'm going to need a secretary soon. Mine just keeps missing more and more, and I'm getting further behind."

"Fire her," I say easily. "Just cut her the two week's check and call it good."

"You ever fired anyone?"

"Nope."

"Yeah. So shut up," he laughs. "I am going to have to do something. But I hate change."

"You'll live." I pilot my SUV into the entrance to my gated community and press the code. The gate rises and I go through. "I'm almost home, G, so I gotta go. You good? Need anything?"

"Nah. Let me know about your shoulder. And for fuck's sake, man, call Dad tomorrow."

"We'll see."

"Talk to you later."

"Later."

Sliding into the garage, I cut the engine and hop out. Stepping over a set of dumbbells, I climb the stairs to the door leading into the laundry room. There's a bounce in my step that even I notice, a little hop that makes me laugh at myself.

I haven't felt like this in a long time. Just happy. Not overcome with a million worries and needing to figure shit out. With her, it's . . . easy. There's no talk of contracts or backup plans or dollar amounts. I'm not sure she even cares. Hell, I'm not completely convinced she wants to see me again. Which is precisely why I have to see her again.

"Danielle Ashley," I say, stripping my clothes to the floor and putting them in the hamper for Rita. "You are one intriguing lady."

***

Danielle

THE WASHCLOTH HITS THE LAUNDRY basket with a splat. I still smell like him. His scent is in my hair, on my skin, and now on the washcloth in my hamper from cleansing between my legs.

I should take a shower, but I don't. Not yet. I just want to feel this little buzz a while longer. I thought maybe when I took off my clothes and put on a robe some of it would vanish, but it didn't. I'm still soaked in Lincoln Landry.

My phone rings in the kitchen and I tighten the tie around my waist and nearly skip in there. I swipe it on with a smile when I see it's Macie.

"Hey," I say happily.

"Wow. What's that all about?"

"What do you mean?"

"Did you get laid?"

My laugh probably confirms something of the sort, but I don't care. I usually try to keep some of my intimate moments private, even from Macie, but not this one. It needs to be celebrated.

"You did!" she exclaims. "It was by the baseball god, right? Please, please let it have been by the baseball god. And please have taken pictures because I want to see his body. I mean, I've seen it online without a shirt, but there are things I'd like to know, and I'm not even sorry I'm saying that about your potential man because *whoa.*"

"Breathe!" I laugh.

"I'll breathe. You talk."

"Okay. Yeah, it was Lincoln. But we didn't have sex," I tell her. "He just fingered me."

"Like in middle school?" she giggles.

"This was nothing like that," I point out. "There was no fumbling, no searching for my clit. Lincoln knew exactly what he was doing." I sigh dreamily. I can't help it. "I mean, it was the most spontaneous, carnal thing I've done in a long time."

"So, details! Fork 'em over, Danielle."

"Lincoln asked me to dinner and I said no. Then he wanted to go play catch and I couldn't think of a reason not to meet Lincoln—"

"You do realize you've said his name like five times in this conversation, right?"

"I have not!"

"You have too!" She smacks her lips together. "You're there, that point where you just want to say his name in a sentence."

"That's not true."

"That is so, so true," she laughs. "It's cute, actually."

I think about that. If it is true, how am I going to feel when this high wears off ? I can't get in over my head here, and I'm aware just how easy that is to do. It's how I do everything, really. I move fast and hard. My therapist told me when I was younger that I wanted someone to love me because I felt neglected by my parents. That I needed someone to protect me from them, not physically, but emotionally. I don't think that's true. I don't search out friendships or relationships. Do I want to connect with someone? Absolutely. But do I bend over backwards for it? No. Still, when I commit, when I go down that rabbit hole, I spiral into the darkness with no parachute. There's no way I'd survive Lincoln Landry.

"So . . . details!" Macie insists. I fill her in on all the things I can make myself say out loud, much to her amusement. "I knew he'd know what he was doing, you lucky duck."

Blowing out a breath, I find myself settling a little. "You know what the scary part is?"

"What's that?"

"That he's fun to talk to," I admit. "He doesn't take himself too seriously and asks questions and seems to care about what I say. He's . . . dangerous to my health," I laugh.

"I think he's perfect for your health. You deserve to have fun, Danielle. Lincoln Landry seems like the answer to your problems."

"Or more problems," I sigh. Already, I want to see him again. I want to hear his voice and smell his cologne and hear him laugh. I want to feel his touch and make him smile and that . . . Is. Not. Good.

"You still here?" Macie asks.

"Yeah, I'm here." I chew on a snagged fingernail. "What's happening with you today?"

She pauses, like she's trying to figure out whether to steer me back to the topic at hand or let me change it. Thankfully, she rolls with me. "Not much. Will is training tonight. They got a new guy in named Pike from somewhere in the South. His accent though," she whistles. "Anyway, he's just training for a few weeks. They think he's going to be something, I guess. It's all I hear about right now."

"Better than baseball."

"Truth," she laughs. "So, what are your plans for Thanksgiving?"

I shrug. "Probably the same as always."

"Want to come to Boston? Julia and I are fixing dinner, and we always make way too much."

"Nah. Thanks, though."

"Did you think about the job? You know, at the foundation with Julia?"

"Honestly, I haven't really given it much thought. Is this a time sensitive thing?"

"I don't think so. She's just getting her ducks in a row."

"Okay, well, let me see what happens at the budget meetings and go from there."

"Sounds like a plan," she yawns. "I'm going to grab a shower and go to bed. Call me later."

"I will."

"Bye."

I end the call, but hold the phone in my hand. For some reason, I don't want to put it down. Realizing how stupid I look standing in the living room, staring at it, I go to sit it down when it buzzes.

My heart leaps when I look at the screen.

Lincoln: Just checking to see if you made it home okay. Let me know when you can.

Hurriedly, I swipe my fingers across the screen.

Me: I made it a while ago. Already cleaned up and getting ready to make some tea.

I watch for his response, but it doesn't come right away. Just as my nerves start to get the best of me, the light goes off.

Lincoln: Thank you for coming tonight.

Me: Is that an innuendo?

Lincoln: Could be. ;)

Me: Well, thank you for having me come. ;)

Lincoln: It was my pleasure. Wait, are we sexting now?

Me: I think sexting includes dick pics.

Lincoln: I'd rather you see it in person. Feel free to send me naked pics of you though. ;)

Me: Yeahhhh. There are no naked pics of me floating in the digital world and I think I'll keep it that way.

Lincoln: Classy. I like it.

Me: I have to make up for letting you finger me on a picnic table today.

Lincoln: I hope you're kidding. That was the best thing I've done in a long fucking time. You're something else, Dani.

Me: It's Danielle. Grr . . .

Lincoln: I like when you growl. And when you moan. And when you get all bossy when you're hot and bothered.

Me: I think I need to go to bed now. LOL Lincoln: Dream of me?

Me: There's a good chance of that since I still smell like you. Lincoln: That's so damn hot. I'm hard again.

Me: Sweet dreams, Landry.

Lincoln: Night, Ryan.

Me: Ugh. Night.

Lincoln: LOL

ELEVEN

DANIELLE

I TYPE THE FINAL WORDS of the email with a flourish and hit "send." It's taken all morning to focus, but I've finally started to get into the flow. That is, until I remember the feel of his hands or the draw of his gaze.

Picking up a pen, I click it against my desktop. The sound ricochets through my office, just like the thoughts of Lincoln ping around in my skull.

I'm a twisted mess. My body is on fire for this man. My brain is on high alert. My heart is desperate to feel the warmth and giddiness of having a man in my life.

"It can't be him," I whisper, rolling the pen against my stapler. "I can't do this with him."

"You can't do what with whom?"

My head snaps to the doorway where my boss, Gretchen, stands. She's looking at me curiously.

"Good afternoon," I say, folding my hands in front of me like I have nothing to hide. "How are you today?"

"Today, I'm curious. What's going on with you?"

"Nothing," I lie.

"Uh-huh." She enters my office and places a set of files in front of me. "Take a look at these when you can. It's the proposed budget. It's a mess, Danielle. If this passes, I fear for our program."

"I really don't see how they can cut us back that sharply. This hospital is known, in part, because of this program. Don't they realize we can't provide the services we do without money?"

"It seems not."

"I'll go over this in a bit," I promise. "I have a few emails to get through and a scheduling issue for next week, then I'll give it a quick look."

With a nod and a half-hearted smile, she bustles out. I'm logging back in to my computer when a knock at the door pulls my attention away.

Lincoln looks almost edible in a pair of loose fitting black shorts and a long sleeved, grey t-shirt. A silver watch sits around his thick wrist, adding a touch of sophistication to his otherwise casual appearance.

Kill. Me. Now.

"Hey," he drawls, his rich, Southern accent pummeling me.

"Hey," I say.

"Can I come in?"

"Sure."

He waltzes in like he owns the place. Every movement is so fluid, so graceful, that I can only imagine what he's like when he's moving over me. Beneath me. Behind me.

When I look at him with flushed cheeks, he smirks. "What were you thinking?"

"That you weren't supposed to be here today," I deflect.

He sits across from me after swinging the door shut. His feet are shoulder width apart, his arms resting on the sides of the chair. "I forgot."

"You did not," I laugh. "You just do whatever you want."

He leans forward, his elbows now on his knees. He peers at me from across my desk, his eyes a potent mix of greens and blues. "Trust me when I say I don't just do whatever I want."

"You do," I shrug. "You figure out a way to get your way."

"If I had my way, you'd be lying on your desk with your ankles wrapped around my back right now, making all those sexy little sounds that I can't get out of my head."

I want to look away from him. I should. But he holds me in place with his gaze, steadying me even when I feel like I'm on the cusp of falling apart.

"Have dinner with me this weekend."

"That doesn't sound like a question."

"Will it help if I demand it?" I flash him a look that makes him smile. "Didn't think so," he laughs.

"I have work to do, you know."

"I have dinner reservations to make. Where do you want to go?"

Sighing, I lean back in my chair.

If I'm honest, I love his determination. I just don't understand *why*. He wants nothing more than a distraction from whatever is going on in his life. It's the off season. He has time to kill. That's how this works, and I'm all for a little sexual recreation, but I know better than to think that's all it will be for me with him. I can't risk that.

"Why are you doing this?" I ask.

"Doing what?"

"Not letting it go."

An easy chuckle drifts across the desk and tickles my ears. "Because I don't want to."

"You're impossible," I say, wanting to be annoyed but just not able to find it.

"What do you want, Danielle?"

"To finish my work."

He tsks me. "I'm not leaving until you answer me for real."

"I want . . ." I take a deep breath. I know exactly what I want, but it's not something I can explain in five minutes. Nor is it something I think matters anyway. "It's more about what I don't want, really."

He watches me, his chin cupped in his right hand. "Well? I'm waiting."

"You know what I don't want? I don't want to get all tied up in something that isn't real."

"Sounds fair. So go to dinner with me. Somewhere public, somewhere that I can't just maul you."

"I might like you mauling me," I point out, pressing my lips together.

His eyes darken. "You have no idea how much I'd love to maul you right fucking now." He leans back, his chin pointing towards the ceiling. "But here's the thing, Dani: as much as I want to maul you, I also want to talk to you. Hear your laugh. Watch your smile. You're making a mess of me over here."

My cheeks hurt from smiling as I fight so hard succumbing to him. "You are too good for your own good," I tell him.

"You haven't seen anything yet."

"Get out of here," I laugh, feeling the last bit of restraint wither away.

"Fine, fine." He unfolds himself from the chair in one simple movement. "I'm going to warn you though: be at Spora's at eight o'clock on Saturday. My buddy, Fenton Abbott, owns it and I'll get us a table. And, Dani—I will show up here every day if you don't. I can be a thorny fucker."

He's out the door before I can get a word out.

TWELVE

DANIELLE

SPORA'S IS BUSTLING. LOCATED ON the bluff overlooking the river, it's the hottest restaurant in the city. I've been here once. It was the only time my parents visited Memphis, not really me. They were here for three days for a convention. We had dinner once.

The front is dark with clear lights twinkling in the front beneath a large, red lettered sign spelling out the name. My heels click against the sidewalk as I reach the door. A man in a suit opens it.

The lights overhead have an antique, industrial look and the bulbs cast a yellow glow over the dark wood inside. My stomach is in knots as I approach the reception desk. "I believe there's a reservation for Landry."

Her eyes widen. "Yes. Give me a moment." She waves a man over from the bar lining the wall on the right. "Can you escort her to the balcony?"

"Follow me," he says, leading me along a walkway at the front of the restaurant to a little elevator tucked on the other side. He pushes a button and the doors swing open. We enter, and as I'm struggling to not let my nerves get the best of me, they pop open again. We're in another hallway with six different doorways spaced evenly apart. We walk to the first one to the right and he knocks gently. He waits a few seconds before pushing it open.

My palms are sweating as I prepare to see Lincoln. We've talked and texted over the last few days. It's been light and funny, and I've found myself laughing more, smiling more, even when I'm not with him. It's the Landry effect. I keep reminding myself this is for fun, for the off season, to keep it in perspective. He makes that seriously hard to do.

Giving myself a quick inspection, I'm confident in the dress I chose. A navy blue lacy overlay atop a silky fabric, the halter top shows off my toned arms, and the way the bottom hits mid-thigh will hopefully give him ideas.

Filling my lungs with precious air, I fight to stay calm. I almost cancelled this a hundred times since he left my office. I shouldn't be here. It's only going to lead to disappointment.

My breath catches in my throat as he comes into view.

Scratch that. It's going to lead to an orgasm and he's not even going to have to touch me.

He's standing at the table, a tumbler of a clear liquid in his hand. Dressed in a pair of slim fit khaki pants, a deep brown leather belt winds around his trim waist. A black dress shirt, rolled up to the elbows and the top couple of buttons undone, and I want to devour him. Throw him on the ground and just go for it.

I wonder vaguely if the rooms are soundproof as he walks to me. It's an unhurried movement, like he knows that every second I have to anticipate his hug or kiss on the cheek gets me one second closer to combusting. The door shuts as the waiter leaves. I force a swallow, my mouth dry and hot. The light catches on the face of his watch and just amplifies how much he looks like he walked off a movie set.

Dear God.

The glass isn't in his hand anymore when he reaches me, and I have no idea where it went. All I can see are his arms reaching for me, and I hold my breath as he makes contact.

His right hand lands on the small of my back as he leans in and kisses me on the cheek. When he pulls back, both spots immediately feel cold.

"You look gorgeous," he says. Taking a step back to see me better, I feel his gaze scorch a path from my eyes, down my neck, across my breasts, all the way to my feet. "Just gorgeous, Dani."

I don't even correct him. I can't. I can't find my voice.

This is the first time seeing him in something other than sweatpants or shorts. I might've thought I was prepared, but I'm not. He's divine. Classy. Sophisticated. Yet, a little rogue.

He takes my hand, his palm wide and warm, and leads me to the table. Pulling out my chair like a gentleman, he waits for me to sit. Once I'm settled, he disappears for a moment before returning with a bouquet of white roses.

"Lincoln! They're beautiful," I say, taking the flowers from him. As I lean in to take a deep breath, I notice one pale pink rose hidden in the midst of the cream ones. I look at him. He's smiling. "I'll bite. Why is there one pink one?"

"Because there's always one that stands out from the bunch, just like you."

My jaw drops as I swoon. "Wow," I laugh. "That's good."

His chuckle joins mine as he sits across from me. "It is, right? I can't take credit for it. I called my sister, Sienna, and she offered it up." His brows pull together. "I hope that doesn't take away from the gesture."

"It doesn't," I say, smelling the flowers again. "Thank you."

A waitress comes in and sits the vase on a wet bar and takes our order. Once we have wine, we're alone again.

"I was afraid you weren't going to show," he says with a twinkle in his eye.

"You knew I'd come."

"I know you'll come if you want to."

We exchange a smoldering look. He tugs at the collar of his shirt. "You really do look gorgeous, Dani. I wish now more than ever I would've picked you up and gotten the privilege of walking in with you on my arm."

"You picking me up would've been pushing it," I laugh. "One step at a time."

"One step at a time," he repeats. "How was your day? Anything interesting happen? Did the asshole doctor stop by?"

"No," I giggle. "What did he ever do to you?"

His head cocks to the side. "He thinks he has a chance with you."

"So do you," I point out with a tease in my tone.

"Damn right I do," he says with zero playfulness in his. "I deserve it."

"You deserve it?" I ask. "Really, Landry? Explain to me how you deserve a chance with me."

He leans in, his features looking sharper, more regal in the light. "I want to know everything about you. The way you feel under my hands as I'm buried inside you, but I also want to know what makes you tick. How to make you laugh. The reasons you stay awake at night. What makes you smile."

How do I respond to that? My heart tugs as I have to deal with his out-and-out declaration of what he wants. This I didn't even try to prepare for. If he weren't so damn genuine, it would help. If only he could give me a glimpse into the athlete inside him, it would help. If he weren't so fucking sexy, that would really, really help.

"If your sister told you to say all these things, she should really start a romance column," I laugh, trying to avoid having to address his words specifically.

"Nah," he grins. "She just helped on the flowers. I'm winging the rest of it, relying on the ol' Landry charm."

"It's working for you." I take a sip of my wine and notice he winces as he picks up his glass. "How does your shoulder feel?"

He sighs. "Honestly, it's a little sore. I haven't thrown a ball since the last one I threw that tore it, so it's a little stiff."

"Oh!" I exclaim. "We didn't have to play catch. Now I feel bad!"

His laugh rolls over the table. "I can honestly say I haven't had that much fun playing ball in a while."

"I'll feel terrible if it messes up your therapy."

"It won't." He takes a long drink. "Did Rocky miss me today?"

I can't help but laugh. "He did. He drew you a picture, but I forgot it on my desk. It's of a bird and a pig, I think. But your Van Gogh reference was a little misleading."

He grins. "I was online last night really late because I never sleep these days."

"Thinking of me?" I say, batting my lashes.

"Some," he winks. "I found a painting class across town on Saturday afternoons. Have you thought about doing that?"

I can't believe what I'm hearing. My hand stills around the stem of the wine glass and I smile at him. "What made you think of that?"

"You said you liked painting. Or you did when you were younger," he blushes, looking down. "Maybe that was stupid."

"That's not stupid at all," I whisper, my voice full of emotion. "I can't believe you remembered that."

He shrugs like it's no big deal, but also like he's embarrassed. I reach out and place my hand on top of his. The contact brings his gaze to mine.

"Thank you," I tell him, hoping my earnestness says what I'm trying to say.

"For what?"

"For listening to me."

He laughs, lacing our fingers together. We both look at our hands on the table, moving them around in the candlelight. His palm envelops mine, the roughness of his in contrast to the softness of mine. He brings them together and kisses them.

"You know, since I got hurt, I've struggled," he says, clearing his throat and sitting our hands on the table again. "I've been a little lost. I mean, I play baseball. It's what I do. Or what I've always done," he says, his voice distant for a split second. "I was really having a hard time. But since I got off that elevator and chased you to your office, things haven't seemed so bad."

"You have to do what you can for your shoulder and let it be," I say. But as soon as the words are out of my mouth, I realize that's not what he meant.

"Life hasn't seemed so bad," he clarifies. "Not that it seemed bad before, but the entire thing was getting old. The parties. The trips. All of it," he says, his cheeks blushing a little.

"You mean the naked pictures?"

He bursts out laughing. "Those too. I shut my 'baseball phone' off, as a matter of fact. But it was like cutting off a part of me and I didn't know how to fill my time."

"So you've filled it with what?"

"Things," he grins. "Ideas. Thoughts."

The waitress comes in again and sets a plate of food in front of each of us, refills our glasses, and disappears.

The moonlight shines behind Lincoln, almost illuminating him. A cool breeze trickles in through the open glass doors, yet we're not cold. I'm not sure if it's from the excitement of being with him or if there's a heater somewhere. Either way, it's so comfortable, so cozy tucked in this little room that I don't want to leave. I just want to sit here and stare at this handsome man.

He slices through his steak, spearing a piece. "Want to try it?"

I don't really want to, but I'm not turning down the opportunity for him to feed me. "Sure," I say, opening my mouth a touch and leaning forward. He gulps, his Adam's apple bobbing as the fork extends over the candles in the center.

My lips wrap around the silverware, my eyes focused on his. His pupils dilate as I pull back slowly, running my tongue along the bottom of my lip.

"Keep it up," he warns, resting his fork on the side of his plate.

"And what?"

"And we will jump to dessert right here, right now."

The authority in his tone goes right to the apex of my thighs. I can feel my muscles pull together, my panties dampening. "Promise?"

He pulls his lip between his teeth, chuckling mischievously. "Careful what you wish for, babe."

"I'm pretty certain I know exactly what I'm wishing for," I say, taunting him. "It involves your tongue running up my—"

"Stop," he laughs, shaking his head. "Even if we leave now, it'll take ten minutes to deal with the check, and I'm going to need to get you out of here in way less than that."

Smiling, I spear a tomato and bring it to my lips. "I'd call for the check now then."

"Damn you, woman," he says, jumping to his feet. The door opens and shuts behind me, and for the first time since walking in this room, I take a long, deep breath.

I both know what's coming and have no idea what's coming. Where will we go? What will he do? All I know is that I want the answers to both those questions. And if it fucks me in the long run, so be it. I just need fucked right now.

The sound of the door opening rolls through the room and his hands are on my shoulders. "Let's go."

"You paid that fast?"

"Fuck yeah, I did. Want to follow me to my house or just ride with me?"

Getting to my feet and grabbing the vase, I look at the most dazzling man I've ever seen. "I'll be riding enough later. I'll follow you."

***

Lincoln

"SLOW DOWN," I REMIND MYSELF. Glancing in the rearview mirror, I see her puttering behind me as slow as molasses. I can't help but laugh at her little law abiding self.

My fingers tap against the steering wheel as I hum along with the radio. I have a rule about bringing girls to my house. I simply don't do it. I go to theirs or get a hotel room because you never know what's going to go down after it *goes down*. But the thought of having Dani in my house seems right.

I'm scared as fuck. I've had relationships before. Serious ones, even. I'm good at them, if I do say so myself. My mom and sisters taught me a thing or two about girls. Even with my past girlfriends, I've never felt like this. Before, they did their thing and I did mine. I'd send flowers when I needed to or make sure they had a cute dress to wear to an event, but that was it. There was no desire to actually get to know them. As a matter of fact, I'm not sure there was much about them to know.

Dani is not that way. She makes it easier to be with her than to be without her. She's not needy and I love that. She asks about things, but not like she's digging for information. It's like she actually gives a fuck.

We've talked late into the night every night this week and when we hang up, I want to call her right back. I tell her stories about my brothers and sisters and growing up in Savannah. She tells me stories about volunteering at a children's hospital in college and how she hopes to do something bigger with her life than just a nine-to-five.

I love that. I respect that. I admire that. I admire her.

I might be screwed.

THIRTEEN

DANIELLE

HE'S WAITING ON ME IN the driveway, leaning against the side of his charcoal grey SUV, his keys twirling in the air. "You are the slowest driver ever," he laughs as I climb out of my car.

"I had to exceed the speed limit by fifteen miles per hour to *almost* keep up with you." I smack him when I reach him. "What's the hurry, Landry?"

His arms fall around me, his hands locking at the small of my back. He pulls me to him. "You are the hurry," he whispers. "Next time we ride together."

We exchange a look and I read exactly what he's saying: that he doesn't want to rush this, even though he does. I'm feeling the same way. The ride over gave me a second to regain some control and I want to keep that. At least for a bit.

He laces his fingers through mine and leads me to the front door. A key switches in the lock and we step inside.

"Bachelor pad much?" I comment, taking in the interior. It's stark white walls and light gold carpeting mixed in with dark hardwood and bright white tile. It's expensive with all the trendy, newer hallmarks yet lacks a feel of being lived in. Even the pictures dotting the walls look like they were hung up there solely to break the vacant feeling.

He shrugs. "I don't live here much. I'm on the road half the year and the other half, I'm usually out with friends or visiting my family." He shrugs again.

"There are no personal touches at all," I note. "This doesn't feel like you, Landry."

He cocks his head to the side. "What feels like me?"

"Well," I gulp, looking around again. "Something more masculine. Warmer colors, maybe. I expected art, for some reason."

He grins. "I agree." He turns away and heads into the kitchen. "Want a drink?"

"Uh, sure." I follow him into a room at the back of the house. Viking range, stainless steel refrigerator, marble countertops—it's a kitchen to die for. But I'm pretty sure it's never actually been used.

After offering me from a basic selection of drinks, he hands me a glass. We both take sips, feeling each other out. Finally, I break the ice.

"What do you do when you're home? I've heard a lot of athletes play video games or work out for hours on end. What's your jam?"

"I lift some. Run some. Play a little video games, but I'm pretty much over that. Some guys do it all the time though. I don't know how they do."

"I've never gotten into that whole thing," I say. "I've heard yoga is really good for athletes. It stretches you all out in different ways."

He makes a face. "I'll be your yoga instructor. Stretch you out in all kinds of ways."

I swipe at him playfully, making him laugh.

"No to yoga," he says. "It's a girlie thing. Unless you're doing it and then I'll stand right behind you."

"Oh, that's what I want you to see! My ass in downward facing dog."

His eyes darken. "I'd love to see you from every angle."

My mouth goes dry from his gaze. This is the moment I've waited on for days now, the situation I've fantasized about. With a slightly shaking hand, I reach for his belt and begin undoing it.

His eyes hood, making me squirm. I yelp as his hands find my waist and I'm hoisted in a circle and sat on top of the cool marble. His hands are on either side of me, caging me in.

"What are you waiting on?" I pant, cupping his face in my hands. His cheeks are rough, the stubble biting into my skin. He watches me, his gaze penetrating mine.

"It's different this time, don't you think?"

"How?"

"I know what you're going to feel like, what you sound like, what you taste like."

"How do you know that?" I pant.

"You don't think I tasted you off my fingers before?"

"Oh, God," I moan.

"But tonight, I get to experience you. Feel you. Taste you first hand. Feel you squirt in my mouth—"

"Stop," I say like I've run a mile.

"Spread your legs, beautiful."

With no hesitation, I part my legs as his hands cup my ass and he slides me to the end of the marble. He wastes no time sliding his tongue into my mouth, caressing mine. I forget about my parted legs until his knuckles brush against the sensitive skin of my inner thigh. I shudder.

His left hand is on the back of my head, keeping my head from pulling away from him. I can barely compute anything; too many fireworks are exploding in too many regions.

My thumbs brush his cheeks before I find the silky strands of his hair. Lacing my fingers through them, I tug slightly. It elicits a moan from his throat and that does it for me. I'm so wet I can feel it coating my legs. He does too because his eyes flash open for one brief moment, a look of pure lust written all over them. And when he realizes I'm not wearing any panties, I feel him melt against me.

He slips one finger, quickly followed by a second, into me. I suck in a breath, only to have it stolen by Lincoln's kisses. He works his fingers in and out as he shifts his weight from one foot to the other.

Just as he's finding a steady pace, he stops. Before I can object, I'm lifted by the waist. My legs instinctively wrap around him, his hands beneath the globes of my ass. The skin almost stings as his fingers kiss into my flesh.

I have no idea where we're going, and I can't even see from the merciless assault of his lips. We bump into walls, into corners, as he makes our way down a dark hallway.

Turning one corner a little too sharply, a picture falls from the wall and crashes on the floor. Gasping for air, I'm laid on a king sized bed with silky silver-grey sheets. Sitting up, I try to work my zipper down in the back in a rush when I hear his voice low and gravelly.

"Let me," he says.

I still. He peers down at me, a small smile on his lips. One knee is on the mattress, then the other. He is behind me in a flash. With a gentle hand, he brushes my hair to one shoulder and tugs on the zipper at my neck.

I shiver, more from his touch than the air hitting my exposed skin. Looking straight ahead, I feel the zipper slowly roll towards the small of my back. It finally hits the end. His hands, so rough and hardened, push the fabric at the shoulders so it falls to my waist. I feel his lips press a kiss at the base of my neck.

Glancing at him over the corner of my shoulder, I watch him unbutton his shirt. As each inch of skin is displayed, I feel my heart-beat pick up until the shirt is tossed on the floor, and I'm on the brink of a heart attack.

He steps off the bed and removes his shoes and pants. I shimmy out of my dress and toss it to the floor, freezing when I catch him staring at me.

"What?" I ask, feeling, for the first time, self-conscious.

"Damn, baby."

"What?" I ask again, feeling my nipples harden under his observation.

"You just make me want to stand here and stare at you, you're so goddamn beautiful."

"Stop, Landry," I blush. "Not that I'm opposed to appreciating the view because your body is seriously . . . You're incredible."

"I know."

I burst out laughing, crooking my finger. "But now's not the time for that. I need fucked."

Using those stellar baseball reflexes, I'm on my back and he's hovering over me before I see it coming.

"It's about time," I say breathlessly, slipping my hand between us and grabbing his cock. "Just like I thought."

"What's that?"

"Size thirteen."

"What?"

"Never mind," I giggle. "I want to feel you inside me."

"You," he says, his mouth up against my ear, "are going to be the death of me."

"Don't die until after you fuck me, please."

He takes a nibble at the shell of my ear, making me shriek and writhe beneath him. He uses my movement against me, or for me, depending, and I feel his girth at my opening.

I still and hold my breath. His arms, those sinewy, muscled arms, cage me in on either side of my head. A sinful smirk plays on his lips as he swirls his hips and drags his cock through my wetness. I move, attempting to get some friction against my needy clit. I dig my nails into his ass to convince him to go.

"Do I need to use a condom?" he asks.

"I'm clean and on the pill," I say.

"I get checked every six months. I'm clean."

"Then get on with it, Landry, I—" My sentence is halted by a yelp as he pushes into me with one long, hard, owning push. "Ah!" I squeal, panting.

"You like that?"

"God, yes," I breathe, my eyes rolling to the back of my head.

He's watching me and I'd like to be able to hold my ground and gaze, but I can't. It's impossible. He knows this. He likes this, the cocky bastard.

"You are so fucking sexy," he almost growls as he strokes his cock in and out of my pussy. "Damn it, Dani. You feel better than I even imagined."

"Do I?" I ask, reaching my hands behind me and gripping the pillows. "Do I turn you on, Landry?"

"You know you do. You feel how hard my cock is."

"For me."

"For you."

"Ah!" I moan as his strokes become harder. "Yes! This!"

My entire body is on fire, my breasts bouncing with each thrust. He drives into me, hitting that spot in the back of my vagina that is a trigger to an orgasm. "I'm going to come."

"Come all over my cock," he growls.

"Fuck!" I scream as my vision is dotted with an array of colors. The build-up starts at my pussy and rolls, like lava, through my body. In a matter of seconds, I feel the energy pulsing through my toes and the top of my head. "Lincoln!"

He doesn't slow down, just massages that spot with his swollen head. When my eyes can open again, I see his skin is broken out in a glisten of sweat.

Pulling his cock out so just the tip sits in my opening, he grins. "Up." He rocks back on his heels.

Confused and still out of breath, I try to sit up. He bends down, touching his lips to mine, before wrapping an arm around my waist and twisting me on my hands and knees. A quick slap collides with my bare ass.

"Hold on, baby," he says.

Before I can hold on or get my wits about me, he's once again at my opening and thrusting in.

"Shit," I mutter, clenching my teeth. One hand grips the bend of my waist, the other sitting on the end of my spine. His thumb plays against my ass, applying concerted pressure over the opening in the back. "I can't," I groan, knowing good and well that I can. And I want to.

He chuckles behind me. "We'll save that for another day."

"One day at a—" I start but am stopped by another smack to my rear. "Landry!"

He laughs again, both hands now digging into my sides, as he builds me up with quick, powerful strokes.

"You feel so good," he growls, finding that spot once again. "I can't hold back for long."

I wait a few thrusts, making sure the rush of the climax is coming.

Once the sparks start shooting through my veins, I yell, "I'm coming!"

He grunts behind me, going harder than ever before. Hearing him come apart only adds to the intensity of my own fall. My arms can't hold up, turning to jelly, and I make it just until his last hiss of breath before I collapse onto my belly.

In an instant, he's curled up behind me, dragging me into him.

I'm going to have to get up and clean myself in a second. But for now, I'll stay right here, tucked safely in the arms of this delicious man.

FOURTEEN

DANIELLE

I SNUGGLE IN CLOSER, ONE arm draped across his chest and dangling off the side. There should be no cuddling right now. I should be in my damn car and driving home. Alas, here I am. Tucked into his side. Feeling him draw what I believe are baseballs on my back with the tip of his finger.

"I'm hungry now," he says.

"Well, I'm not cooking."

"Damn right you're not."

"And why is that?"

"Because I had to fight like hell to get you into my bed. You aren't wasting time by spending it in my kitchen."

I just snuggle into him more.

"I like when you do that," he admits. "It makes me feel . . . happy, I think."

"You think it makes you happy? That's a weird thing to say."

"Maybe." He kisses the top of my head. "Things feel different these days."

"How?"

His chest rises as he fills it with air. "I'm not sure," he says finally.

"Before this injury, I didn't have time to think about much. I just went from game to practice to game to a party. I didn't just lie in bed and contemplate the world, you know?"

"So you're lying here considering world peace?" I tease. "Good to know."

"The only *piece* I'm thinking about right now is this one," he says, turning onto his side and looking at me in the eye. "I've just had some time to myself without anything to do. It's made me think about things."

"Sounds dangerous."

"It does, doesn't it?" He gives me a grin I haven't seen before. It's sweet and soft and I want to lift up and press a kiss to his parted lips. So I do.

Nestling back against him, I'm falling hard and fast just like I knew I would. He's too easy to be around—too kind, too sexy, too sweet. I can try to play like I don't realize it, but it would be a big, fat lie. I don't know that it's love or just unbridled lust, but whatever it is, it has me wrapped up tight.

"You know you're all I've been thinking about right?" he whispers.

My heart stills. I let my fingers drift up his bicep and back down again, watching the goosebumps pop up in their wake. "Sounds about right," I joke.

"Who's cocky now?" he laughs.

"Cocky? I call it logical. You think about me. It happens. But prepare yourself: you'll just think about me more now that you've had me in the sack."

"That's the truth."

I feel him quiet against me, his palm lying flat against the top of my ass. It's a long couple of minutes before he outlines what I think are baseball bats.

"Where does this put us?" he asks. Hope drips through the question and lands right on my heart.

I pull away and look up in his eyes. My own hope is reeling all too high and I have to be smart. "Let's just take it one day at a time."

"I told you," he says, "I'm always a step ahead. We call it a bird-dog step in baseball." He lets his head burrow into the down pillow and he pulls me up under his chin again. "Why won't you just admit you want to be with me?"

"I will admit it," I say simply. "I want to be with you."

"You are the most confusing woman I've ever met."

I smile. "I'm not confusing. I'm fairly simple, actually."

"Then help me out here, Ms. Simplicity. If you know you want to be with me, and it's obvious I want to be with you," he says, rolling his hips against me so I can feel him, "why aren't we together?"

"We are." I swing a leg over his hips. "Feel me? I'm here. With you. Together."

He sighs in frustration. "Okay, let's try this another way. Most women are all over me."

I roll my eyes, even though I'm sure it's true.

"I can't help it," he winks. "But you—I feel like I want you more than you want me and that's really fucking weird."

"I don't think that's true. Arrogant on your part, but not true," I laugh.

"Then help a guy out," he groans. "Fix my ego."

"Your ego is fine."

"And you're deflecting, babe."

I roll away from him so he can't see my face. "You bring things way too close to home for me. That's the truth," I tell him.

"Go on . . ."

"Getting involved with you puts me one step closer to becoming my mother, and that's the one thing I've promised myself I won't be."

I've never admitted that out loud before and it's a damn personal thing to admit to the man that's pretty much from the perfect family. It's also embarrassing.

"Hey," he says. His arm drapes over me. "What's this all about? You don't want to be like your mother? What's that have to do with me?"

"My father was in sports," I say, glossing over the topic. "My mother ended up losing both him and herself to the game. Professional athletes are where they are because it's their passion, the one thing that matters more than any other. You wouldn't be where you are if that weren't true."

"Dani . . ."

I turn so I can see him over my shoulder. "I promised myself I'd never be like them. I'd never put those I love second to a game, and I'd never let another person take the game over me."

"I'm not taking anything over anyone."

"But you would," I say, fighting my voice from breaking. "I get that. I respect it even. You can do something only a handful of people in the world can do. You have a giant opportunity in front of you. But I don't want to be crushed as you go crushing the world."

"I'd never crush you."

"I know you wouldn't," I say, touching his cheek. "At least not on purpose. But it's more than that." My hand falls and I take a deep breath. "It's not being crushed but it's not having a life like my mother too. Waiting on my guy to come home. Hoping he calls. Listening to statistics over dinner and trying to get your man to squeeze some time for you in the middle of a couple of hundred games. It's not the life I want. That life broke her. I watched it. I don't even really have parents because of it. What I want out of life is the polar opposite."

His features crease, his eyes darkening, as he takes that in. The soberness of his expression makes me think maybe he realizes how right I am, just how much I know what his life is like. And how this thing between us can never deepen too much.

"I like the way things are between us," I say, my voice soft. "You are so much fun. Smart. Sexy as hell. But we really need to try to keep it on this level."

"I feel like this is completely unfair," he says, a sort of laugh in his voice that doesn't mean he's amused. "Out of all the chicks that want me, I have to like you."

Slapping at his chest, we both laugh. He pulls me in close again. There's a tenderness in his eyes that tugs at my heart and if I let myself, I could fall right in. I also know I can't do that. As much as it hurts to claw my way back from the ledge of doing just that.

"Don't take this the wrong way, Landry, but you'd be impossible to watch leave."

"You don't like the view of my ass?" he teases.

"Not as much as I like the view of your face."

He takes a deep breath, his eyes troubled. "I like you. I really fucking like you. You make me remember what it's like to be . . . more than me."

"You don't need to be anything more than you are."

His grin hits me in a soft spot deep in my heart. "See?" he says softly. "Right there. That's why I want to lock you up." He peers into my eyes, like it's going to drive his words home.

"Damn it," I sigh, trying to keep this light before I succumb to his words. "You make it so hard to resist you."

"So don't."

I consider this. "Do you know Weston Brinkmann?"

He makes a face like he just sucked a lemon. "Why?"

"He wanted to date me a year or so ago and I turned him down."

"Smart girl. He's a complete fucking cocksucker."

I laugh, squeezing him tight. "I turned him down even though I kind of liked him just because he played baseball. For the same reasons I'm telling you about."

He just watches me.

"See, that's the thing," I say. "I turned him down. I can't tell you no. I don't know what that means, exactly, but it scares me."

"You shouldn't be scared alone. It's like drinking when you're sad — have a partner," he winks. "Let's hang out. Take some batting practice. Have dinner, breakfast if things go well. I promise to use all my Southern manners."

My leg slings back over him again, this time so my pussy is lined up with his cock.

"I can feel your heat," he says, his breath picking up. "Want round two?"

"Only if you promise not to use those Southern manners."

"Deal."

FIFTEEN

LINCOLN

She's gone.

When I woke up and she wasn't beside me, I hoped she was in the shower. Or living room. Or kitchen. But I've thoroughly inspected every room and come up with nothing, save a little note written on the back of a takeout menu.

Morning, Landry.

Thanks for last night. And you're welcome for it, too. I had some things to do this morning, so I went ahead and left. You probably need to go grocery shopping. You have no coffee. Who are you?

Xo Danielle

"Sure you did," I say, holding the note in my hand as I pull a gallon of milk out of the refrigerator. I give it a quick smell test before drinking straight from the carton. "You left because you had things to do. Right."

She left because she didn't want to have to deal with the fact that she slept all night in my arms. That we were together three times from the time we got home from the restaurant until she snuck out of here sometime after six a.m. That she liked it.

If she didn't like it, she wouldn't have smiled in her sleep or slept right against me like a log. She wouldn't have let me kiss her while she slept or snuck out this morning.

She's lame. The girl does have a flaw after all.

Grinning, I spy the mail from yesterday and sort through it. A letter from Arrows' management is included in the pile of bills and junk and I rip it open and scan the contents.

"Blah, blah blah," I read aloud, my eyes searching for words that mean something. "We expect . . . blah, blah, blah . . . a final assessment on Tuesday, November 25th. We will meet with you about your contract after the Thanksgiving holiday."

I test my shoulder, rolling it around and around. It feels better, stronger, but not strong enough to fire one from two hundred feet out. Not strong enough to ward off this sick feeling in my stomach.

"Damn it," I say, mentally rolling through therapy dates and schedules. How much harder can I press it? Can I speed this up in any way? What if this doesn't work? What if—

The buzzing of my phone interrupts my errant thoughts, and I scamper into the bedroom and pick it up hastily to see it's Graham.

"Just the man I was wanting to talk to," I say, heading back into the kitchen.

"Why does that concern me?"

"Because you're smart, G. Super fucking smart."

"Well, let me go first," he sighs. "Ford called this morning. He'll be officially out in a few weeks and home for good. He wants to put together a new branch of Landry Holdings. Details haven't been hammered out yet, but it would basically involve security for individuals, companies, things like that."

"Sounds smart," I chime in, detouring into the living room. Picking up a baseball from a chair next to a bookcase, I toss it in the air. "Why do I need to know this?"

"Since we are all shareholders of Landry Holdings, we all get a vote whether to branch off. It's a potential risk and, on the other hand, a potential reward, for all of us."

Considering this for a half a second, I toss the ball back in the air. "I have no problems with it. Ford knows what he's doing. I say let him have at it. He's probably taken the least out of our inheritance out of us all. What does everyone else say?"

"Barrett's in. I'm in. If you're in, that's majority. But I really don't see Camilla against it, even though she's acting a little odd these days."

My interest is piqued. Nothing ever happens with Camilla. She's as boring as a loaf of plain white bread. It's not a bad thing—her predictability is something I count on. But if something is up with Miss Perfect, this I must hear.

"Sienna will be in," I volunteer, speaking for the sister that could've been my twin spirit-wise. "But tell me more about Camilla. What's going on?"

Graham blows out a hefty breath, his office chair squeaking in the background. "I'm really not sure. You know how she's always around? Always available? Always completely put together like Mom?"

"Yeah."

"Well, that stopped a couple of weeks ago. She's not around as much, doesn't return calls. I've left her one message about the security company and another about an event Mom is planning that I need her input on and nada. No call back, no quick text. Nothing."

"She's all right, right? I mean, you've seen her lately? She's not kidnapped or some shit?"

My brother laughs. "She was at dinner on Sunday. She's around. But, get this—our little sister was in sneakers."

"Camilla?" I ask, my face contorting in confusion as I try to picture her slumming it. "Are you sure it wasn't Sienna?" I laugh.

"It's weird as shit," Graham remarks. "But she's a big girl. Maybe she's decided she doesn't want to be someone's trophy wife after all."

"Maybe," I say, getting impatient. "My turn. This is actually a two-parter."

"Great."

"Don't sound so excited."

"Trust me, I'm reeling it in as hard as I can."

"Asshole," I mutter. "First thing is I got a letter from management. I go in for my final test on the Tuesday before Thanksgiving. After that, we renegotiate."

"All right . . ."

"All right . . . Can you please make me feel better about this?"

His laugh booms through the receiver. "You want me to coddle you? Sorry, Linc. I draw the line at giving you the warm and fuzzies."

"I don't want the warm and fuzzies," I huff. "Just tell me pragmatically how this is going to end well."

I roll my eyes at his sigh, feeling like a needy asshole. Finally, after a long enough pause that I really start to consider he might've hung up on me, he speaks.

"How's therapy been going? How do you feel?" he asks.

"Good."

"This is going to be fine. You're an athlete so you know injuries happen. Management knows that too. Just keep rehabbing it and see what happens."

"What if they don't sign me?"

"There is a chance, as there always is, that you will move cities. You know that."

My head hangs. "Yeah, yeah, yeah."

"But you're going to have a job. And, even if you don't, you have me managing your money. You're not going to have to worry about it." He's right, but that's not the problem. It's not that I'm afraid I won't be able to eat or buy a house. It's more like—what am I if I don't play ball? I can't announce. I don't have a business or marketing degree.

I'll just be another has been before age thirty and the biggest letdown to my family.

"Okay, enough of that," I say, flopping on the sofa, shoving base-ball out of my brain. "Next topic: I need a plan."

"For post-baseball?"

"No," I gulp. "Don't laugh."

"If it's coming from your mouth, I reserve the right to laugh."

This is going to be a tough one to live down, the fact that I, the best looking out of the family, is having a struggle getting the girl I want. If I tell G, he'll tell Barrett and probably Ford, and then I'm fucked. Holidays at home will never be the same. Knowing I'm fucking up my reputation with Graham, I still need him.

"Fine," I mutter. "I met this girl. The one I was telling you about the other day, remember?"

"Yeah," he says, sounding entirely too amused for my own good.

"She doesn't want to see me."

Grimacing, I wait for the chuckle at my expense. It doesn't take long before Graham is snickering on the other end. Tossing the base-ball onto the sofa, I wait him out.

"Sorry. I thought I just heard you say she won't see you," he says finally.

"I did. I don't mean it like she won't see me at all, because I fucked her three times last night and she slept in my bed. But unlike most women that won't leave the next day, she won't stay." My voice drifts off as my mind goes to more sinister places. "Is this what my life will be like if I don't get resigned? Will I become a loser?"

"You'll get resigned."

"But if I don't, is this what I can look forward to? Is this how you live?"

"Fuck off," Graham snorts. "I'll have you know I have no problem getting a woman. I've never called you for advice, have I?"

"That's because you have a plan for fucking everything," I laugh. "You give your own advice."

"True. Now what kind of advice are you after with Miss I-Don't-Want-You?"

"You don't have to say it like that, asshole," I buzz. "I need a plan to win her over. I think what I need to do is convince her I'm more than an athlete. She's all anti-baseball-god. Weird, right?"

The line stills as my brother formulates his proposal. "Okay, so tell me about her. Besides her physical attributes, please."

"So you think I was going to start with her banging body?"

"Absolutely."

"Well, you'd be wrong. I was going to start with her smile."

"Her smile?" Graham balks. "What the fuck have you done with my brother?"

"Funny," I say, rolling my eyes. "She's into kids. She coordinates events and shit at the hospital where I get therapy. That's all I really know about her. That and she has a disdain for athletes, baseball specifically. She won't open up to me much."

Graham's tongue clicks off the roof of his mouth as he dissects that information. His chair squeaks in the background again, the sound of something tapping distant.

My feet move, walking a circle on the navy blue wool rug on the floor. I watch the impressions my bare feet make into the runner, trying to find some rhythm in my steps.

"You're a family guy. So if she likes kids, she'll probably be drawn to that," Graham says finally. "Is she close with her family?"

"No, actually. Her father is a cocksucker and her mother is pretty much a dick too, I think."

"Even better."

"G, there's nothing good about that."

"Okay, let's do this." He's standing, I can hear it in the increased tempo of his voice. He has so many of Dad's mannerisms and that's one. "This is going to sound crazy . . ."

"We're off to a good start," I joke.

"Women love seeing a man with kids. Especially this one, I bet."

"But she's already seen me with kids. I've painted with them at the hospital. This is not new information."

Graham laughs. "Do you trust me or not?"

"Go on."

"Okay," he says, warning me not to interrupt again. "We need to tweak your image, much like we had to do with Barrett during the election. We need her to see more to you than just a baseball player that wants to fuck her senseless."

"Yes. I. Fucking. Do."

"Here's what you do." He stops himself and snorts, mumbling under his breath, "I can't believe I'm even suggesting this."

"Suggest it," I demand. "Use Huxley."

"What?"

I'm sure I'm not hearing him right. *Use my brother's girlfriend's kid? Is that even moral?* I laugh out loud. *Do I even care? No. No, I do not.*

"Use Hux," he repeats, obviously as amazed by his suggestion as I am. "Think about it. You can show her you're a well-rounded guy, one that's responsible and capable of solid relationships with those you care about. It's different than the kids from the hospital because she could possibly think that's an act. But if you have Huxley, that's different. That's a piece of who you are outside of anything she is. Get it?"

"Yeah. I get it," I say, mulling this over.

"Barrett is on his way to Tennessee anyway, I think."

The beauty of the plan glitters in front of me like a well-timed curveball. If you can just get a hold of it, you can hit a home run. And this particular home run might feel even better than hitting one out of the ballpark.

"Graham, you're a genius."

"Glad I could be of service. Just do me a favor, okay?"

"What's that?" I mumble, already trying to figure out how to phrase this to Alison.

"Don't tell Barrett this asinine idea was mine."

I look at myself in the mirror and smile. "G, I gotta go."

SIXTEEN

DANIELLE

SHOULDN'T YOU FEEL SHAME DOING the Walk of Shame? In the past I have had that feeling of "Don't look at me" while I trekked the sidewalk back to my dorm or to my car. This morning, I waved at his stupid neighbors.

Where is my class? Where is my dignity? I fight the smile on my lips as I realize both are somewhere curled up in Lincoln's sheets on the floor of his bedroom.

Showered, blow dried, and a little achy, I notice the spring in my step as I turn the corner towards the Smitten Kitten. Each step is accompanied by a throb between my legs. I wonder exactly which position caused it. Reverse cowgirl? My legs on his shoulders? On his benchpress? The corkscrew?

My body hums as I imagine that one: me resting on one hip and my forearm near the edge of his chaise lounge, thighs pressed together, him straddling me from behind.

I'm wet again.

Entering the Smitten Kitten, I see Pepper behind the counter. The place is dotted with patrons enjoying croissants and chicken salad sandwiches. "Hey!" she says as I approach. "You're early."

"I am, aren't I?"

She frowns. "Why?"

I contemplate whether I can get away with lying to her. It's quickly apparent I can't.

"Fine," I say, looking in my purse like there's something I really, really need buried in the bottom. "I might have stayed the night at Lincoln's."

"You did not!"

"Hush," I say, blushing. "This is one of those things you don't scream, Pepper."

One hand goes to her mouth as she surveys her diners. "Sorry," she says in a more reasonable tone. "But what did you expect me to say? You stayed all night with Lincoln 'Lick Me' Landry."

"Nice."

"Did he?"

"Did he what?"

"Lick you."

My jaw dropping, I half laugh. "Either get me something to go or I'm out of here. Damn. Do you have any couth?"

"Do I ever?" she laughs.

"Let's pretend you do today. I need a little time to process this."

She leans on the counter. "Was it amazing? Just give me that. Throw me a scrap."

I lean in too. "It was incredible."

Her eyes light up as she fist pumps the air. "Thank God because if he was mediocre in bed, every fantasy I've ever had was going to be ruined." She disappears in the back and returns with a paper bag. "Here you go."

I hand her my credit card and she swipes it before handing it back. "Thanks," I say, taking the bag.

"Where are you going now?"

"Home."

"I just packed you breakfast for two."

Peering in the bag, I see she's not lying. There are two chocolate croissants, two Styrofoam containers, and a container of strawberries. Sighing, I look at her hopeful face. "I'm going home. Want to make me a bag for one?"

"Why are you going home, Danielle?"

"Because . . ."

"Because he had an appointment this morning?"

"Something like that."

"You fucked and fled, didn't you?"

"My God, Pepper."

"You did! Damn it, Danielle."

The bag raps as it's plopped back on the counter. "Don't 'damn it, Danielle' me. I'm trying to go with the flow but keep my head above water, all right? He's my kryptonite. Attractive, cocky, confident, sweet, great in bed, and a fucking baseball player. He's every sin I want to make wrapped up in one delectable body."

"So, what's the problem?"

"Ugh," I huff. "Aren't you listening to me? Don't you know me?"

She appears unfazed by my outburst. "I do, actually. Which is why it makes me happier than a lark to see you with some spark right now. To see your eyes all lit up and some fire in your ass. You need to get rid of these crazy fears you have that everything will end in heartbreak."

"It's not crazy. It's like . . ." I look at the ceiling for inspiration. "Imagine this: you grew up with a family that loved sugar. It was their weakness, okay?"

"I did."

"Follow along," I reprimand her. "Let's say they were so addicted to it that they couldn't stand for any of it to be in the house. They'd eat it all. All of it. Gone."

"Okay . . ."

"So you move out. Start your own bakery. You're safe because they aren't there to eat your sugar, right? Then imagine you fall for some guy. He's perfect . . . except he too is a sugar addict."

She looks at me blankly.

"Don't you see what I'm saying?" I ask.

"Yeah, but if he looks like Lincoln, I'd just handcuff him to the bed."

Rolling my eyes, I grab the bag and turn towards the door.

"Hey," she calls after me. "I want details. Don't think you're getting out of it that easy!"

The bell chimes as the front door closes behind me. I'm to my car in record speed. I need space. I need air. I need to think. When my phone buzzes right before I pull out of the parking lot, I know it's Pepper and she's not going to quit until I give her something to occupy her mind.

"Fine!" I nearly shout into the phone. "His cock is about ten inches, if I'm guessing, and he fucked me in about every position I could explain. My favorite, though, was the corkscrew. Not sure what that is? Google it."

My finger goes to swipe off the call when I see the name on the screen and drop the phone. "Shit!" I cry, digging through the items on my passenger's side floorboard until I find the glowing device.

My heart is pounding as I try to decide whether to end the call or talk to Lincoln. Mortified, I bring it to my ear and squeeze my eyes shut. He's silent.

Maybe he didn't hear. Please, God, don't let him have heard that.

"Hello?" I eke out.

"I'd say ten inches is fair and I've made a note about the corkscrew. Glad I called," he chuckles.

"Hey, Landry." I want to slink into the seat and melt into the leather.

"That's one way to make me a little less pissed that you snuck out on me."

"I didn't sneak out on you. I left a note."

"For the record, the note didn't help. But hearing you talk about my cock—who were you talking to, by the way?—that helps. That really helps."

"Fuck off," I say, smiling. Ready to change the subject, I flip on the Bluetooth and pull onto the street. "Why did you call? Hoping you'd overhear me embarrassing myself ?"

"Baby, there is nothing embarrassing about having a man hear you talk about how much you liked being with him."

I don't know what I swoon harder over, him calling me "baby" or the husk in his voice. Sure, he's called me that before, but hearing it when he's not inside me is different. More meaningful. Maybe more like a word choice instead of a reaction.

He clears his throat. "I called because I need a favor."

"Really, Landry?"

"Really, Dani," he mocks. "My brother needs someone to watch his girlfriend's kid overnight tomorrow night. They have something to do in Nashville and want to take the kid with them, but he can't go with them that night. And Alison, my brother's girl, doesn't believe in nannies."

"What do you need my help with?"

"Come over and have dinner with us. Help me entertain him. He's ten or eleven or something and is a pretty cool kid. His name is Huxley and he's a big baseball fan. So, naturally, we hit it off."

"So why do you need me? Sounds like you have this figured out."

"I've never been left alone with a kid all night."

"I'm not staying the night with you and your nephew, Landry."

"I'm not asking you to," he says, mocking me again. "I'm asking you to come for dinner, watch a movie, build Legos, or whatever. Just hang out with us."

I blow out a breath as I turn onto my street. Again: kryptonite. I can't say no to this man. Even though I should back away slowly from the predator he is, I can't. I like being his prey.

"What time?"

"Six," he says and I know he's grinning. But that's fair. So am I.

SEVENTEEN

LINCOLN

MY WEIGHT POUNDING DOWN THE hallway causes the pictures hanging to knock against the wall. "I'm coming!" I shout as the doorbell chimes again. Like a kid at Christmastime, I pop open the door.

"Hey!" "Uncle Linc!" Huxley lunges forward, wrapping his arms around my waist.

Chuckling, I rub my knuckles across the top of the Arrows cap I gave him. Then I look up and wink at Alison. "Why'd you bring that guy?"

"Because that guy is her fiancé," Barrett says, a smile thick in his voice.

"Officially?"

"No," Alison sighs, rolling her eyes. "He better ask me soon or I might just up and leave him."

"Try me," Barrett growls, making her laugh.

I untangle myself from Hux and pull my brother into a quick hug. "How are you?"

"Ready to spend a few uninterrupted minutes with Alison."

We both turn to the woman at his side. A red dress skims her curves, her lips painted the same color. I've seen this monochromatic look done a million times, but on her it looks different. Classy. Distinguished. *Not mine.*

It's a running joke that I have a crush on my brother's girl. It *is* a joke. I wouldn't touch her if my life depended on it. As a matter of fact, I'd thrash any jackass if they tried it. Alison's different. She's smart. Funny. Nurturing. She's a lot like Dani.

"What's that look for?" Alison asks, just before she kisses my cheek.

Her fingers find my face and she wipes the lipstick away. "What look?"

"That look like you're thinking of something, or someone, else." Tossing her a wink, I spread my arms to encourage her to follow Barrett and Huxley into the house. Once inside, I shut the door behind us.

"Can I explore?" Hux takes in the living room. "Please?"

"Better not," Barrett warns, looking at me out of the corner of his eye. The look of potential horror on his features makes me laugh.

"Go ahead, Hux."

"Yay!" he says and takes off.

"Don't touch anything! Don't open drawers!" Barrett calls after him.

"And don't look in his phone," Alison adds, jabbing me in the side with her elbow. "Lincoln Landry, you have no idea the conversation I had to have with my son after he got ahold of your texts."

I grimace. "It was one text and it wasn't even a picture text—"

"It was a very, very descriptive—"

"—that she never followed through on. But that's not the point," I grin. "He didn't even get to the good stuff. I told him she was talking about a kitten at the pound. He believed it."

Alison's hands go to her hips. "And I had to buy a cat."

"And I hate cats," Barrett adds, shaking his head. "Just keep the phone out of his sight. Got it?"

"Yeah, yeah, yeah. Geez, you make it sound like you regret agreeing to leave him with me."

"We only agreed because we need a night to ourselves," Barrett sighs. His hand finds the curve of Alison's hip and he brings her to his side as her head falls against his shoulder. "We've not had a night alone in forever. We need a break."

Smirking, I start to retort with how I'd spend a night alone with Alison if I was him, but am silenced by Barrett's warning glare before I can get a word out. Instead, I laugh and head into the kitchen. "You guys want a drink?"

They turn down my offer, but follow me into the next room. Hopping up to sit on the island, I look at my brother. He looks at me. We exchange a smile. It's a gesture that's loaded with a feeling I've never been able to find with anyone but my siblings. A look of comfort, of understanding. Of "I don't know what in the hell you're doing, but I'll do it with you."

Barrett looks at Alison like that. Ford looked at his girlfriend like that too before they broke things off when he went overseas. I've never been close to feeling that way with someone else who wasn't a Landry.

"Tell me about her," Alison says softly.

I grin like crazy because Barrett rolls his eyes, earning him a nudge in the side from Alison.

"She's . . ." I watch my bare feet swing. It's easy to joke about things, about women, with my brothers. I'm the goofball of the family; I can play everything off. But with Alison, it's different. She picks up on so much more. It's like she has a bullshit meter that dings when my mouth opens.

"Go on," she encourages.

"Her name is Danielle. I met her by accident. She's . . ."

"Not a whore?" Barrett offers.

"She's not a whore. She's beautiful and smart and funny as hell. She reminds me of you, Ali."

"And she's also impervious to your abs, I recall Graham saying," Barrett adds.

Alison laughs, wrapping her hand around Barrett's arm as I wince. "Fuck Graham."

"Hey," Barrett shrugs, amused. "That's the word on the street."

"I think that's a very good thing," Alison whispers, swatting my brother. "Never take a girl seriously that just wants your abs, Linc."

"But they're great. Wanna see?"

"No, she doesn't," Barrett glares.

It's my turn to shrug. "Just being nice and offering. She's been with you a while. She's not seen something like this in a long time."

Barrett begins to fire back, a grin on his face, when Huxley ambles in the room. "This place is nice. I put my backpack on the bed with the boxes on it. We can move them right?"

Furrowing my brow, I make a face. "Yeah. I wonder what's in the boxes?"

"How do you not know?" Alison asks.

"Rita kind of does her thing and I sort of live around it. Stay out of the way."

"But it's your house," Hux points out.

"Weird, right?" I shrug.

Barrett taps at his watch. "We need to get going. Troy is waiting in the car. We'll be back tomorrow afternoon sometime."

"Sounds good," I say, following them to the door. They say their goodbyes to Huxley and then turn to me.

"Please don't warp him," Barrett mutters before looking at Alison. "Are you one hundred percent sure this is a good idea?"

Alison kisses me on the cheek again. Looking into my eyes, she says, "I am. I trust him."

"See? She trusts me."

"She's gorgeous but clearly not very smart," Barrett sighs.

"Will you please go?" Huxley butts in, bouncing on the balls of his feet.

Alison and Barrett laugh. They open the door and Alison blows her son a kiss. "I'll see you tomorrow. Take care of him, Linc."

"Let's be real—take care of him, Hux," Barrett calls over his shoulder.

"I got this. Just enjoy yourself," I sigh.

They leave and Huxley turns to me. "Now what?"

Why I feel put on the spot by a kid is beyond me. But I do. The little shit starts a smirk that seems to flip our roles.

"What are you laughing at?" I say, heading into the living room and flopping down on the sofa.

Huxley climbs onto the cushion beside me. "I'm not laughing at anything. I'm just wondering what we are going to do. That's all."

"That's all, huh?"

A grin that he seems to have picked up from Barrett, a sly little twitch that makes him seem so much older than he is, slips across his lips. "Well, kind of. I mean, I do want to know what we are going to do. But not because I'm bored or something."

"So you're suspicious?" I tease, kicking my feet up on the coffee table.

"I'm a cool kid," he laughs, "but, yeah, I'm suspicious."

"Maybe your mom and Barrett just wanted to be alone," I shrug.

His face twists in disgust. "They kiss . . . All. The. Time."

That's not all they're doing. My mouth pops open to say that, but my senses kick in first and I shut my trap. It doesn't really matter though. Huxley gives me the ol' side eye. I burst out laughing.

"What?" I tease.

"Adults are so gross." He removes his hat, his fingers rolling around the brim. "Can I ask you a question, Linc?"

That question is as loaded as my cock when I'm looking at Dani's bare ass. This is very much above my pay grade. I mean, I can explain . . . things . . . to him. But in a way that my uptight brother and Ali are going to appreciate? Probably not so much.

Still, when I look at the kid, I know I gotta say something. It's taking a lot of balls to even bring it up and I don't want him thinking he can't talk to me. With Barrett as a stepdad, the kid may feel a little uncomfortable asking about sex. I couldn't ask my dad. Not that I needed to ask anyone. With three older brothers and the best looks in the family, I figured shit out quick.

"Sure," I say, playing it off. "What's up?"

He gulps, which makes me gulp. "I know what they're doing when the door is locked, but . . ."

"Yeah?"

We look at each other, both fidgeting. I'm not sure who's more nervous.

"Well, I was wondering, you know, kind of like, what are they doing?"

"Oh, shit," I mumble, looking anywhere but at him. Stretching my legs in front of me, I try to figure out how to explain sex to a kid that can't even say curse words yet.

When my eyes finally drift to his, I see the little kid that he is. Not the kid sitting in front of me, but the little boy that lives inside him. The six-year-old that lives in every man, regardless of how old we really are. It's the voice in our head that reminds us we don't have our shit together half as well as we present it to the world. It's the sound of questioning every move we make. The little boy inside every man in the world holds on to fear of something and reminds us of our vulnerabilities, whether it's the monster in the closet or the General Manager's call. Or, in this case, a mother that now loves another man.

That's what he's asking me. That's the fear. This has nothing to do with sex, thank God, but more to do with his insecurity. This I can handle.

"Let me ask you a question." I take the hat out of his hand and toss it onto the coffee table. "How are things going with Barrett? And you can be honest with me. He's my brother, but you know, *he's my brother*," I wink. "There are times I'm not his biggest fan."

Hux's shoulders rise and fall. "I like him. He always asks me what I think about things." He bites his bottom lip in thought. "I think he likes me too."

"No doubt he likes you. You're the coolest kid ever." He blushes, his little cheeks splitting into a grin.

"Here's the thing, Huxley. When Barrett and your mom spend time together, they're getting to know each other. See, you know how your mom loves you every day? No matter what you do or what you break or what you tell her you saw on my phone . . ."

A laugh breaks out across the room as Huxley tries not to look at me.

"You're a little shit, you know that? I took so much hell for that," I say, laughing too.

"You let me have it!"

"Once. I let you have it once when I was half asleep. Won't happen again."

Hux grabs his hat and jostles it back over his head. Shaking mine, I wait until he's settled down before continuing with my explanation.

"You and your mom have that," I say finally. "You're a family. She gave birth to you. But when adults marry each other, they're picking that person to love. It's a different thing."

"I get that."

"And your mom had to pick more carefully because whoever she loves will be around you. And you are the most important person in her life."

Inch by inch, the anxiety in his eyes melts away. "You think?"

"I know," I say.

He sighs, resting back against the sofa. Gazing out the window, he seems to be caught up in his thoughts. Slowly, he turns to me. "So, about what they're doing in the bedroom . . ."

"You really want to know?" I laugh.

"Nope."

"Thank God."

EIGHTEEN

LINCOLN

"ARE YOU SURE IT TAKES all this stuff to make dinner?" I survey the kitchen. It looks like the grocery store threw up on the floor, counters, and table.

"How do I know? I'm a kid."

"You were the one that read off the ingredients from the app. I need a little confidence here, Huxley."

"There were about seven ingredients on the list. We got . . ." He looks at the golden plastic bags overtaking the kitchen. "We got way more than that. We should start putting this stuff away."

I start opening cabinets and looking inside. "What are you doing, Lincoln?"

"Trying to figure out where this stuff goes."

I think he sighs behind me, but I don't double check. We're running out of time. The app says it will take almost an hour to make the pasta and I wanted to try to make sure the wine was chilled and put the cake from the bakery on a plate of some sort like my mom does when she tries to pretend like she's baked something.

"Can I ask you something?" Hux asks.

"Sure."

"Why are you going to this much trouble to make dinner for a girl? Do you like her or something?"

My hand stills on the bag of frozen spinach. "I do. I like her a lot."

"What's her name?"

"Danielle."

He nods, organizing all the ingredients from the recipe beside the stove. Then he goes to work putting things in an empty cabinet.

"I'm going to need your help tonight," I say, sticking a container of coffee next to my brand new coffee pot.

"How?"

"I need you to help this girl think I'm awesome." He peers at me over his shoulder.

"You're my wingman."

"Wingman?"

"Yeah. Wingman," I say, putting three different flavors of coffee creamer on the door of the refrigerator. "That means it's your job to be adorable and to say nice things about me when you can. But, you know, don't force it. Just when the time is right. And don't say anything about the texts on my—"

"I get it. You need me to make her fall in love with you."

"In love with me?" I balk. "No, no, no. You don't get it at all."

The little shit smirks at me. If I didn't know better, I'd think he was Barrett's kid with that look. "I think I get it better than you do."

"Fuck," I sigh, opening a box of plates. They're navy blue and heavy.

"We should wash those first."

"What?" I ask, looking at him. "Where do you get this stuff?"

"Life. Haven't you ever moved? You always wash things before you use them if you haven't used them in a while." He watches me before laughing. "Did you buy glasses too?"

"Yeah."

"Didn't you have glasses?"

"I'm not sure how many."

He glances at the clock. "What time is she coming?"

"In about an hour."

"Do you have any idea how to cook? Have you ever cooked at all?"

"Some," I say defensively. "Look, I'm the adult here. You're the kid. You put this shit away and I'm going to . . ." I pull up the recipe on my phone. "I'm going to bring a large pot of lightly salted water to a boil. Add pasta and cook for eight to ten minutes or until al dente, whatever that means, and then drain and reserve."

Hux sighs. I do too.

LINCOLN

THE CAKE LOOKS PRETTY GOOD on the plate. Some of the icing got knocked off as I tried to slip it out of the box, but I fixed it with my finger. Then licked it off. That got me a look of disapproval from Hux.

"So you know what to do, right?" I ask, drying the glasses and setting them on the table beneath the lit candles.

"Yes. Be cute. Say nice things about you. And don't talk about what's on your phone or what I heard you say to the girl on the phone after Barrett's election at the Farm."

My brain races to remember what I would've been saying. "Did you mention any of that conversation to your mom?"

"No," he grins. "But I Googled it."

Putting him in a headlock, I rub my knuckles over his head. "You're gonna get me in so much trouble."

"Hey, Linc? I think the sausage is burning."

As soon as he says it, I smell it. "Fuck!" I hustle across the room and start fumbling with the knobs on the stove. "That oil got hot fast."

"Take it off the burner for a minute," Hux suggests. "It's what my mom does when the eggs start burning in the morning."

I try it. It works. The sizzle quiets down a little and by the time it's cool enough and I can put it back down and break it up with a big plastic spoon, it doesn't look too bad.

Huxley starts to say something when the doorbell rings. Instead, he raises a brow. "You want me to get it?"

I'm flustered, my hands reaching for the onions and garlic and then looking at the door again. How can I crack a homerun with full count and not break a sweat, yet I don't know which way to go right now?

"Um," I stutter, unsure as to what to do.

Huxley's hand lands on my bicep. "I'll get the door. You need to get yourself together."

Before I can respond, he's skipping out of the kitchen. I busy myself trying to take the skin off the onion and eavesdropping on Huxley and Dani as much as I can. I don't hear much. Finally, I glance up and they're standing in the doorway.

Huxley's wearing a huge grin, his eyebrows lifting up and down. I chuckle and then stop when my gaze lands on Danielle.

She's wearing a pair of jeans that are tucked into a pair of boots. A mustard-colored sweater sits snugly around her curves, which are showcased even more with her hair pulled into a messy bun on the top of her head.

My mouth goes dry. I can't take my eyes off of her. Something about the way she looks in my house, so casual and easy, has my brain fogged.

"Hey," she says finally. "I think you're burning that."

"Shit!" I exclaim, turning around to see the sausage meat frying again. Pulling it off the burner, my jaw locked, I remind myself I can't mess this up. This is my chance to prove I'm more than a bachelor, more than a baseball player, more than the athlete types she knows. And I'm burning fucking dinner.

Her hand lands on my back and I relax on contact. Her vanilla perfume wraps around me as she peers into the skillet. She must sense my anxiety because she lifts her toes and kisses my cheek. "Why don't you go get cleaned up and I'll finish."

"Get cleaned up?" I say, standing there holding a pan in the air. "Do I not look good?"

I'm slightly offended. I've busted my ass to make this night as perfect as possible and everything is going wrong.

"You have grease and chocolate icing all over your shirt," she whispers. I look down and see that she's right. "Let me help."

"You don't even know what I'm making."

"Huxley will help me." She looks over her shoulder. "Right, Hux?"

"Sure."

She pats my ass. "Go on. Get a new shirt on and breathe a little, Landry. He's just a kid."

I hide my smile. "Yeah, why I'm so nervous about a kid is beyond me."

Turning on my heel, I pass Hux and give him a wink. He responds by sticking a hand out that I high five on my way out.

NINETEEN

DANIELLE

LINCOLN'S LAUGH FILLS THE AIR. It's a different laugh than I've heard from him. It's completely relaxed, like he doesn't have a care in the world. I watch him reach over and bump Huxley's shoulder. The boy looks up at him like he hung the moon.

He was so great with Rocky, but seeing him with Huxley is a new level of amazing. They're natural together, like brothers or a father and son. For a split second, I imagine Lincoln as a father. It wouldn't take much work to imagine us having dinner as a family.

A warmth like I've never felt before stretches through my chest, burrowing into little cavities that have been empty my entire life. Places I didn't know were there. I don't want this feeling to end.

"This was really good," Huxley says, setting down his fork. "Thank you for making it, Linc. And thank you for coming to dinner with us, Danielle."

"You are so welcome. Thank you for inviting me."

"My mom would really like you."

"You think?" I ask.

"Yeah. You're smart and nice and you make Lincoln laugh a lot."

"Well, Lincoln makes me laugh a lot too."

Lincoln watches us banter, a huge smile on his face. He's leaned back at the head of the table, his blue workout shirt nearly painted on his body. I can see every line of his muscles, every ridge of his frame.

Huxley tries to hide a grin. "I think Lincoln likes you."

I burst out laughing. "You think?" I ask coyly. "What makes you say that, Hux?" I hold my finger in the air as a warning for Lincoln to stay out of it when he starts to interrupt.

"Because you're really pretty," he says, his cheeks pinking a little. "And Linc usually just laughs at girls."

"Does he now?"

"Huxley . . ." Lincoln warns, making Hux burst into a fit of giggles. "He does. He doesn't take them seriously. But," he says, cupping his hands around his mouth to direct his voice to me as he whispers, "they are pretty dumb."

"Good to know." I pick up my glass of water and take a sip so I don't laugh.

"Also, he went to all this trouble for you," Hux continues. "We bought all this food and he got coffee because he said you like it."

My eyes flip to Landry.

"And he bought plates and cups because he wanted you to like it here."

My heart mushes. I have to force myself to take my gaze away from the handsome man at my left and look across the table at Huxley. "That was awfully nice of him."

"Yes, it was. So you should be super nice to him, okay? He's a nice guy. He—"

"Laying it on a little thick now, Hux," Lincoln chuckles. He clears his throat as he dabs his mouth with a napkin.

"Okay, okay." Huxley looks at me. "Can I go get a shower and maybe lie down? We traveled all day and Barrett bought me a book in the airport and I really want to read."

"Sure," I say. "Let me know if you need anything."

"I will." He stands and heads to the doorway. I'm not sure what he does as he stands there, but it makes Lincoln nod and laugh.

Once he's sure Hux is out of earshot, Lincoln reaches under the table and takes my hand. He laces our fingers together, his nearly swamping mine. His thumb caresses my palm.

"So, you going to be super nice to me tonight?" he teases. "I can think of super nice ways for you to show me you like me."

"Can you?"

"Since I know your favorite ways to come, thanks to your little declaration on the phone today, I thought we could start there."

"Don't embarrass me," I say, tucking my chin.

"There's nothing to be embarrassed about, baby." He squeezes my hand until I look at him. "Want some wine?"

"Sure," I nearly whisper.

"Red or white?"

"White."

He brings our interlocked hands to his lips and presses a kiss against them before letting mine go. My normal wit is long gone, sitting in a puddle along with the rest of me on the floor. I watch him uncork the wine and pour us both a glass. "Come on," he says, exiting the kitchen. I follow him into the living room where he gets comfortable on the sofa. A fire is burning in the fireplace, the crackling of fake logs making the room feel intimate.

"Sit," he instructs, motioning with his chin for me to land beside him. He doesn't have to tell me twice. I curl up next to him, his arm stretched along the back of the brown leather couch as I tuck my head into the crook of his shoulder. He hands me a glass of wine. "This is nice."

"It is." I take a sip of the full-bodied liquid and feel every stress in my life float away. A niggle in my subconscious tries to remind me not to get too close to him, but it ends up on the stress-exodus and vanishes. It's too easy with him. It's too much like what I've always wanted.

Sitting with him and Huxley tonight had such a feeling of family, something I've never experienced.

"What are you thinking about?" he asks.

"What a nice time we had tonight."

He kisses the top of my head. "I'm glad you liked it. I almost had a fucking nervous breakdown."

"You could've ordered takeout," I giggle. "Or I could've brought something."

He stills, his heartbeat loud against my ear. "I wanted to do something for you. I wanted you to feel special, to know I wanted to make you happy."

"Damn it, Landry. Don't go getting all swoony."

"Why?" he laughs. "Isn't that a good thing?"

"Not when you look like you," I giggle. "That makes you impossible to forget."

"Good. Unforgettable is what I was going for."

"You gave me a taste of something tonight," I whisper. "I'll never forget how it felt to sit at the table with you and Huxley. It was so welcoming, like I belonged in this greater plan."

"You do. You belong here."

I look away. I don't want him to see the emotion in my eyes because he's too good. He'll capitalize. He doesn't miss a thing.

Is he right? Do I belong with him? Or is this just a really good time in between seasons?

"Hey," he says, reaching forward and sitting his wine glass on the coffee table. He takes mine from my hand and places it next to his. In one swift motion, he lifts me onto his lap sideways. "Your shoulders just got all tense."

"That happens," I say.

"Not with me. I don't want you stressed with me. I thought you were enjoying yourself."

"I was. I am," I correct myself. "I just can't shut my brain off."

"You overthink everything. I think your brain is the only part of you I have a love-hate relationship with."

I press my lips together. "So you think you have a solid love relationship with the rest of my body?"

"Uh-huh. I love every," he says, his fingertip touching the center of my lips, "fucking," the pad of his finger trails down my chin, in between my breasts, "thing," it descends across my stomach and landing between my thighs, "about you. And I'm certain your body loves me just as much."

His palm sits on my pubic bone, his hand cupping my vagina. I shiver, flexing my hips for more contact. He laughs. "See? I'm right."

"Maybe."

"Whatever," he says, rolling his eyes. "I just have to win over your brain now. I tried tonight to convince it I was more than an athlete. I even borrowed my broth—" He cringes.

"What was that?"

"Nothing."

"You borrowed your what?" He looks at the ceiling. "Talk, Landry."

"I borrowed my brother's kid. Or stepkid. Or whatever. I borrowed Hux," he gulps.

"You did what?"

"I just wanted to show you, not tell you, that I'm not just a base-ball player. That I'm not an athlete that only loves the game," he gulps. "I have a family. A big ass one. And we are all pretty damn tight. They're important to me. I balance that with the game, with my commitments. I do charity stuff with my mom—all kinds of things. I just, I wanted you to see that."

My hand shakes as I touch his cheek. "I can't believe you went to all this trouble."

"I don't know what this is between us. Not exactly," he says, his Adam's apple bobbing. "I know it's all happened pretty fast and I feel like I don't know what would happen tomorrow if you didn't want to see me."

"I feel the same way about you. I just don't know if it can work long-term."

"I'm not saying it has to. Not yet. I just know that it really seems like, with you, it's the right time, right place, right face."

Bursting out laughing, I kiss his cheek. "Did you make up that rhyme?"

"I did. It was a good one, huh?"

"Something like that." I stretch out on the sofa, my head in his lap. I'm not sure what this means, but there's nowhere else I want to be right now than right here.

TWENTY

DANIELLE

HIS CACKLING GIGGLE STREAMS DOWN the hallway, and before I even turn the corner, I know it's Rocky. Peeking around the bend, I see his bright-red hair flopping as he hoists a basketball in the air. It rolls along the rim of the portable hoop before cascading down the side and into the net that keeps the balls from bouncing every which way.

"Almost!" I say. "Flick your wrist a little more."

"What do you know about basketball?" he asks, his little button nose crinkling.

"Hey, now," I giggle, ruffling his hair. "I grew up hearing all kinds of sports conversations."

He shoots me a look that tells me he's not quite convinced. "All right. But hey," he says, his eyes sparkling again as he throws his little arm haphazardly across his buddy, Tommy's, shoulders. "We were wondering if we could do balloons again? You know, the ones that twist like animals and stuff."

"Yeah," Tommy says, picking up Rocky's enthusiasm. His head is bald now, but the nurses are saying he might be released soon. "I missed it last time. Can we do it again? Please?"

"I'll do my best. Now it's time for you guys to head to your rooms."

"But before we go," Rocky interjects, sticking a finger in the air, "one more question."

"Make it quick," I laugh.

"When is Lincoln coming back?"

Hearing his name makes my heart skip a beat. Rocky smiles wide and it's a long moment before I realize he's mirroring mine.

"I'm not sure, Rocky," I admit. "But I think he's planning on dropping by soon."

"Yay!" Rocky shouts, before leading Tommy down the hall. "I told you he would be back! Just wait 'til he comes . . ."

The rest of the conversation is buried under the sound of sneakers squeaking against the tile and the racket of a medicine cart being wheeled down the hall. Glancing at the mail in my hand, I head back into my office.

The phone is ringing as I enter and I toss the envelopes on my desk and pick it up.

"Danielle Ashley," I chirp.

"Hey, Danielle. It's Gretchen."

"How are the budget meetings going?"

A short laugh rips through the phone. It's one of those laughs that isn't a response to humor, but more of a cover-up for something else. Something less funny. "Shit," she follows up. "My God, the board wants to hack us down to nothing!"

"You're joking." Reaching blindly behind me, I find the armrest to my chair and slide it beneath me. "What are they doing?"

"What are they *not* doing is the real question," she huffs. "If they get their way, our budget going forward will look like a third of what it does now."

"A third?" I nearly shout. "We can barely operate as it is! They can't be serious."

"They're serious, Danielle. Dead serious. I just . . . I'm at a loss for words." She ends her statement on a sigh, the weight of her battle landing on me.

This department was completely overhauled by me and Gretchen, made into something truly special. Parents fight for their kids to come here because of the atmosphere. We keep the kids lively, engaged. We keep them from remembering they're sick.

A lump swells in my throat. "What can we do?" I ask.

"I'm doing everything I can, Danielle. Just send good vibes and a prayer if you can." Her voice nearly breaks. "We can't lose the funding. I'll do everything I can."

"I know that," I whisper.

"I'm going to go. I need to get some numbers together before we resume our meeting this afternoon. You'll have some minutes in your email if you want to take a look. I sent them this morning."

I nod, even though she can't see me. Before I find my voice, she's said her goodbye and the dial tone blares in my ear.

Letting myself fall back into my chair, I survey my office. It's bright and playful, a testament to the kids that have been through our program. My gaze lands on a picture taken a couple of years ago, a young family with a little girl with pigtails. Her mother came to my office the day she was released and told me her daughter made little progress in the two other facilities she was in before here. Here, she rebounded and she could never thank the program enough. I get updates from her every six months or so.

Flicking the mouse, I wait for my computer to fire up. When it does, I see a number of emails. The one from Gretchen is bolded and shines at me, begging to be clicked. But another one sits right above it, the name staring me in the face. It's that one I click on first.

Dear Ryan,

Your father and I will be leaving for St. Thomas in a couple of days. We'll be staying through the Thanksgiving holiday and will, for the most part, be unavailable until the second week of December.

Joyce has offered for you to join her family for Thanksgiving dinner. I told her I would pass along the invitation.

We will be spending Christmas with the Spencer family in Aspen. I will leave your gift under the tree when we leave. Give Joyce a call and she can stick it in the mail.

Take care and talk soon.
Mom

The lump in my throat just doubled and it's difficult, if not impossible, to work around it. I wait, unmoving, to see how I react. Every time it's different. Sometimes I cry, unable to push away the rejection of my own parents. Other times, I laugh at their self-absorption and wonder how miserable they must really be. And then there are times where a numbness settles over my soul and I can't make any headway on how I really feel beneath it all. How am I supposed to internalize the absurdity of a second-hand invitation to a holiday with their housekeeper? It's like I'm not good enough to be with them, just their help. An afterthought, as always.

It's moments like this I'm grateful that the numbness is stronger than the hurt. That somehow I've trained myself to block out the most agonizing moments, like holidays, and just embrace the alternative: un-feeling. Maybe shock. Either way, it's preferable.

Easter two years ago was the last time I was invited to my parents' house and that was only because they needed me to put in an appearance. I went along with it because it was easier than being on the receiving end of their wrath. Or so I thought.

"*You seem like such a sweet girl,*" *a wife of one of my father's associates coos, swirling an absurdly-priced wine around in an overpriced crystal glass.* "*Your mother was telling me that the two of you don't quite see eye to eye on a lot of things.*"

"*That's true.*" The explanation is on the tip of my tongue, how my *mother only cares about appearances and my father's acceptance. That I don't spend time with them because they don't want me.*

"*Your mother told me how you refuse to accept their help.*" She eyes me carefully, the wine blushing her cheeks. "*It's too bad you won't let your mother get closer to you, honey. She has so many connections. I would love a daughter to shop with, go to the spa with,*" she sighs. "*It's such a shame you and she are so different.*"

"No, it's such a shame she wants nothing to do with me," I say aloud, startling myself. I jump again when my cell hums on my desk and am grateful to see Macie's name on the screen. "Hey," I say, blowing out a rickety breath.

"Hey! What's happening?"

"Oh, the same old stuff. What about you?"

"What's wrong, Danielle?"

"Nothing."

"Are you okay?"

"Yeah. Of course I am," I promise, although it isn't completely true. "I'm fine."

"You get like this every year around the holidays . . ."

"What do you expect when your parents take off for vacation and never invite you? I mean, I'm shocked they remember to email me," I snort. "God knows they wouldn't call me. Or text me."

"Your parents are assholes."

"That they are," I agree weakly. "But still . . ."

"But still nothing," she retorts. "They don't deserve you. They're two of the most self-obsessed people in the world."

I don't respond because there's nothing to contribute. And the longer this conversation happens, the worse I feel. Macie picks up on it, like she always does.

"Come here for Thanksgiving. Julia and I are cooking a huge ass meal. It'll be fun."

"Nah . . ."

"You are welcome here. We'd love to have you," she says softly.

"I have too much going on here." My eyes drift to my calendar and the blank slots surrounding Thanksgiving and the emptiness that fills the time around the holidays makes itself apparent. I cringe.

"We'll chat about this later," she warns. "But I need to go get back to work. My lunch break is over and I can't even remember why I called. I'll call you later if I remember."

"Sounds good."

Replacing the receiver on the cradle, I bury my head in my hands. My heart swells, causing the pain buried there to sweep up my throat and to my eyes. I try to blink back the hot, salty tears but one lone, solitary tear drips down my cheek. When I reach for a tissue, my hand stalls over the box. Lincoln is standing in the door, his face washed with some unnamed emotion. He doesn't ask for permission to come in. He just does. The door latches softly behind him. He also doesn't ask what's wrong and he doesn't wait for me to tell him. He just storms around my desk and nearly lifts me out of my chair and pulls me into the deepest hug I've ever felt.

That does it. The tears stream, wetting his white t-shirt. He holds me against him, not saying a word. We stand like that for a long time. I couldn't pull away if I wanted. He wouldn't let me.

He reaches behind me and I hear the tissue box being moved. It's only then he lets me lean back.

"Baby . . ." he says, his eyes full of trepidation. "What's wrong?"

"Nothing." I take a proffered tissue and turn away, cleaning up my face. "Just a bad day."

"This isn't how you do a bad day, Dani. Something's wrong."

His hands are on my shoulders, rolling them gently. It feels good to have him here, to have the physical and emotional support so available. I don't really know what to do with it.

"Please talk to me," he pleads.

"I'll sound like a baby," I laugh, the sound barely above a whisper. "This isn't the Danielle I want you to know. I want you to see the strong, confident Danielle. Not . . . this."

He whirls me around until I'm facing him. Our eyes are level, his jaw set in defiance. "I want to know every side of you. The confident side, the part of you that's a little bitchy," he grins, "the sweet one, and the baby one, if it exists."

I wrap myself around his waist, needing to feel him. He smells like expensive cologne and sweat. My eyes close and I allow his scent to calm me. Once I'm sure I won't lose control, I explain. "My parents sent me an email with their holiday plans."

He stills. "And they are?"

"Their usual—St. Thomas for Thanksgiving, Aspen for Christmas."

"Are you going?"

"I'd have to have an invitation to go," I sniffle. "Don't worry though. Their housekeeper will mail my Christmas present."

"Are you fucking kidding me?" he barks. "Tell me you're joking."

I shrug helplessly. "It's been this way my whole life. Even in high school, I'd find a friend to stay with for the holidays because they'd leave. It was that or stay home with the help." My chest tightens as I remember watching the snow fall on Christmas Eve while the microwave counted down the minutes until my hot chocolate would be done. All of my classmates loved the holidays and would come back from break with stories of dinners and vacations and gifts and pranks. I'd spend my break making up the stories I'd tell. No one ever knew I'd really spent two weeks watching re-runs alone.

"I fucking hate them," Lincoln insists.

"You don't even know them."

"I don't have to and it's probably better that I don't," he says, kissing the top of my head. "You're coming to my house for dinner tonight. I'll order something," he chuckles. "But this isn't up for nego-tiation, Dani. You're coming. End of story."

I don't even fight it. I don't want to. "I'll be there."

TWENTY-ONE

LINCOLN

"HEY, G." I STRIP THE sheets off my bed and toss them to the floor. Balancing the phone against my bare shoulder, I find a clean white set in the hall closet and begin remaking the bed.

"What's up?"

"Two things. One, are you coming home for Thanksgiving?"

"Yeah. Why?"

"I have some papers for you to sign for the security company. I didn't know whether to mail them or wait for you to come home."

"Nah, I'll be there. What's number two?"

"In a hurry?" he chuckles.

"Kind of." I start shoving pillows into new pillowcases.

"What are you doing?"

"Making my bed."

"Okay, you're scaring me now. Where's Rita?"

I plop the final pillow against the headboard. "She's not here today. You had two things to talk about?"

"I suddenly don't remember what the second thing was."

An irritated sigh slides out of my mouth. "So we good to go then?"

Graham doesn't respond for a moment. Finally, as I'm walking into the kitchen and wondering if the cake should've gone into the refrigerator, he speaks. "What's wrong, Linc?"

Deciding the cake is fine having sat out, I slump against the counter.

"I have a lot on my mind. That's all." My hand squeezes my forehead, the headache that creeped in on the way home from therapy intensifying. If I could stop clenching my jaw, I'm sure it would help. I glance at the clock.

"Is it your shoulder?" he asks.

"Nah. I had therapy earlier today. My range of motion is about 60% better than it was."

"That's good . . ." He gives me an opportunity to respond, but I don't. "Seriously, all joking aside, are you okay?"

"I'm fine. This isn't about me." I scratch my chin. There's more stubble dotting my face than I usually let add up. "I don't think it's about me, anyway."

My brother blows out a breath. "If you don't want to discuss it, that's fine."

"You know what it is?" I say, shoving off the cabinet. "I'm fucking pissed off."

I can hear it in my tone, the sharpness that's been needling my gut since leaving Dani's office. Graham hears it too because he doesn't push me. He gives me a minute to get my thoughts together.

"I swing by Dani's office after therapy and she's all tore up."

"What do you mean?"

"She's crying, G. I can't deal with her crying, man."

Her beautiful face, stained with tears, slays me again. The feeling of her back heaving as she tried to hold back the hurt makes my fingers itch to find her and pull her to me again.

"Did you do something stupid?" he asks.

"No. It's worse."

"Who?"

"Her fucking parents, G. *Her parents.*"

"What?"

There's no doubt he's having as hard of a time envisioning this as I am. Coming from a family like ours, it's nearly impossible to imagine someone hurting you on purpose. We go to battle for one another. Our dynamic isn't perfect—we have issues just like everyone. But, at the end of the day, we are Landrys. One family. One team. To think her parents hurt her like this is unfathomable. It makes me want to come out of my skin.

"I don't really know the whole thing," I say. "I just know they go off on vacations and never invite her, not even for the holidays. She's their only kid. She said they've never really Included her in shit and she's always been a disappointment to them."

"She's not a prostitute or drug addict, right?"

"Shut the hell up, Graham."

"Just asking. I know some of your haunts," he laughs, trying to break up the seriousness. It doesn't.

"She's kind. Sweet. Sincere. How could anyone hurt her like that?" My fists clench at my sides. "I want to hurt them. Bad. Take a fucking weighted bat and swing for the fucking fences."

"Easy there, slugger."

"Fuck!" I'm pacing the kitchen, my bare feet slapping against the hardwood. My body temperature is rising. Despite being in just my boxer briefs, I'm boiling. "I can't take it, Graham. I can't. I can't see her cry because of some crazy fucking thing like this!"

I think Graham is holding the phone away from his mouth. I think he might be chuckling. I think I might kick his ass when I see him next.

"So my little brother is in love."

"I am not," I counter. "What the fuck do you know about love, anyway?"

"I know it when I see it. And I'm looking at it, I'd say."

The cake is sitting on the table. The smell of Columbian Roasted coffee fills the kitchen. I have three bottles of creamer plus regular milk sitting beside a brand new pink coffee mug with paint brushes on it.

Is this love? Am I in love with Danielle Ashley?

The heat turns to a stone-cold chill.

"I haven't known her long enough to be in love with her," I say.

"You don't have to convince me," Graham says, not bothering to stifle his chuckle. "Work on convincing yourself."

The doorbell rings and my eyes skirt to the clock. "She's here. I gotta go. Call me back if you remember the second thing."

He doesn't say goodbye, just laughs as I hang up. My phone goes sailing across the kitchen table as I jog to the front door.

***

Danielle

I'VE NEVER BEEN SO HAPPY to see him and, this time, it's not because he's basically naked or that his body looks like it was sculpted by the hands of a saint. It's because I just need to be in his arms.

I don't have to wait long. At all, actually. As soon as it registers that it's me standing on his porch, he pulls me inside and into him. My arms wrap around his waist, his skin warm against my face. We don't speak for a long time, just stand in the doorway in the midst of a pile of sneakers and duffle bags.

"How are you?" he whispers against the shell of my ear.

"Better now."

His lips twitch; I feel his smile against my neck. It makes me smile too. Pulling back, I touch his cheek. I fight back the wetness in my eyes. So I don't fall victim to the mushiness I feel sneaking up on me, I stand on my tiptoes and pucker my lips. It takes him all of two seconds to touch them with his.

"Thank you," I whisper against his mouth.

"For what?"

"For being here for me. Let's go sit down. I want to cuddle."

"Cuddle?" he asks, his brows raising. "If all I get for this is a cuddle . . ."

I laugh as I make my way to the living room, leaving him to follow me. I wait for him to sit so I can use him as a pillow.

My head in his lap, looking up into his eyes, I feel relief. Relief from the loneliness that saturates my life, especially this time of year. A break from feeling like no one cares. A reprieve from fending for myself.

I'd forgotten, or maybe I've never known, this little smidgen of peace in my soul. Even if it doesn't last forever, I'm grateful it's here today.

"I was worried about you," he says, his eyes full of concern. "I didn't know what to do."

"Why?"

"Because you were upset. You were crying."

"Haven't you seen a girl cry before?" I laugh.

"Yeah, but usually because of some dumb shit that I really can't feel sorry for them over. But you, today, that was fucked up."

"It's just a part of my life," I shrug.

He brushes a strand of hair off of my forehead. His touch is gentle, caressing, and I close my eyes and just enjoy being at the receiving end.

"Do you have other family?" he asks. "Besides your parents?"

I shake my head. "I'm an only child. So were both my parents, so no aunts or uncles or cousins. My father's parents are alive, but they live in Washington State in some kind of nursing home."

"Your dad put them in a nursing home?" He seems shocked by this, almost flinching as he says it.

"Yeah, I guess. We were never close with them anyway. I saw them sometimes in the summer when they took a vacation near us. But that was maybe six or seven times in my life that I remember." I think back to the weird moments with them. Stifled tea hours. Odd conversations. No hugs, no kisses, no little presents like my friends' grandparents brought them, even though mine had way more money and means. "They're in their eighties, probably. They had my dad when they were older in life. So once they couldn't live alone, Dad signed papers for them to live in this center. I remember hearing my parents discuss it."

He whistles through his teeth. "They're hard core."

"Why do you say that?"

"Because unless you cannot physically care for your family, you don't put them in a nursing home, Dani. They're your blood. Their sacrifices got you where you are, in part." He cringes, as if maybe he's overstepped. "I just didn't grow up like that, I guess. My mom's mom lives in a little guesthouse behind my parents. And if I have to take care of my mom when she gets old, I will. I won't lock her up somewhere." He chuckles. "Graham gets Dad though."

I can't help but laugh at the look on his face. "You really don't see eye to eye with your dad, huh?"

"Nah, we get along. I'm just the most like my mom, I think. Dad is all about work and success and the Landry name. Mom is more about enjoying life, making a difference if you can." He strokes my arm. "You know, when I first got signed by the Arrows, I remember thinking, 'Maybe this will make Dad proud. I'm a professional. I'm an asset to our family.'"

"Lincoln . . ." I say softly. "I'm sure he's proud of you either way."

He just shrugs. We both sit still, lost in our thoughts, and, before I know it, my eyes are closing and sleep settles over me.

TWENTY-TWO

LINCOLN

SHE STIRS. IT'S A SLOW process. At first her hand wiggles, then her feet start to rustle under the sheets. Her head goes back and forth and she yawns softly before her eyelashes start to slowly flutter.

It's fascinating. I realize how creepy this may look—me lying on my side in my bed, watching a girl sleep. I don't give a fuck. I want to be here when she opens her eyes. I want to be the first thing she sees.

Her lips press together as her lids lift. She startles for a half a second before realizing it's me. "Hey," she whispers, clearing her throat. "How'd I get in your room?"

"I carried you. Did you sleep well?"

"Yeah." Her brows pull together. "What time is it? And when did you get new sheets?"

"I changed them today."

"I'm impressed." She yawns again. Her face looks pale, the start to bags evident under her eyes. Her normally smooth features are tight and I wonder what she was dreaming about. "Thank you for letting me come by."

"Of course."

She gives me an odd look, tugging the blankets around her. "What time is it?"

"It's still pretty early. Want me to order some dinner?"

"I better get home. I'll just grab something on the way."

"Why?" I ask. "Why don't you just stay here?"

"I work tomorrow."

Kicking myself for missing such a huge point, I scramble for a solution. "Want me to stay with you?"

"You don't have to do that. Thank you for taking care of me today. Thank you for being there for me."

"Of course. I'm always here if you need me."

Something I said hits her wrong and her eyes widen. She wiggles beneath the blankets, dragging in a deep breath.

"What?" I ask. "What did I say?"

Her head shakes from side to side. "Nothing."

"Tell me the truth."

After what feels like an eternity, she looks at me. "You are amazing. More amazing than I even imagined and that was a lot."

"Naturally."

A start of a smile slips on her lips. "I needed you today."

She says it like those words say it all, like I should understand everything from the simple sentence. Furrowing my brow, I look at her. "I'm glad," I say cautiously. "You should need me. That's what I'm here for."

"It's not." She climbs out of my bed, messing with her long, dark locks. "Things between us have been fun. Great, actually. But today when you walked into my office, I can't even tell you the relief I felt."

"I'm sorry," I say, scrubbing my hands down my face. "How is that a bad thing?" I follow her into the living room where she slides on her shoes.

"Me needing you like I did today is another step into something I'm not sure I can handle," she says, straightening up and facing me. "We are fun, Landry. This thing between us, whatever it is, has made me so happy."

"Me too," I say, feeling a little seed of unease settle in my gut.

"But it's a short term thing. You are going to head into the preseason soon and then you'll be off for two hundred games."

I don't know what to say to this, so I say nothing and hope she clarifies.

"I told you before I don't want to be a baseball girlfriend. I won't, as a matter of fact," she says, pulling her gaze from me. "I somehow convinced myself I could keep it light between us and enjoy it for what it was and let you go when the time came. But I'm in too far."

"There's no measuring stick to what's too far," I say, reaching for her. My heart plummets when she starts to retreat. "What are you doing, Dani?"

"I think I need to take a little step back, Lincoln. For my sanity."

"What are you talking about?" She won't look at me and I swear I must have misheard her. There's no fucking way she just said that to me. I bounce back and forth from being confused, to pissed, to what might just be hurt. "I'm sorry, what did you just say?"

"You heard me," she whispers.

I run my hands through my hair. "Why do we need to *take a step back*? What the hell does that even mean?"

She looks at the doorway. "It just means I don't want to get to a point where I'm dependent on you or need you when I'm feeling crummy."

"You're fucking joking, right?" I repeat. My mind buzzes with a million thoughts, a thousand questions, a hundred replies to that. But I can't get any of them to my tongue.

"When you came in my office today, right after I got my mother's email, I was so happy to see you. And then you told me to come here, and Landry, I didn't even hesitate. This is right where I wanted to be."

"Great. Good. That's what I was hoping for. That's how it should be."

"I know. I think I was too, but," she says, frowning, "I can't do this with you."

"You've already done this with me," I glare.

Her lips press together and I can tell she's warring with herself. I have to bite my tongue, sit on my hands, because I'm two seconds from losing my temper . . . just like I'm two seconds from losing my girl.

"I disagree with all of this," I say. "You are my girl, my girlfriend, my lady. I don't care what you call it, but that's where we stand."

She backs away towards the door, her eyes wide. She's scared. But I can't let her leave here without knowing exactly how I feel.

"When I saw you so hurt today, it changed the game for me. I knew as soon as I walked in your office that it was a watershed moment. I couldn't go back." I stalk through the room until I'm standing in front of her. "I want to see where this goes. I've never felt this way about a girl before. Well, no guys either, for that matter."

Her face slips and she starts to smile. I take it as a good sign.

"I want to lock you down. Be there to make you smile. Make you mad. Make sure you're protected and know how awesome you are."

"I'll still come over and fuck you, Landry."

She says it to get a rise out of me, to deflect from the topic she doesn't want to discuss. It's how she rolls. Instead, I flip it back on her.

"You bet your sweet, round ass you will. And you'll come over and let me make love to you too."

She moves down the hall to the front door, thanking me again for being there for her today. I can barely hear her over the roar in my ears. I put my hand on the door, closing it.

"I can't get wrapped up in you," she says, looking straight ahead. "I'm going down a rabbit hole and I have to pull myself out."

"You can't get wrapped up in me?" I ask, my voice a little louder than I care to admit. "You'll wrap up in my sheets. In my arms. Around my cock. But you can't get wrapped up in my heart because I play fucking baseball? Really, Danielle?"

"It's not like that."

"It looks just like that standing here."

She stands on her tiptoes and kisses me gently against the lips. "You are so amazing. Too amazing for your own good," she smiles. "I just need a little time to work this out in my mind, okay? I'm sorry."

I don't respond as she walks out the door.

TWENTY-THREE

DANIELLE

"YOU'RE KIND OF FREAKING ME out right now." Pepper stands at the edge of the table and watches me like I might start screaming at any minute. "I'm not sure soup will fix this."

"I don't think so," I sniffle. The napkin has a giant hole in the center from my tears. I toss it to the side and grab another one. "I don't know what will fix this. Maybe a time machine so I'm not working the day he ventured off that damn elevator."

Pepper sinks into the booth across from me. "What happened?"

"I broke it off."

She gasps, her hand hitting her thigh with a slap. "You better have a damn good reason." When I laugh, she narrows her eyes. "You broke it off with Lincoln Landry. Listen to that out loud: *you broke up with Lincoln Landry.* Hear that? Hear how stupid that sounds?"

I drop my hands to the table. "I never intended for it to get this serious with him. I have to get a handle on this while I can. Get what I'm saying?"

"I get you're dumb."

"Thanks, friend." I shred the napkin, making a pile of equal strips in front of me. "It would be easier if he was a jerk or had a little dick or was self-centered. But he's not." I look at her. "He's perfect."

"I so don't understand you."

"When my parents got married, they were so in love. My dad adored her. I found this trunk in the attic when I was a teenager and it was filled with letters he wrote her while they were dating and right after they got married. He doted on her, Pepper. Whatever she wanted, he got her. Whatever he could do to make her happy, he did. He even had a plane fly over a picnic with a banner telling her he loved her. I mean, how sweet is that?"

Pepper gives me a thumbs-up. "I'm waiting on the point."

"They had what seems like the perfect relationship. And then my dad got signed to play pro. I could hear the change in the letters, which went to post cards from different cities. Eventually, there were no more." I grab another napkin. "I don't remember him being home much in my early childhood and, when he was, I was a distraction. My mom was a distraction. I was a pain in her side because I took away from her energy to entertain him."

"That was their choice, Danielle."

"It happened to every one of their friends. Their wives sit at home, bored, while the men do what they really love. It's like the sport replaces the love for their wives. I just . . . I promised myself I wouldn't end up like that, Pepper. Since I was a little girl, at home with a nanny that I didn't even know or like, I said I'd never end up like them, no matter what. I would have a huge family and hug and kiss them all the time and not make my children feel like they had to cower in the corner when I walked in the room."

"But Lincoln has been nothing but fantastic." She narrows her eyes. "What spooked you?"

I look away from her.

"What happened that you aren't telling me, Dani?"

Sighing, I feel my heart tug in my chest. "My mom emailed me. I felt that loneliness and my first instinct was to go to Lincoln. I woke up in his bed and realized how bad it's going to hurt when either a) he leaves me or b) I end up like my mom. There's no other end to this love story. Trust me when I say I wish there was, but there's not."

Pepper's shoulders fall forward. "This entire thing makes me so sad. You were so happy lately. I was hoping this was a good thing for you."

"It was good. But I need to end it on my terms while it is good, Pepper. I needed him today. I can't need him."

"You're just scared."

"No, I'm terrified. But it's over now, more or less." I look up at the confection display and smile as realistically as I can and do what I do best: deflect. "Can you make me those pumpkin cupcakes for Thanksgiving? I draw the line at baking for one."

"You can come with us."

"Pepper," I laugh, sitting back in my seat, "you couldn't pay me enough money to have dinner with your mother-in-law."

She laughs too. "I feel you there. Yes, two pumpkin cupcakes for Thanksgiving. Consider it done."

One broken heart? That's done too.

923

TWENTY-FOUR

LINCOLN

BRINGING THE BOTTLE OF BEER to my lips, I take a long, steady draw. I hold the neck between two fingers, twirling it a bit as I try to figure out my fucking life.

My shoulder throbs. I haven't felt it hurt like this in a while. It's a little disconcerting, but I tell myself it's from therapy. That Houston pushed me too far. That it'll go away in the morning. There's relief in that. There would be more relief in knowing my fucking heart won't feel like this when I wake up.

The cake still sits on the table. Her pink mug, the one I bought just for her, sits by the sink. Both make a small smile play on my lips, even though I feel hollow.

Flipping off the coffee maker, I grab my phone from where it sits next to the cake and hold it. Finishing the beer and tossing it towards the trash, I watch it bounce off the lip and hit the floor.

I don't even care.

Scrolling until I find the name in my Emergency Contacts, I place the call. It rings a few times and I almost hang up when she answers.

"Well, if it isn't my long lost baby boy!" my mother trills on her end. "Can you hold on just a second, Lincoln?"

"Yeah."

I listen to her talk to someone and recognize Paulina's voice. She's one of my mother's oldest friends, one that Barrett used to bang off and on. Ford maybe too. Soon, she's back.

"I'm sorry about that. We were wrapping up the plans for a coat drive for our women's club."

"How's that going?"

"Good. There are so many needy families this year. The requests were double what they were last year. It's so incredibly sad."

"Can I send a check or something?"

"Such a sweet boy," Mom gushes. "Why don't you come down this winter and help us with a fundraiser. Maybe we could do a food drive. Put some baskets together for needy families for Christmas. With your name attached to it, I bet we could stock some pantries for the winter."

"I'd love to. Tell me when and I'm there."

She pauses and I hear a quick breath. "Linc, what's wrong?"

"What do you mean?"

"You don't sound like yourself. There have been no jokes, no cracks, no baseball analogies, and we've talked for two whole minutes."

I chuckle, but even that sounds sad. "I don't feel like myself either."

"Is it your shoulder?"

"Well, it's hurting like hell."

"Watch your language."

"Sorry, Mom," I sigh. "I go in for a battery of tests in the morning. Then I meet with the GM and team docs and things after Thanksgiving to see what they have to say."

"It's going to work out."

"Yeah." I place my elbows on the counter and sigh again.

"Give me one moment," she says. "Paulina! Just one more thing . . ."

I wonder what Dani is doing. If she's okay. If she misses me half as much as I miss her.

How can she do this? How can she just write this off like it's nothing? This is something. Something possibly great and she knows it. Why wouldn't she want this? I look down at my abs.

"Okay, honey. I'm so sorry," Mom says, coming back to the line. "Now tell me what's really wrong."

"I just did."

"No, you just lied to your mother."

Chuckling, I stand up and walk around the island. "I met a girl."

"That's great!"

"She hates me."

"I have a hard time believing that," Mom laughs. "No one could hate you, Lincoln."

"Okay, maybe she doesn't hate me, but she doesn't want me."

"Do you know why?"

"Does it matter?"

"Of course it matters."

I head to the sink and pick up her cup. The paintbrushes remind me of how I finagled my way back into her office to paint with Rocky. Out of all the contents of this house, this cup is the only thing that I feel a connection to. That feels dumb.

"Lincoln?"

"She has this hang up with me because her family are complete dicks. Sorry, Mom," I apologize for the language before she can call me out on it. "Her dad was an athlete and kind of ruined their family, I think. I'm losing her and it's nothing I did. Nothing I am, other than exactly what I am."

"That's tough."

"You think? She likes being with me, likes me doing little things to try to make her like me, yet she panics about it. She flipped out on me today because I tried to take care of her. How do you get around that?" I ask. "How can I fix her not wanting who I am as an athlete and not wanting me to, you know, love her? Not saying I do, but you know."

I know my mother is smiling. She's probably standing in her massive dining room with her diamond-laden finger sitting right on her heart. I said the L-word. She's a sucker for that stuff.

"I don't mean I love her," I clarify. "Don't go planning weddings and stuff."

She laughs. "I won't."

"This is why I don't date seriously. It's too much of a headache."

"You don't date seriously, Linc, because you haven't found a woman that makes you want to see her every day. No offense, but you don't typically choose women that have much to offer you."

"Oh, they offer me—"

"Lincoln Harrison Landry, don't you even go there with me!" she nearly yells over me. "I do not want to hear about your escapades. Save that for your brothers."

I can't help but laugh, and before long, she's laughing too.

"I think she's scared," Mom reasons. "From what you told me, she doesn't have a safety net to fall on. She's probably learned to be her own protection system. Think about it. You are handsome and smart and wealthy and talented . . ."

"Keep going," I grin.

"You are a prize, honey. And she knows that. Think about this from her perspective: she is alone in the world. She finally breaks and lets you in and then something happens and it doesn't work out."

"But that's true of any relationship. Not just with me."

"True, but you're an athlete. Like her dad. It's human nature to stay away from things that remind us of other things that have hurt us."

I hate when she makes sense. "So that leaves me shit out of luck?"

"That's a disgusting choice of words."

Ignoring her, I press forward. "So I'm supposed to just suck it up because her dad ruined her life? That's not fair, Mom. I don't accept that."

"Then don't," she says softly. "You just struck out. What do you do when you strikeout in a game?"

"I hit a homerun at the next at-bat."

"That's right," she sings. "Just be patient with her. Pretend like the pitcher is a little off his game and you have no idea what's coming down the pike."

"The pipe, Mom. What's coming down the pipe."

"Whatever," she laughs. "You get the picture. Now, tell me when you'll be home."

"I have the assessment in the morning. I'm supposed to leave the day after."

"I can't wait to see you."

"Love you, Mom."

"You too."

Placing the cup back on the counter, I walk across the room. When I get to the doorway, I stop and look at it sitting on the counter over my shoulder.

Batter up.

Me: Hey.

It takes more than a minute for her to respond, every second feeling like a year. When I hear the ping announcing a message, I can't swipe fast enough.

Dani :Hi.

Me: How are you?

Dani: Good. In the bathtub.

Me: Are you fucking with me?

Very slowly, a picture loads on my screen of one bent knee in a pool of bubbles. A wine glass is on the ledge, along with a row of little candles.

Me: You better be alone.

Dani: Of course.

I erase every response I type out. I'm not sure which emotion to use to inspire the follow up. When hers pops up, I let out a sigh of relief.

Dani: *I'm good. Thank you for checking.*

Me: *Out of all the words you've ever said to me, and you've said some things that have been borderline offensive, those are the ones I hate most.*

Dani: *Which?*

Me: *Thank you.*

Dani: *How is that?*

Me: *Because it implies I'm doing you a favor. Or going out of my way when I ask if you're okay or checking on you.*

Dani: *Ok. I appreciate you doing those things.*

Me: *That's better. Sort of.*

Dani: *How does your shoulder feel tonight?*

Me: *Sore.*

Dani: *Ice it.*

Me: *I don't want to talk about my shoulder.*

Dani: *I know. I was just thinking about it. The wine is starting to make me sleepy. I need to get out of here and get to bed.*

Me: *I'm here if you need me. You know that.*

Dani: *I do. Goodnight, Landry.*

Me: *Night, Ryan.*

Strike one.

TWENTY-FIVE

DANIELLE

"YOU LOOK LIKE SHIT."

"Gee, thanks, Gretchen," I sigh, heading to the doorway.

She surveys me before following me down the hallway. "I take that back. You look worse than shit."

"Do you have something productive to say to me or are you just here to insult me?" I laugh.

I'm more than aware I don't look my best today. Hell, I don't even look mediocre today. My eyes have dark circles, my face crinkled with lines from sadness and wine and lying on the side of my face while I cried last night.

I woke up not sure what decision was right. Letting myself get involved with Lincoln, even when I felt like I was getting in too deep? Or pulling away because I'm scared? Which is worse—being extra risky or overly cautious?

All I know is that I thought of him as I fell asleep and when I woke up. I miss his voice and his stupid texts and wonder how his shoulder feels. There's a part of me that feels dead not knowing when I'll see him again . . . if ever. This is impossible.

Gretchen sighs, pulling me back to the present. "The budget is ripped apart."

"No," I gasp, my eyes going wide.

"Unfortunately. The official papers will come through next week, so enjoy the holiday. You might want to make plans for another job though, Danielle. I can't promise you anything right now."

My face falls as I try to keep this in a little box in my brain. If not, I'm going to be completely overwhelmed.

"I have a meeting and then I'm heading home to nurse this migraine. Take the day off tomorrow—paid. Extend your holiday weekend before the chaos of next week hits."

"Gretchen?"

"Yeah?"

"I'm so sorry."

"Aren't we all?" With a sad smile, she turns down the adjacent hallway and disappears.

Maybe this isn't the worst thing to happen. Everything seems so bleak here. I could use this as an opportunity to move. Maybe somewhere warm. Or maybe Boston. I should call Macie.

The elevator dings and I glance over my shoulder and stutter-step before stopping. His eyes light up in the way I love, his body looking strong in a fitted black workout shirt and shorts. Lincoln makes no effort to move, to wave, to insinuate in any way that he is happy to see me besides the flicker in his eyes. As the doors close, we exchange a small, almost-smile, and then, before I'm ready, they swing shut.

A whimper slides through my lips, my eyes wetting immediately. "Stop this," I hiss to myself and dart to the bathroom. It's empty.

"This was your decision and it was a good one." I straighten out my rumpled yellow dress. I'd hoped the color would brighten my spirits, but no luck.

I head back to my office, my heels clicking against the tile. "Take the job with Macie. Get out of here and make a fresh start," I whisper to myself as I watch my feet step in the center of each tile.

I flick the door behind me to my office and nearly yelp. "Lincoln!"

He's sitting across from my desk, the twinkle in his eye replaced with a look of . . . fear? He forces a swallow as I grab the corner of my desk for support.

"What are you doing here?" I ask.

"I needed to see you."

"Why?"

"A number of reasons," he says, a smile ghosting his lips.

"I thought you went down on the elevator," I whisper, still not sure I'm really seeing him here.

His face lights up as a full-blown smirk drags across it. "I did. Then I came back up."

My cheeks ache from the smile I'm giving him and I tell myself to stop it before I give him a false idea, but I can't erase it. There's no way to turn off the light he ignites in me.

He holds a tube up in the air. "I brought a signed poster for Rocky. Think I could take it to him?"

Some of my hope wavers. "Rocky was released two days ago. His cancer is undetectable."

The joy on Lincoln's face hits my heart. This is part of what I love about him. His genuineness. His sweetness. His thoughtfulness.

"I can take it and mail it to him though," I offer.

"Please."

I take the tube and our fingers touch. I jerk mine away. "I have a favor to ask," he says tentatively.

"The last time you asked a favor, it was a trick." I sit across from him, grateful for the support.

"It might be a trick this time too," he laughs. "Can you blame me?"

"Yes."

"I'm leaving in the morning for Savannah for Thanksgiving."

"So?"

"Go with me."

"What?" I squeak. "Landry, are you nuts?"

"Nuts about you."

I collapse back in my chair with a huff, hoping I sound more irritated than I am. I have to power through, not succumb. Protect myself. "I can't go with you."

"Can't or won't?"

"Does it matter?"

I expect an argument, at least a little fight, but get none. He just shrugs his broad, thick shoulders. "Fine."

My brows pull together, but I keep my features otherwise smooth. He's watching me too carefully. He's looking for an opening and I'm not about to give him one.

"Should I bring dinner to your house or should we cook it together at mine?"

"Excuse me?"

"Look," he says, sliding his hands down the legs of his shorts, "if you don't want to go to Savannah, I get it. My family can be a little overbearing. So we'll stay here. We'll—"

"I'm not having Thanksgiving with you."

"You have plans I'm unaware of ?"

"Maybe."

"You better fit me in."

My eyes wet again and he grips the armrests. He's obviously fighting to keep himself from jumping the desk and grabbing me, but he doesn't. I'm both thankful and a little disappointed he doesn't.

"You need to see your family," I counter. "It's your thing. You've told me stories about football with your brothers and everything."

"Yeah, they'll be pissed if I don't come. But I'm not leaving you."

"Why do this? I've told you this won't work out between us in the long term. We're just setting ourselves up for a lot of heartache later."

"Because," he says, leaning forward until his elbows rest on my desk, "I care about you. And I know you care about me too. So maybe you are afraid to trust me. I hate it, but I'll deal. But we're friends. Hopefully with benefits," he winks in only the way he can.

My heart nearly explodes as a warmth extends throughout my veins. The twinkle is back in his eyes. Slowly, his hands reach across the desk for mine.

And just as slowly, mine take them and give them a squeeze. "This is what I was telling you," I say, our gazes locked together.

"What's that?"

"You'd be impossible."

"So you'll go with me? Or are we staying home?"

I open my mouth and then close it. Then, against the screaming of my brain, I let my heart do the talking. "Let's go to Savannah."

As good as it feels to say that out loud, it's even better to be met with Lincoln's smile.

TWENTY-SIX

DANIELLE

MY HEAD RESTS AGAINST LINCOLN'S shoulder as the car, driven by one of Barrett's staff, rumbles down the road. The plane ride to Savannah was fast, uneventful, and quite frankly, the best trip I've ever taken. First class and sitting next to him, breathing him in, feeling his touch, watching women beg him for attention while he held *my* hand was pretty much the stuff dreams are made of.

Lincoln squeezes my hand, our fingers interlocked as they have been since we got in the car. "You okay?"

I'm not sure if I am okay. Right now, I'm perfect. I haven't felt this excited about something since I was a little girl and I'm not even sure what it is I'm excited about. Spending time with Lincoln? Being a part of something bigger on a holiday? Feeling this happiness in my heart? Maybe some of all of it. But with the good, comes the bad. There's the unknown of what happens when we get home.

This feels right. Being with him always feels right. But how do you trust your heart when your brain is screaming you know better? When as soon as you start feeling good about things, a photo essay flashes before your eyes highlighting the resemblances in past mistakes and this situation?

The uncertainty of what's ultimately right, not what feels right at this moment, keeps me wobbly. So I do what any crazy person does: I don't think about it. Pasting on a smile and reminding myself I'm enjoying this weekend for what it is, I squeeze his hand back.

"I'm good," I say.

"I hope so. I'm just really glad to have you here." He brings my hand to his lips and presses a kiss to the top. When my phone rings inside my purse, I think about not answering it because it means taking my hand out of his. He seems to figure that out and laughs, using his free hand to unlace ours. "Get it."

With an exaggerated sigh, I dig through my bag and pull out the glowing device. "Hello?"

"I'm so sorry to call you while you're on holiday," Gretchen rushes, "but I have news. Big news!"

"Really?" I squirm in my seat. This can go one of two ways. "What is it?"

"I just got a call from the business office, Danielle. There's been a donation to the department. Big enough that we don't have to worry about anything until mid-year next year! We can stay fully staffed and under normal operations for the time being."

I can hear the emotion in her throat and it causes my own to clench shut. My mind races with all this means—continued service to so many children and their families. A job. I hope.

How did we get so lucky?

"I'm in disbelief," she chokes out. "I haven't slept in nearly two weeks. I'm drinking a mai-tai to celebrate and then I'm passing out."

"Who made the donation? We need to thank them somehow." I glance at Lincoln as he shifts away from me ever-so-slightly. "I feel like a load of stress has just evaporated from my shoulders."

"We don't. It was made anonymously this morning."

A twitch pinches my gut, hidden away in that place that only triggers when you know something you don't know you know. It crawls out, over my heart, making it tingle, and to my brain. "We don't, huh?" I look at Lincoln's profile, all angles and scruff. He refuses to look at me.

"No. But whoever it is deserves a huge hug. And a kiss." She rattles on and on while I watch Lincoln pointedly not look at me.

"Are you still there, Danielle?"

"Yes," I laugh, shaking my head. "Such great news. Thank you for calling. I'll see you at work on Monday!"

"See you then. Happy Thanksgiving." The phone goes back in my bag as I continue to wait for Lincoln to look at me. "Guess what?"

"What's that?" He faces me, his eyes cautious.

"Someone anonymously donated enough money to keep our program going for a while. Isn't that nice?"

"That's awesome, Dani."

"You, uh, you wouldn't know anything about that, would you?" Instinctively, he leans away. It's so slight, so barely noticeable that I know he doesn't realize he's done it. And therefore, given himself up.

"Why would I?"

"I think you do, Landry." My hand rests on his knee, and with even pressure, I run it up his muscled thigh to the bend of his jeans.

"I think you're crazy," he gulps, nodding towards Troy as if he's reminding me he's there.

"Don't act innocent. No one believes you."

"Oh, don't get me wrong," he grins, "I'm happy to fuck you right here."

"Landry!" I exclaim, my cheeks burning.

He chuckles in return while Troy, ever the professional, pretends not to notice. The car pulls up to the entrance of the Farm. It is beautiful. An ornate gate opens, and a long, winding driveway extends in front of us. Hedges block any visibility from the road, and it's not until we are rounding a bend that I can see the house.

Why they call it a farmhouse is beyond me. That word paints an image of a little white house with a chicken coop. This is a Southern plantation. A huge, wide porch with pillars looks to encompass the entire place. Mums line whiskey barrels and give the clean exterior pops of burgundy, orange, and yellow. It's breathtaking.

"This is gorgeous," I breathe as it comes into full view. "Not what I expected."

"This is my second favorite place in the world," he whispers against my ear.

"Second? What could be more perfect than this?"

"Inside you."

Before he can pull away, I turn my face so my lips capture his. He deepens the kiss, our lips working against one another in perfect harmony. As we pull away, breathless, he grins. "Thank you for coming."

"I'll ensure you come later," I promise.

"Naughty girl," he chuckles as the car rolls to a stop. "I like it."

"You will."

Looking around the fields leading to a spectacular tree line of evergreens, I feel my heartbeat pick up. I practice my even breathing technique so I don't panic. "Who are all these people?"

A swarm of people seems to pop out from all directions. A regal couple stand on the porch, and I figure them to be Lincoln's parents by their age. Another man comes out the front door and down the steps towards the car. He looks like Lincoln, just more distinguished in his navy button-up and open collar. I vaguely recognize him as Barrett Landry from random magazine articles.

From the side of the house comes a stockier, clean cut version of the same cloth. With his black track pants and long-sleeve white shirt, he looks military. At his side is a female, younger than Lincoln, in ripped jeans and an orange off-the-shoulder shirt. Her long, blonde hair is purple at the ends.

"My family," Lincoln smiles the widest I've ever seen. "Come on!" Without waiting for Troy to open the door, Lincoln slides out, nearly pulling me along with him. His excitement is contagious and, despite the tinge of panic, I find myself smiling.

"Hey," Lincoln calls, pulling one of his brothers in a bear hug. "How are you, Barrett?"

"Good. How was the trip?"

"Great. Where's Alison?"

"Fuck off," Barrett laughs, stepping to the side. "Who is this?" He heads my way, his eyes sparkling. "I'm Barrett. Nice to meet you."

I tuck a strand of hair behind my ear before extending my hand to him. "I'm Danielle Ashley. Nice to meet you."

He walks right past my hand and pulls me into a quick hug. "We don't shake hands in this family," he laughs.

"Easy with the hug," Lincoln laughs, shoving him gently.

Barrett chuckles as the other siblings reach us. Lincoln greets them both before standing beside me, his hand around my waist. "Danielle, this is Ford and Sienna. Guys, this is my girl."

My reaction to his declaration in front of his family is pasted on my face. Sienna laughs right before she, too, pulls me into a hug. "It's so great to meet you," she says, her eyes shining. "He treats you right, right? Because if not, I'll take care of him."

"He's great," I blush.

"Don't say that," Ford says, stepping to me and rolling his eyes. "You'll make his ego even bigger. I'm Ford." We hug. Naturally.

"Tell us about you," Sienna says. "Forego the normal introduction stuff. Tell us what you enjoy. What you love."

"She loves my cock," Lincoln interjects.

"Oh my God," Sienna says, her hands covering her ears.

"That's great, Linc! I'm so glad the surgeons could create one from your pussy," Ford jokes.

"Fuck you guys," Lincoln laughs.

His fingers dip into my skin. I'm not sure if it's to remind me that even though he's conversing with his family, his mind is on me, but that's what it does. My heart fills with warmth and as I try to fight this feeling, of maybe falling in love, the sensation takes over.

"Let's go say hi to Mom and Dad," Lincoln says.

He guides me to the porch, his brothers and sister bantering back and forth in a way I've never seen before. The love that fills these siblings is so apparent, so dynamic. I could watch their facial expressions and listen to their stories for days.

"There's my baby boy!" The woman has her arms out for Lincoln before he gets there. She's dressed in beige slacks and a purple top with a long gold necklace that catches the sunlight. Her hair is perfectly coiffed. She's beautiful. "I've missed you. I'm so glad to have you home." "Missed you too." Lincoln kisses her cheek and smiles at her more warmly than I've ever seen him look at anyone. The love between them tugs at my heart. He turns on his heel and extends a hand to his father.

He takes it, pulling him in to a quick, more formal embrace. "Hey, Dad."

"Hi, Son. Good to see you. How's that arm feeling?"

"Pretty good. A little sore, but therapy keeps it that way."

"You're gonna be fine, Lincoln. You're gonna be fine."

Lincoln nods stiffly before turning towards me. "Mom, Dad—I want to introduce you to Danielle Ashley. Dani, these are my parents."

"Hi, Mr. and Mrs. Landry," I say, hoping I come across way more cool than I feel. I've met distinguished people a hundred times in my life. Why the nerves are kicking my ass now is beyond me. "It's a pleasure to meet you."

"Oh, sweet girl," Mrs. Landry says softly, her hand patting my back as she leans in. "It's Vivian. Mrs. Landry was my mother-in-law." She sends me a quick wink before turning to her husband.

"It's nice to meet you," her husband says, shaking my hand. He gives me a kind smile, but I can tell he's distracted. "Lincoln, want to take a walk with me?"

I grab on to his bicep as he looks warily at me. "Go on. I'll be fine."

"You sure?" he asks, his brows pulled together.

"I'm sure. I'm a big girl."

Vivian places a hand on my shoulder. "Go on with your father," she tells her son. "I'll take Danielle inside and we'll get her some food. You hungry, dear?" she asks me.

"A little." I'm not, but I want Lincoln to go. He needs to, I think. "I'll be inside when you get back."

He kisses my cheek, much to his mother's amusement, and takes off down the stairs with his father.

"Do you like soup?" she asks.

I almost laugh. "Soup is great."

TWENTY-SEVEN

LINCOLN

THE WIND IS COOL AND steady as we step off the porch and away from the house. I let my father lead me. We amble down the driveway for a bit before he takes a detour off the asphalt and towards a little bench near the tree line.

My stomach knots and twists as I try to read his body language. He's said nothing, indicated nothing, and it has me wanting to just ask him outright what he has to say. Because there's something. There always is.

Looking towards the house as I take a seat next to my father, I wonder what Dani's doing. If she's okay. If she's nervous or anxious. This kind of thing is new to her, and I have no clue how she's feeling, and that adds majorly to the chaos inside me.

I want to be with her. My hand around her waist. My ears picking up her giggle, making sure she's happy and comfortable.

"Lincoln?" Dad's voice pulls me back to the cold, iron seat. His eyes are on me, but the fire I expected in them isn't there. I breathe a sigh of relief.

He's always treated me like the youngest boy in the family. True, I am, but I'm capable. I've never needed him, not like Barrett and

Ford have. I've never asked him for a dime, for a job, or for anything more than a piece of advice and that was only when there was not one other person in the world that knew what I needed to know. Yet, he always seems like I'm hanging by a thread or on the cusp of destroying everything. Sure, I might have wrecked a couple of cars and got tossed from a game . . . or two. But I'm not whatever he thinks I am.

"How are you doing, Son?"

My head bobbles around. "Good. Fine. Everything is chugging along."

"Therapy going well?"

"Sure." I toe a rock with my sneaker. "I meet with the management when I get back about the assessment I did yesterday."

He nods, taking in more than my words. He already knew this, but what he didn't know is how I feel about it. I'm careful with him. I project what I want him to take away. The way he's looking at me now has me nearly squirming. He's putting together every cue I'm emitting.

"I talked to your agent about that briefly yesterday. What's your plan, Lincoln?"

"For what?"

"For your career." He blows out a breath, fixing his gaze on something across the lawn. "I'm assuming you want to re-sign with Tennessee."

"Definitely," I say without hesitation. "I love it there. They love me there. I'd love to be a franchise player for them."

"Have you given any thought to being traded?"

The knot winds tighter. "Yeah."

"And?"

"And I'll have to go," I nearly bark. When I see his eyes narrow, I relent. "I'm just worried, Dad. I've had this over my head for weeks now. I just need an answer so I can get comfortable. Does that make sense?"

His hand clamps on my shoulder, giving it a gentle squeeze. "It does. It's hard to not know what the future holds. It causes a lot of stress." His hand falls back to his lap. "That's the hardest part of elections. You gear up for these things for months, even years sometimes, and have to wait it out. It's not good for a man's sanity," he chuckles.

"How did you handle it?"

"Well . . ." He tosses around the words in his head before speaking. "To tell you the truth, it's why I stopped campaigning. It's why I took Landry Holdings to another level. The nerves couldn't handle it anymore. And neither could your mama."

"Mom can handle anything," I laugh.

He shrugs, a smile still on his face. "She's a tough one. She's handled this life with the dignity and class of a saint, especially considering who she's married to," he winks. "But after my last campaign, we had a sit down. She was really over it. She never once asked me not to run again. She wouldn't do that. She loves me too much, understands this is in my blood. But she stood beside me and supported me for years, Linc. There had to come a time when I decided to do what was right by both of us."

This is news to me. I always thought my mom loved the publicity as much as my father. And I also always thought my dad did whatever he wanted. How weird.

"Sounds like you made the right choice then," I say. "But why did you push Barrett into politics?"

My father takes a deep breath. "From the moment you all were born, I tried to find your strengths. Then push you into areas I thought you might like and things I thought you might excel doing. Barrett is a natural politician. Did I push him too much there? Did I hang too many of my own aspirations on his shoulders? Maybe."

"I think you did. You know I think that."

"I know," he sighs. "And you're probably right." His lips press together, the lines on his face deepen. "You want to know what your strengths are?"

"I'm definitely the best looking."

He rolls his eyes. "You're wrong. I am," he deadpans, making me laugh. "You can do anything. You can do everything you want to do with such ease, it's crazy."

I still. I have never heard him talk like this before and I'm not sure whether he means it or if he's going to start laughing.

"You are one hell of a baseball player, Lincoln. Watching you on the field, reading your name in the paper gives me so much pride . . . You'll never understand it until you have a son of your own."

"I just hope I haven't fucked it up," I say through the tightness in my chest.

"Here's the thing," he says, his hands on his knees as he watches a car come towards us on the driveway. "Regardless of what happens in your career, you're going to be fine. There are seasons of our lives. Look at me. I was a businessman. Then a politician. Then a businessman again. Now, I'm thinking about retiring altogether."

"You are?"

"Ford's coming home. The company is branching out. Graham is doing a fine job." He smiles softly. "I'm tired, Linc. I want to sit back and maybe have some grandkids driving me nuts. I want to take your mother on some vacations and have my phone stop ringing so damn much. I'm getting old, kid."

My jaw is hanging open. I barely register the car has stopped and someone is walking towards us. I just look at him and watch him laugh at my reaction.

"What I'm saying is this: don't worry too much. What's done is done. We don't always see eye to eye and part of that is because you're a lot like your old man, Lincoln," he chuckles. "You're hard-headed. You're a man's man. You're opinionated, and while that makes me want to strangle the life out of you sometimes, I also respect that."

"Wow," I whisper, exhaling a deep breath.

"Graham's coming, so I want to say this quick and be done," he says quickly. "Out of all my children, you are the one I worry about the least. Yes, I may second guess you and question your decisions, but it's only because I want to make sure you've thought it through.

But, like me, you'll figure out a way to succeed. Nothing will hold you back."

He pats me on the leg, stands, and heads across the lawn to meet Graham. I just watch, speechless, unsure as to what the hell just happened.

TWENTY-EIGHT

DANIELLE

"MAKE YOURSELF AT HOME." VIVIAN Landry taps the side of a stool facing into the kitchen as she makes her way to the refrigerator. "How was your trip?"

"Good," I say, not sure whether to sit or stand. She indicated to sit, but maybe I should stand. "Do you need help with anything?"

She glances at me over her shoulder, a warm smile splashed against her porcelain skin. "Don't be silly. You've been traveling all day. Sit down and let me get you something to refresh you."

Sienna waltzes in and joins her mom in the kitchen. She, however, hops on the counter top just like I've seen Lincoln do a million times. It makes me grin as I climb onto the stool.

They make me nervous. Not because they're Lincoln's family—I've met a guy's family before. Not because they're wealthy or so beautiful. It's because they're different. They are a family. They like each other. It leaves me a little uncertain how to proceed.

"What do you like?" Vivian asks. "Water? Hot cocoa? Tea?" She looks at her daughter. "When do we sit on counters, Sienna?"

"Come on, Mom," she sighs playfully. "It's the Farm. Not your house. I'm not tainting your counters with my as—behind."

Vivian flashes her a warning glance. "Careful, little girl."

Sienna reacts with a bubbly laugh and picks a piece of celery off a plate beside her. Twirling it in the air, she looks at me. "It's nice to have you here, Danielle."

"Thanks," I blush. "It's nice being here."

"Will your family miss you for the holiday?" Vivian asks, pulling a tray with two pitchers on it from the refrigerator. A little bubble of panic floats to the top of my throat as I try to figure out how to tell these people I'm nothing like them. I'm more than relieved when she keeps talking and doesn't wait on an answer. "I hate when my kids can't come for Thanksgiving. It's our favorite holiday, the one not marred by gifts and cards and money," she says, shooting Sienna a look.

"I don't ask for money," Sienna shoots back. "Daddy just gives it to me."

Vivian lets it go and instead pulls three heavy glasses from a mahogany cabinet. "You are spoiled rotten."

"That's why I've had a job since I was fifteen, right?" Sienna asks, crunching on the celery. "Because I'm so spoiled."

"A little work never hurt anyone," Vivian retorts, handing me a glass of dark liquid. "If you want something else, just ask. I got side-tracked here with my mouthy daughter."

Sienna blows her mom a kiss. Vivian walks across the room, grabs her daughter's face, and kisses her cheek.

They're so easy with each other. Mother and daughter, yes, but something more. Something I've never really seen before. Maybe this is unconditional love.

"Danielle?"

"Oh, I'm sorry," I say, fidgeting as I come back to the present. "It's just been a long day."

"Do you need to lie down?" Sienna asks. "I can take you up to your room. Lincoln always tries to take mine, but since I got here first, y'all are at the end."

I can't help but laugh at the smug look on her face. "That's okay. I think Lincoln wanted to show me around when he gets back. He was pretty excited to bring me here."

"It's our favorite place," Sienna smiles. "Our parents don't live here, so we didn't grow up here in that sense. But we've celebrated every holiday except Christmas morning, every big occasion, every summer break here."

"I can see why."

"What about you?" she asks. "What does your family do for holidays?"

I swallow a lump in my throat and fidget in my seat. Vivian's perfectly executed brow lifts ever-so-slightly. "My parents travel. Holidays really aren't a big deal in my family," I say as nonchalantly as possible.

"What?" Sienna almost barks. "How are they not a big deal?"

"Sienna," Vivian breathes, giving her a look to shush her. I'm grateful for it, yet nervous because she senses my unease. That will lead to questions and it's not something I want to get into.

These people are Americana. They're as red-white-and-blue as apple pie. They'll never understand my life. To them, I'll be the black sheep of my family and I'm sure they'll think I'm blemished in some way. Isn't that how it will look? Why else would a set of successful, socially prominent parents have nothing to do with their only child?

"It's fine," I lie, smiling gratefully at Vivian. "My parents are just super busy." Sipping my tea, I gather myself. "So, Sienna, what do you do?"

"I'm a fashion designer." Her eyes sparkle as she grabs another stem of celery. "I live in Los Angeles, but am considering a move to Paris."

"You just think you are," Vivian scoffs, pulling various boxes and cartons from a pantry. "You are not moving overseas, Sienna Leigh-Ann." Sienna rolls her eyes behind her mother's back, making me laugh.

"No, I should move home and live with Camilla. We can wear

matching rompers and attend all your social functions like the girls in *My Best Friend's Wedding*."

A giggle escapes my lips before I can stop it. Vivian looks at me and smiles. "She's a handful."

"At least I'm not a weirdo," Sienna says, chomping on the vegetable again. "Like my dear twin sister. Where is she, anyway?"

Vivian releases a long, heavy sigh. "She's supposed to be here," she says, looking at the iron clock on the wall. "An hour ago. You need to talk to her, Sienna. See if you can find anything out."

"What's going on?" I ask before I stop myself. "I'm sorry. I just way overstepped my bounds."

"No, honey, it's fine," Vivian says, swiping a manicured hand in the air. "My other daughter is usually the first one to all family functions, an ever present fixture in all our lives."

"We call her Swink because she's always in our business," Sienna points out. "But all of a sudden, she's gone. I mean, she's here. She's around. But she doesn't call me anymore. She's not answering Graham's calls. She's not—"

"—showing up as usual," Vivian sighs. "I'm sure she's fine. She sounds fine. She's just going through something, that's all."

As if she can't think about it a moment longer, Vivian turns back and works to form a tray of little sandwiches and fruits. And that's the end of that.

***

Lincoln

MY FATHER GREETS MY OLDER brother quickly before heading back to the house. I stand, still a little perplexed, and walk towards the car. Graham is standing at the hood of the car waiting on me.

"Hey," I say as I reach him.

"Good to see you." Graham pulls me into a quick, one-arm hug.

"How was your flight?" He tugs on his green tie, loosening it from around his neck.

"How do you wear that shit every day?" I ask, watching him unbutton the top button. "Don't you feel like a monkey in a suit?"

He rolls his eyes. "Don't you feel like a giant little boy playing ball every day?" he teases.

"A giant little boy a lot of chicks want to fuck."

"I'll tell you a secret," he says, heading to the driver's side door. "Chicks might like ball players. *Women* like suits."

Climbing in the passenger's side, I laugh. "Whatever you say."

"Speaking of women, did you bring Danielle?"

Her name sparks a warmth inside me. "Yeah. She's inside with Mom and Sienna."

He flashes me a look. "Is that safe?"

The car slides down the driveway towards the house. "Why wouldn't it be?"

"Um, Linc. Your normal girlfriends make Sienna want to brawl. Remember the one that wore fishnets to Barrett's birthday party?"

"She wasn't a girlfriend," I scoff. "Don't give her too much credit."

"You brought her."

"Kind of. I *kind of* brought her," I say in defense. "Seriously, why do we always bring her up?"

"Because it's so easy," he chuckles. "Just like I'm guessing she was."

"Dude, she used to take my—"

"No. Just no," Graham laughs as the car comes to a stop in front of the house.

"Pussy," I wink.

We exit the car and I breathe in a lungful of clean, Savannah air. It smells different this time. Tastes different. Feels different.

Cleaner, maybe? Crisper? I can't figure out what it is, exactly, but something seems like a page has turned.

"What?" Graham asks, furrowing his brow as we climb the steps to the house.

"What what?"

"You're thinking something."

"How do you know?"

"Because you only have one face you make when you are thinking about something. And because you rarely think, it's a look all its own."

"Fuck off," I laugh, opening the door. Graham goes in first and I hesitate a moment before stepping over the threshold. I wait for it, anticipate it, and the door isn't closed behind me before I feel it: the sense of being home. It's the same feeling I'd get when I was a little boy and had been to baseball camp too many days. It only happens here, at the Farm. It's the warmth of the lighting, the perfect temperature, the smell of cinnamon and vanilla, like a fleece blanket has been draped over me.

This is what I compare every place I've ever lived to. My college apartment. The little place I had in Milwaukee right before I was traded to Memphis. The starter house I had there before I moved into the one, deemed safer by my agent, I have now. They never come close.

Although I've seen them a million times, I take in all the little things as I pass by. The photographs of my siblings and I peppered on the walls, the glass of marbles my grandmother collected sitting on the mantle. The ding right above the baseboard as we enter the hallway, a mark from a wild toss one day that was intended to hit Ford in the head but missed, both regrettably and thankfully.

Graham disappears around the corner in front of me, yet my feet falter. I uptake a quick breath, feeling like the time Sydney Fettingberg was my date for junior prom. She was the "it girl" of school and I felt like I had scored a grand slam when she agreed to go with me. I did hit a grand slam later that night, but it wasn't all I thought it would be. I ended it a couple of weeks later.

This is that on steroids. Danielle's laughter blending with my mom's and sister's, hearing Graham introduce himself to her, makes my chest feel like it's going to explode.

I could stand here all night and listen to them. It feels better than any homerun I've ever hit, any ridiculous catch I've ever made in center field. This is better than any accolade I've gotten from the baseball league or any magazine cover I've been on and this isn't even about me. It's about her.

Maybe. Maybe it's about me and her. Maybe it's about us in a way that's feeling more real with every passing minute.

"Hey," I say, turning the corner. Everyone stops and looks at me. I see Mom first, a twinkle in her eye. Sienna gives me a thumbs-up. Graham looks slightly impressed and Danielle looks beautiful.

She's sitting at the bar, Graham to her right and Sienna across from her, as naturally as if she'd been here a million times. She gives me a soft smile, an ease in her shoulders that makes me want to grab her and kiss the fuck out of her.

Walking up behind her, I put my hands on her shoulders and give them a gentle squeeze. "What's happening?" I ask.

"I've made an order from Hillary's House for dinner. It should be here in an hour or so," Mom says. "How was your talk with your father?"

"Good," I laugh. "What do y'all think of my girl?"

Dani stiffens under my touch, but I massage it out of her. I wish I could see her face, but I can't.

"You don't ask that in front of me," she says, swatting at my hand.

"Normally he shouldn't," Graham agrees. "But I think he's safe this time." My brother looks at me and winks. "I have no idea how you've managed to convince this one to like you, but you should keep her."

"I plan on it," I say, kissing the top of her head. "Now, if you guys are done, I'd really like to show her around."

"Sure. Thaaaat's what you're wanting to do," Sienna laughs, getting a tap on the leg from Mom.

"Go ahead," Mom says. "Enjoy yourselves."

Danielle steps off the stool and I immediately clasp my hand around hers. She looks at me, her big eyes lit up.

"We'll be back." I lead her into the hallway and my plan is to take her outside, but we don't make it. As soon as we're out of sight, I pin her to the wall.

"Linc," she breathes, her hands finding the small of my back. She scrambles to find my skin buried under my shirt.

"Thank you for coming," I whisper against her lips. I follow my words with the most reverent kiss I can manage. When I pull back, she's smiling.

"Thank you for bringing me. Your family is amazing."

"They're all right," I joke.

She doesn't say anything, just cups my cheek with her hand. She searches my face for something, but a long moment passes before I can tell if she finds what she's looking for.

"What's wrong?" I ask.

"I'm just thinking how handsome you are."

"Get a good look at this face."

"Why?"

I can't help the smirk that tugs my lips. "This is the face you'll be sitting on later."

She falls against the wall, her mouth gaping open. Looking at me like she's ready to skip the walk altogether, I step away. She gasps.

"What are you doing? You can't say that and leave me hanging," she complains. She reaches for me and I step back farther, laughing.

"Sure I can. I have things to show you first."

"I hate you, Landry," she groans, shoving off the wall with her shoulders. "I need the bathroom."

"A little wet?" I say, bumping her shoulder. She's not amused, which only makes me laugh harder. "The door at the end of the hallway. I'll wait here."

She grabs my cock and squeezes it through my pants, then she walks away.

TWENTY-NINE

DANIELLE

THE DOOR CLOSES A SPLIT second before my back hits it and I heave out a frazzled breath. I practice breathing deep, focusing on counts of eight. I realize this is Lincoln's baseball jersey number and that makes me laugh and my heart to swell again.

I can't win. Not with this man.

The excitement of everything is taking its toll. I could feel the adrenaline start to wear off right before Lincoln and Graham walked into the kitchen.

Graham. *Holy shit*. He's like a darker, more brooding version of Lincoln. He doesn't look at you. He assesses you. He doesn't flippantly decide he likes you. He decides. Chooses. Everything with him seems so calculated and it leaves me scattered. He's a force, the eye of a hurricane, and his power is felt not just by me, but by the whole family. They jab at him, tease him, but there's a respect with Graham that makes me wonder who he really is behind the scenes.

I make my way to the sink and check myself out in the vanity. My reflection smiles back. My cheeks are flushed, my eyes almost shining in the light. I look . . . happy.

Rinsing my mouth out with a handful of cool water and

smoothing out my hair, I open the door and flip off the light. Making my way down the hallway, I almost laugh out loud. It's like walking through a commercial for greeting cards. Everything is so cozy and inclusive, just like the Landry's have made me feel.

Lincoln isn't standing where I left him. I peek into the kitchen and don't see him in the mix. Turning, I catch the outline of two bodies, one of which is undeniably Lincoln's, on the front porch through the window. I pitter across the hardwood and have my hand on the doorknob when I hear his voice on the other side.

"Yeah, Sienna," he says, his voice low and smooth. "I do. I like her a lot."

"I like her too."

I smile and know I should open the door and not eavesdrop. But when I hear their voices again, curiosity gets the better of me.

"She seems really nice," Sienna continues. "I think she really likes you too."

"What's not to love?"

Sienna laughs at him as I stifle my own.

"I didn't say she loves you, asshole," Sienna jokes. "I said likes you. But, since you brought it up . . ."

My heart slams so hard I'm afraid they hear it. My free hand clamps over my mouth and I drop my other from the handle. I'm not about to open the damn door now.

"Do you love her, Linc?"

Shoes squeak against the porch before what sounds like a chain rattling. Then it rattles again. When Lincoln answers, his voice sounds a bit farther away.

"I think so." His words, even though a touch distant, are as clear as a bell. Both in volume and in meaning, and my heart wraps them around itself. "I think I love her."

"Why? Why her? Not that I don't like her, but I'm curious."

"She's such a great person," he says. I know without looking at him that he's smiling and looking out across the lawn. "Dani's smart and funny and she cares about shit. Not just how she looks or how I look or my contract. She never asks about it. She asks about my shoulder, but not about the game. Not ever."

"I like that," Sienna say softly.

"Me too." The chains rattle again. "She's one-of-a-kind, Sienna."

"What are you going to do about it?"

My throat constricts as I wait for his response. My hand trembles at my side and I'm tempted to barge through the door because I don't know if I'm ready for his answer—either way.

"It's like this," he says. "Meeting her has put me in a position."

"Like doggy style?" Sienna laughs.

"No," he sighs. "Like . . . I'm standing at the plate in the championship game. We're down by three and bases are loaded. Full count. The perfect pitch is coming and I'm a fucking idiot if I don't swing."

I hear my gasp. I look behind me to see if anyone else did. The room is vacant, the laughs from the kitchen trickling into the foyer. Tears dot my eyes as my hand lies across my heart.

"Wanna define swing?" Sienna giggles.

"Yeah," I whisper, then clamp my hand harder around my lips. "Just . . . I can't be tentative up there, Sienna. I can't think about it too much, rethink my decision. Yeah, it could be a ball. There's no guarantee. But every fucking indication is that it's a fastball and that's my jam. It could be a curveball. I could strike out in a blaze of glory. But it's still a blaze of glory. It was still worth that chance."

I brush my eyes with the back of my hands. My heart feels like it's bursting in a Fourth of July finale.

For some reason, it means so much more that I heard him say it to someone else. With Sienna, he didn't feel compelled or pressured to say these things. It wasn't said in the heat of the moment. He means it. I'm sure of it, and I can't take it. I shove the door open. I need to see him. I need to hug him. I need him to know I feel the same way before I start thinking about curveballs and change-ups.

"Hey," I say, probably a little too loudly as I step onto the porch. Lincoln is leaning against the railing, his body facing his sister who is sitting on the porch swing. "Sorry that took so long."

Sienna rises, flashes her brother a knowing look, and then comes my way. "No worries. It was nice having a minute to catch up with Linc. I'm going to head in and see what Ford's doing. I haven't given him enough hell yet."

"See you in a bit," Lincoln calls after her. Once we're alone, he extends a hand to me. Without a second thought, I go to him. But I don't take his hand. Instead, I wrap my arms around his waist and bury my head against his chest. He smells faintly of the cologne he put on hours ago mixed with the pines spattering the landscape around us.

One hand finds the small of my back, one caresses the back of my head. It's the safest, most adored moment of my life. I'm not sure how because he's not saying a word. He's not saving me from anything. There's no declaration promised or insinuated.

Maybe it's just the love I feel pulsing through the Farm. I suppose it could be infecting my brain somehow. Pulling away from him, I look into his eyes and I'm wrong. It's not the love in the air. It's the love buried in those green eyes.

"Let's take a walk," he whispers. Taking my hand and interlacing our fingers together, he guides me down the steps. The sun hangs barely, sending a final farewell with a burst of purples and pinks.

"Where are we going?" I ask. We take the corner of the house and then veer away from the lights and down what looks to be a wellworn path. It extends down a little hill and into the trees. "There aren't bears or wolves in here, right?"

He rolls his eyes and mocks me. I shove him off the path, making him laugh. Before I can press the issue, the trees break around a pristine little lake. It's not big, maybe covering a few acres. There's a dock to the right and a slide beyond that. In the fading light, I can also see what appears to be a zip line crossing over a portion where the water fingers inland.

If I close my eyes, I can imagine a bright, sunny summer day. The Landry faces are all smiling, their voices full of laughs, the water splashing as they swim and relax and enjoy the water. And each other.

"Hey," Lincoln says, moving me so I'm in front of him. He peers into my eyes. "How are you? For real. This can be a little overwhelming."

"It's great, Landry. Honestly. I've never seen anything like this." "The lake? The house? Never seen anything like what?"

I shrug. "All of it, I guess. Mostly your family though. They're amazing."

Pride washes over his face. "They are, huh?"

"It makes me want to hope for a house full of kids someday."

His throat bobs as his fingers rewrap around my shoulders. "Maybe little Landry's?"

"I . . ." I laugh, a defense mechanism as old as time. "Lincoln, I . . . Did you really just say that?"

"Too soon?" He plays it off, like it's one of his usual ribbings, but it's not. I see the anxiety hidden in the lines on his face. Things are about to get real.

"You love kids," I say. "That's why you donated the money to the hospital."

His head cocks to the side. "I have no idea what you're talking about."

"Don't lie to me, Landry."

"I'm not. I—"

My fingertip presses against the center of his smooth lips. "Don't lie," I whisper. "It was you."

"How would you possibly know that?" he asks, his mouth moving against my finger. It sounds garbled and silly and, as I laugh, he nips it with his teeth.

"Because I know you," I whisper.

The sun sets behind him, dropping below the tall evergreens. It makes the angles of his face that much more severe. I shiver, not just because the sun's warmth is missing, but because of the way his gaze intensifies in the fading light.

"You do know me," he says, trailing the back of his hand from my temple, down the side of my face, before dropping to my waist. "And if you think you don't know something, I want you to ask me."

This conversation is picking up pace. Lincoln's determination to get to wherever he's going is evident. I just try not to pass out.

A million thoughts swirl in my head. Am I ready for this? Do I go with my brain and breathe, thinking of logic and risk assessment? Or do I follow my heart and just go for it?

He smirks and one thing is certain: I can't follow my vagina. "Do you think you know me, Dani?"

I nod. Or I think I do. I'm not sure. I'm lost in his gaze and a chorus of crickets chirping around us.

"The last time I said this, you tried to break up with me," he laughs. It's not real though. It's a choked version, broken up by a set of nerves I don't see often in him. "But I want to say it again. And I want you to consider it."

He steps towards me, closing the distance between us. Without a thought, my arms reach up and dangle off his shoulders as his own find my waist and pull me up against him.

"That's why you brought me out here, isn't it?" I tease. "You brought me into the forest where I can't run away."

"Damn right," he laughs, kissing me gently. "I didn't bring you here to convince you that I'm the guy for you. I really want you to enjoy the holiday and relax and have fun with this bunch I call family. But I'd really, really, like it if you'd think about maybe . . ."

"Maybe what, Landry?"

His face blushes. "You're going to make me work for this, aren't you?"

"Totally."

Blowing out a breath, he looks at everywhere but me. When his eyes finally find mine, I'm smiling. There's no way not to.

"I would like it if you'd think about taking this thing between us to the major leagues," he says. His shoulders go back, like he's proud of his little proposition. The entire thing makes me giggle. "You're laughing at me?"

"The majors? Really, Landry?"

"Yeah," he scoffs. "We're in the minors now. We're practicing, getting our timing down. But, sweetheart, our timing is impeccable. If it gets any fucking better, I'm just not letting you out of my bed."

"Don't tempt me with a good time," I wink.

"I want to move us up to the majors. *Charge the mound* whenever I want."

"Oh my God," I laugh.

"Have some day games, maybe a double header or two. And I'll slide in head first whenever you want me to, baby."

"You aren't talking about baseball, are you?" I say, feeling my thighs clench together.

"Nope."

His fingers skirt the top of my waistband, leaving a trail of fire in their wake. My body temperature elevates quicker than Pepper changes her mind about soup.

"Landry . . ." I all but beg.

"Say yes." His breath is hot against my cheek.

The harder I try to focus on the request, the harder it is to do just that. My body riots for this man. My heart leads the charge. My brain, even though it still blinks a faint red light of warning, gives in.

"You win," I say, working to dig my hands beneath the elastic of his boxer briefs.

"Does that mean yes?"

"Damn it, Landry," I pant, taking his girth in my hand. "Didn't you hear me?"

He skims up my abs and removes my breasts from my bra, leaving them sitting on the cups. The cool evening air causes my nipples to form peaks.

"I heard you," he says. "And I didn't hear a yes."

He squats in front of me. My shirt is raised to my chin. His tongue darts out, flicking against one nipple before doing the same to the other. "Yes?" he asks.

Taking both a deep breath and his face in my hands, I pull him back just so I can see in his eyes. "Yes, Landry. But I'm going to need you to hit me home *now*."

His lips hover over my breast. "It'll be my pleasure."

THIRTY

DANIELLE

I CRAWL INTO THE BED layered with down comforters and crisp white sheets. Fresh from the shower and wearing one of Lincoln's Arrows t-shirts, I don't smell quite as much like dirt as I did when we got back to the house. Nestling deep in the mountain of fabric, I wait for Lincoln.

I hear his laughter trickle from the stairs, a voice with his that I think is Ford's. Some inside joke was shared between him and Lincoln when we came up the path and saw Ford standing there. I'm not sure what it was about, but the way they teased each other made me wish I had that rapport with them.

The door squeaks open and Lincoln walks inside. A pair of dark grey shorts is the only thing covering his delectable body. His hair, still damp from the shower, shines in the light radiating from the desk lamp across the room.

"I had needles stuck everywhere," he laughs, setting a glass of ice water on the table beside the bed. "I'm not sure why we thought that was a good idea."

He flips the lamp off and slips out of his shorts and climbs into bed next to me. I cuddle up beside him.

"I don't think we were thinking much," I giggle. "Well, not about the ramifications."

"Speak for yourself." His hand trails down my spine until it lies flat in the small of my back. "I was securing our contract."

"Well, Mr. Landry, I like the way you deal."

My cheek bounces with his chuckle. "And I like the way you sign on the dotted line," he says.

A knock raps against the door. I yelp, burying myself under the blankets as Lincoln chuckles.

"I'm not dressed appropriately," I hiss, looking at him for help.

"You're covered," he doesn't quite whisper back. "Come in."

A head full of blonde hair peeks around the corner and flips on the light.

"Hey, brother!"

"Hey, Camilla." Lincoln sits up against the headboard. "It's about time you got here."

"I'm sorry. I should've been here earlier. I just got tied up."

"Doing what?"

I don't know this girl at all, but it doesn't take a rocket scientist to figure out what's going on. She's nervous, careful, and obviously in love. I grin at her, despite my state of undress. Her eyes register my expression and her return smile, while cautious, is warm.

"I apologize," she says to me. "I'm Camilla. And you are?"

"Swink, this is Danielle," Lincoln says, "Dani, this is Camilla."

We exchange greetings and she appears a little relieved that Lincoln forgot his line of questioning. When his mouth opens and I see that tug between his eyes, I talk first.

"Is your mom baking already?" I ask.

Camilla's shoulders slump in relief. "Yes, she is," she says hurriedly. "Sienna and Ford are helping her. I think she put a butterscotch pie and a pumpkin pie in the oven and a coffee cake for breakfast."

"Wow. I love coffee cake," I say.

Catching on to what I'm doing, Camilla giggles. "Me too. I'm going to grab a shower and get some sleep. I'll talk to you guys in the morning."

The door closes before we can say much more. "She seems nice," I say, yawning.

"She needs to work on her game."

"What?" I laugh.

"She's a terrible liar. I have no idea how my family is so confused as to what's going on with her."

"What's your guess?"

"Swink has a boyfriend Daddy won't approve of."

"You think?" Of course, he's right. That's exactly what's going on. I'm sure of it. But how does Lincoln know this?

Lincoln laughs, maneuvering himself in one swift move so that I'm straddling him. "Isn't it obvious?"

"Yeah," I giggle. "I think so."

"Graham is getting to the bottom of it. Of course, she can do whatever she wants . . . as long as it's safe."

"Such a big brother thing to say," I laugh.

He just shrugs. "You know what else is obvious?"

"What's that?" I say, feeling him harden beneath me. Bunching up my shirt, I move so that my opening sits against his shaft.

His pupils dilate as he holds my breasts again. "I don't remember."

"Ah, come on, Landry. Focus," I joke.

"Oh, I'm focused all right."

Swiveling my hips in a circular motion, I let him feel just how wet he's made me. "You haven't even touched me yet, but do you feel that?" I ask, a little moan escaping my lips as the velvety length slips across my clit.

He pushes against my belly, rocking me back. His fingers slide against my flesh. The pressure is just enough to elicit a want, no, a *need*, for more. Rocking my hips against his hand, angling for some relief from the intensity pulsing through my body, he denies me. I begin to object, to outright beg, when his stare takes my breath away.

"I'm going to stretch your pussy wide open and watch you try not to scream my name," he says, a hint of a smile on my lips. "How does that sound?"

"Please." Every ounce of desire I feel is tinted in the word. The hunger in his gaze intensifies. Like gasoline on an already blazing inferno, the look he gives me nearly sends me over the edge.

Lincoln reaches for the glass he carried in here and reaches his long, able fingers inside. A piece of ice glistens between his thumb and forefinger.

Once the chill hits the side of my thigh, I gasp. It's cold and wet against my skin, a stark contrast to the temperature everywhere else.

"Landry," I half-warn, half-moan. He glides the cube slowly against my skin in lazy circles, and then trails it towards the apex of my thighs. "I can't. You're killing me."

He just smiles. The cube is melting fast, the water trickling down my leg and against his side. He doesn't seem bothered. His eyes never leave mine.

My eyes flutter closed, the sensations of my burning core and the cool kiss of the frozen water are nearly overwhelming. My vagina tilts against his cock, gliding up and down the length.

"Ah!" I breathe in as another, colder, cube lies against the inside corner of my leg. This time, he drags it down, torturously slow, until it's almost at my knee. Then he pops it in his mouth.

"Tastes good," he grins mischievously. "But not as good as it can."

"What are you doing?" I groan, losing my composure. "Damn it, Land—"

My words are cut off by a giggle as he flips me to my back. My knees are over his shoulders, his hands parting my thighs. His mouth is against my opening before I can even compute what's happening.

He blows out a breath. It's fire-hot, his own desire nearly melting my skin. Just as I adapt, a chill follows behind from the ice cube still in his mouth. The mixture between the two, hot and cold, against my sex, fires me in overdrive.

"God," I moan as his tongue touches me. He rolls my clit

around with the pad of his tongue and I feel both the heat and coolness as different parts come into contact. It's electrifying and all I
can do is let my head fall deep into the pillows and thrust my hips
forward.

He licks down my slit gently, then more roughly as he retraces his
line. His thumbs push into my thighs as he holds me wide open just
for him.

"This tastes so much better," he nearly growls, the words rever-
berating against my opening. My eyes open, my mind still foggy from
the onslaught of sensations, but one thing is crystal clear: he's. So.
Fucking. Hot.

He watches me from between my legs, his tongue darting out and
swiping against his lips. "You taste so fucking good, baby."

I want to give him some witty comment, tease him back, but
seeing him with his face inches from my body renders me speechless.
He must realize this because he winks.

One finger, then two, slip inside me. He moves them in and out,
never taking his eyes off me. "What do you want, Dani?"

"I want you to fuck me." "Do you? Are you sure?"

"Yes," I say, but then he drops his head and his lips cover my clit
again. He sucks the swollen bud into his mouth, flicking it with his
tongue. His fingers never stop their assault, working me into a height-
ened frenzy.

"You sure?" he mumbles against me, flicking my clit hard again
before taking it back into his mouth.

"Yes," I moan. "I mean no. God, no. Keep doing that. Oh, God . .
." My hips move with his pace, trying desperately to increase the
urgency. Up, up, up I go until I can only see a haze of colors when—
he stops.

He sits up on his knees, wiping his face with the back of his hand.
"Come here," he instructs. His cock is in his hand as he strokes it
from base to tip. "Sit on me."

I've never scrambled across a bed faster in my life. I sit on his lap
facing him. Rising up so he can slide inside me, I wrap my legs

around his back. He slips in with one long, hefty push. The burn rips through me, filling me in every way.

"Shit," he breathes in, his eyes rolling into the back of his head. "It just feels better every damn time." His hand cups the roundness of my ass, guiding me up and down as I get used to his length. "You feel so good stretched around my cock."

"You feel so good inside me," I say, watching him react to me.

Enjoy me.

His hands bury against my backside, his mouth fallen slack. Those beautiful green eyes are squeezed shut as a moan, the sexiest thing I've ever heard, pierces the air.

Cognizant of the fact we aren't alone in the house, I swallow the sound with a kiss. The vibrations tingle in my mouth, dance through my body. My hair is wound in his fist and he kisses me like his life depends on it. Like a desperate man looking for a drink and I'm the oasis.

He pumps in and out of me, his body telling me just how badly he wants me. As if that's not enough, he makes it clear.

"I want you, Dani. I want you in every fucking way," he whispers against my ear. His hands roam my body, finally ending on my breasts. He palms them, rolling my nipples between two fingers and that's it. That's the button, the trigger that sets off a wildfire.

"Landry . . ." My head falls back, my ankles unlocking. My shoulders sag and I can feel the ends of my damp hair touch the top of my ass.

"Come on my cock."

His pace quickens, our bodies working together and I couldn't care any less if anyone hears.

"Landry," I moan, the volume increasing as the syllables stretch out. He strokes harder, his mouth finding mine and making it impossible for me to scream out. My hands are on his muscled shoulders as I bounce up and down on him. "Ah!" I say, but it's a muffled moan. My body tilted so that he runs across my clit as he fills me, the fuse is lit.

His hands squeeze my breasts before digging into my ass. The burn of the flesh. The bite of his mouth against my neck. The swell of his cock inside me as he finds his own release.

It's all too much. It's all not enough.

I slam myself onto him, grinding my body against his pubic bone. His head falls back, his Adam's apple bobbing in his throat. The bomb explodes.

My body trembles, my legs shake, as I find my orgasm. My head falls to his shoulder and I clamp down on my bottom lip to keep from screaming as I am overtaken. His lips are by my ear and I can hear him whispering through gritted teeth, but I can't make out what he's saying. I can only focus on riding through this bliss.

Our breathing is ragged, our bodies coated with a sheen of sweat. We sit facing each other, my head on his shoulder, his fingers drawing a series of designs on my back.

The house is quiet, the moon low and bright out the window. Sitting wrapped around Lincoln in this farmhouse, everything seems absolutely perfect in my world for the first time ever.

THIRTY-ONE

LINCOLN

"DAMN, THE MILITARY GETS YOU in shape, huh?" My hands on my knees, I'm bent over in front of the farmhouse dragging in breaths. "Fuck, Ford. Remind me to never run with you again."

The asshole stands, looking barely winded, and watches me with amusement. "And they pay you to be in shape? Hell, maybe I'll forget the security company and just go play baseball."

I don't even dignify that with an answer. Besides, I still can't breathe.

"Ford kick your ass too?"

Looking up, I see Graham heading our way. In jeans and a green polo shirt, he looks as casual as Graham gets in public.

"Does he make you run with him?" I ask, finally able to stand up.

"Once. I ran with him once," Graham laughs. "I'll run alone rather than be run so hard I want to die."

"Pussies, both of you," Ford laughs. "I'm heading in to shower. Don't eat all the pie before I get out." We watch him go up the stairs and into the house.

"He's a beast," I laugh. "Damn. Why didn't you warn me?"

"Because it's fun to watch you get schooled. What can I say?" He pushes his hands in his pockets. "Where's Danielle?"

"Getting ready." I think back to how she looked standing in my room, wearing one of my old robes, a coffee mug in her hand. "Unless I can get up there and unready her before she comes down."

Graham laughs, his watch catching the morning sunlight. "Is Barrett here yet?"

"Yeah, he and Ali and Hux are in the kitchen."

"I need to talk to him later."

"No business on Thanksgiving, G," I snort. "Give us all a day without talking shop, okay?"

"I wish." He makes a face. "My assistant has decided she and her new guy are moving to Maine of all fucking places."

"Why would they go there? It's cold."

"Apparently they're opening a bed and breakfast. Bad idea, if you ask me. She's known him for like two months now and she's tying up all her investments and accounts with this guy. But what can I do?"

"Nothing."

"Exactly," he sighs. "It's hard to watch. Anyway, she quit. No two-week's notice, no courtesy call. Just picked up her check and said she won't be back after the holiday."

"Shit. That sucks. What are you going to do?"

"Fuck if I know," he sighs again. "I hate temps. I'd rather do it all myself than have to explain every little thing. I'm hoping Barrett has someone that I could hire."

"Hire Paulina," I say and brace for the shove that's undoubtedly coming. It does. He knocks me back a few paces.

"You're an asshole," he laughs.

I look over my shoulder and see the window of the room Dani and I share. A bubble of excitement creeps through my veins. "Hey, I'm going to go get showered. I'll see you in a bit."

"Don't lie," he jokes.

"Okay," I say, jogging to the steps. "I'm going to find my girl, get dirty, get a shower, and then I'll see you."

I hear his chuckle behind me as I enter the house, wave to Barrett as I skip up the steps, and land at the end of the hall. Shoving the door open, she's standing in front of a full-length mirror in the corner.

"Hey, gorgeous," I say, coming up behind her. Our reflections look back at us. She's a head or more shorter than me, her dark hair pulled back from her face. She's dressed in a long floral dress and a denim jacket.

"I'm nervous," she whispers, worrying her bottom lip between her teeth.

"Why?"

She shrugs. "I can hear them all down there. What if . . . What if I don't fit in? What if I feel weird today?"

"Then we will come up here and I'll bury myself inside you until it's time to leave," I shrug. "Sounds easy to me."

She swats at me as she turns around, giggling. "You have a one track mind."

"What's your point?" I grin. "I like it."

I kiss her and then grab the robe she was wearing earlier. "I need to grab a shower."

"What should I do?" she gulps.

"Wanna watch?"

"Yes," she sighs happily.

I laugh, picking out a pair of jeans and a red collared shirt to wear to dinner. "Go talk to my family. Just jump in the mix."

"I don't know . . ."

"I do," I say, kissing the top of her head. "They'll love you, but don't believe everything they say. Now go make yourself at home."

If I stand here and talk to her about it, she'll end up coming into the bathroom with me. And if that happens, I'll end up getting her naked. And if that happens, we'll fuck and that means we'll be late to dinner. And that means I'll have one very upset mother and we all avoid that at all cost.

So I leave her standing in the middle of our room and head down the hall.

∗

Danielle

I CAN DO THIS. I can do this. I can do this.

My anxiety builds the closer I get to the commotion in the kitchen. So many voices, music, laughs, even the sound of a game on television mix to create an atmosphere that's a little overwhelming to someone used to silence.

Instead of heading into the kitchen, I turn left and onto the porch for a quick breath of fresh air. No one is out here, just a line of expensive cars along the teardrop driveway in front of the house.

Sitting on the swing, I take a few quick, deep breaths. The air is so peaceful here, filling my lungs with tranquility. I've never felt something like this before. It's not like this in Memphis or Boston or where I grew up in San Diego. I like it.

The door opens and makes me jump. Graham steps out and spots me and gives me a reassuring smile. "I didn't mean to scare you."

"You didn't," I say.

"Everything all right?"

"Of course," I smile. "I'm just . . . this is all a little new to me."

His brows furrow. "What's new to you?"

"This whole family thing you all have going on. I'm an only child. No cousins or grandparents, really. It's a little . . ."

"Overwhelming?"

"Kind of."

"It can be, even for me." He walks across the porch and leans against the railing. He's not quite as tall as Lincoln and not as muscular, but I'm sure he's his own brand of spectacular without a shirt on. He gazes across the yard like Lincoln does when he's thinking.

"Maybe I should be the one to ask if you're all right," I note.

He glances at me over his shoulder and smirks. "I'm fine. Unless you need a job. Then I'll be great."

"This sounds like a touchy subject."

He blows out a hard breath. "I need to hire someone right away. My secretary just walked out." He sighs again.

"That was nice of her," I wince. "Did she retire? Get sick?"

"Worse," he says, spinning to face me. "She fell in love."

"Ah," I laugh. "Good for her!"

"Maybe, but it's terrible for me," he chuckles, shaking his head. "I don't see the need to traverse the country because you're finally getting laid. People fall in love and do the stupidest shit."

My breath hitches in my throat as I try to figure out if he means any of that towards me in any way.

"I don't mean you," he snorts, a grin still on his face.

"How did you know I was wondering that?"

"You mean besides the way you just looked like you saw a ghost?" he laughs.

"Was it that obvious?"

"More or less." He turns around and faces me, leaning against the railing. His eyes burn into mine and I squirm on the wooden swing. The toes of my boots scoot against the ground, halting the leisure back-and-forth. He doesn't make me uncomfortable, just on the spot. Graham Landry can switch from casual conversation to interrogation faster than anyone I've ever seen. "Can I ask you something?"

"Sure," I say, not at all feeling that way.

"Why do you like my brother?"

His question renders me speechless. My lips part, then close, as I try to figure out what he's getting at. "I'm sorry, Graham. I don't understand."

He almost smiles. Almost. "You know what? Never mind."

"No," I say, shaking my head. "You asked. Now clarify."

"Look, I'm going to say this and it might come out wrong. But hear me out."

"Careful," I warn, a touch of a grin on my lips.

He looks away as he tries to stop his laugh. "Fair enough." He clears his throat and looks at me again. "I'm a critical guy. I'll also go out on a limb and say I'm the most serious of the bunch. So when one of the rest of them bring home a new girl or guy, it's usually a face I don't get to know too well because they won't be back."

"So your siblings are flakes?"

"Yes," he admits good naturedly. "But you, Danielle, are different. I can see you sticking around a while."

My heart leaps in my chest, but I stay composed. You have to with this guy. "Why do you say that?"

"You fit in here," he shrugs. "You make Lincoln laugh. Relax. Hell, you make him think about things other than pitch counts and that's no easy task," he kids. "You bring out something different in Linc that I haven't seen in years. I have a feeling you're pretty special to him."

"I hope so. He's pretty special to me."

"Lincoln has a meeting coming up about his contract," Graham says.

And then it hits me. I stand because sitting makes me feel at some sort of a disadvantage to him. I'm not angry at the insinuation—I get it. I was raised with some of the same issues. But I am going to make myself clear. Crystal clear.

"I get what you're saying," I say, making direct eye contact. "And, for the record, if he gets dropped and never plays baseball again, I would probably be happier."

Graham's eyes widen just a bit, his mouth dropping ever-so-slightly. "I take that back," I backtrack, pulling in a breath. "I think Lincoln would be beside himself and I don't want that for him. He loves the game."

The words come out and I ignore how hard they smash against my chest, remind me of reality. Of the pecking order. Of the insecurity I have as to how I compare to a game with a wooden stick and a piece of leather.

"I think he loves you too," Graham says.

I shrug because now I'm thrown off my game. I fight my brain for control over my emotions, to stay focused and enjoy the weekend. I don't know what the future holds, but I want us both to be happy.

"What about you?" I say, attempting to pivot this conversation back around to him. "Will you have a girlfriend or wife here today?"

He laughs full-out now, sending a flock of birds finding refuge in the trees. "I don't date."

"You aren't one of those that don't believe in love, right?" I tease.

"I absolutely believe in love," he says. "I've seen it. Hell, I'm looking at someone in love right now." We exchange a smile before he continues. "But loving someone means giving them some control of your day, your life. That's not something I'm good at."

"But doesn't it make things seem so much better to share your day, your life, with another person?"

"Certain times of the day, yes," he winks. "I don't have extra hours free to dote on someone. That's the reality of it. I've spent so many years getting to where I want to be career-wise, getting plans in place to take our company to the next level. I love it. It's my passion. And it works because I have a system."

"You're a control freak."

"I'm okay with that."

His mouth opens to say something else when the door creaks and Lincoln steps outside. His hair is styled, kind of swept up and to the side. The wine colored shirt stretches across his lean body and his legs are showcased in dark denim. I almost whimper.

"Hey, now," Lincoln teases, coming to my side. "Don't get any ideas, G."

"Welcome to how Barrett must feel," Graham laughs. "I'm heading inside for a drink."

He disappears and Lincoln pulls me into a hug. I breathe him in, letting his scent settle over me and calm my frazzled nerves.

"Want a glass of tea?" he asks against my hair.

"Yes, please."

Instead of heading into the house, he just pulls me closer. "I want you to know," he gulps, "that I really like having you here. I was in the shower and thinking about you here with my family today, and well, I haven't felt like this ever."

I lift my chin and look at his face in the early morning sun. There is no joke teasing his lips, no distraction in his eyes. It's just a simple emotion that I've never seen before. A pure sentiment that I think I can read and I definitely feel.

I shouldn't. Things like this need to be thought out. Yet he strips me of all logical thinking and my mouth opens before I can sort through all the chatter in my head. "Lincoln, I—"

He kisses me before I get the rest out. I gasp, taken aback by the gesture I didn't see coming. It's a bit of a letdown that I didn't get it out. But when he pulls back, his eyes shine.

"Dani," he roughs, his tone gravelly. "I know what you were going to say."

I try to look away, embarrassed. *Oh, God* . . .

Attempting to pull away, I hear him snicker. The embarrassment turns to anger and I flip my eyes back to him, ready to light him up, but I stop in my tracks. His smile is so soft I stutter.

"I wanted to be first," he whispers. "I love you, Ryan Danielle." I do the only thing I can. I kiss him.

THIRTY-TWO

DANIELLE

"I COULDN'T EAT ANOTHER BITE," Sienna moans, lying flat on her back in the middle of the living room floor. A football game is on the television mounted on the wall. Even though this room is large, with this many people, it feels crammed. It's wonderful. Maybe even perfect. I sit on Lincoln's lap on a love seat next to Ford. Graham and his father stand behind the couch, each with a tumbler of dark liquor, discussing something in detail. Camilla is stretched out beside her sister, her phone in her face, while Barrett and Alison are curled up on the couch. Huxley is leaning against a giant Arrows pillow with a game in his hand.

Vivian enters, looking no worse for the wear after cooking what can't be described by any other word than *feast*. A tray of snacks in her hands, she sets it on the table in front of Barrett and Alison. "Anyone need a nibble?"

"Mom, really?" Lincoln asks, rubbing his stomach. "I don't even want to look at food."

"I get everyone home for a few days a year. Pardon me for wanting to feed you," she says. Taking in the scene in front of her, she smiles proudly. "I love having you all here."

"We love being here, Mom." Sienna blows her a kiss then groans. "But really, get that food out of here. Ugh. So. Full."

"What do you think?" Vivian looks at me. "Do you need anything?"

"No, thank you. I'm great. Can I help you with anything?"

She looks at Lincoln, then at his hand on my knee, then back to me. "Just make my baby boy happy and let me know if he gets out of line."

"Her baby boy," Ford mocks, grabbing Lincoln in some kind of head lock. "Aw, mommy's baby."

"You're just jealous," Lincoln laughs, somehow maneuvering out of Ford's hold.

Ignoring her rowdy boys, Vivian lifts the tray again. "No one wants anything? Huxley? Want a cookie?"

"Are they those chocolate ones with the little candies in them?" he asks, setting down his game.

"Of course. They're your favorite."

He jumps to his feet and takes three. "Thank you, Vivian."

"You are so welcome."

Barrett reaches up and plucks a bunch of grapes off the tray before Vivian disappears into the kitchen again. "Look, Alison. Your favorite."

She immediately turns as red as the pillow on her lap. Barrett holds them in front of her before whispering something in her ear. His hand wraps around her wrist as she giggles and refuses to make eye contact with anyone.

"No secrets," Lincoln says to his brother. "What's making her blush like that?"

"Trust me, it's a great story," Barrett grins like the cat that ate the canary. "Maybe one day I'll tell you."

"Stop!" Sienna squeals, her hands over her ears. "I can only guess and I do not want that visual—no offense, Alison."

Alison laughs, tossing the pillow at Barrett and heads towards the doorway. "I'm going to use the restroom."

"I bet you are," Barrett teases her.

Vivian comes back in again and stands by her husband. She seems completely unfazed by the noise level or mess strewn around the room. Shoes, jackets, cups, glasses, notepads and laptops are nearly covering the carpet. If I would've seen this picture before, I would've cringed.

But that was before I experienced it. I get why Vivian loves this so much. I could get used to it too.

"Lincoln," Harris says to his son. "What day do you and Danielle go back?"

"First thing in the morning. As a matter of fact, we'll probably be gone before you all get up."

"Will you be home for Christmas?" Camilla asks. She gives me a sweet smile and I return it. "We have a huge cookie bake on Christmas Eve. We'd love to have you, Danielle."

Lincoln squeezes my thigh, but I can't look at him. I'm afraid of all the things I'll see in his eyes and how I might reciprocate that.

"I'm not sure what I'm doing," I say truthfully. "The cookie bake sounds fun though."

"We'll definitely try to be here," Lincoln interjects. "You coming, Barrett?"

"Don't even come if you aren't engaged, Barrett," Sienna says, sitting up cross-legged.

"Sienna!" Vivian chastises her.

"What? Alison isn't in here. I'm not embarrassing her. I'm just saying, time to put a ring on it, brother."

"I agree." Camilla sits up too and shrugs. "Ring it, Barrett."

"Does no one trust me?" he asks, feigning horror. "Besides, little ears are listening."

Huxley smashes a cookie in his mouth with one hand, his other flying across the video screen on his lap.

"He's not listening," Camilla says. "At least tell me you have a ring and tell me it's vintage."

"No," Sienna gasps, looking at her twin like she's crazy.

"Modern, Barrett. Trust me. I have the degree in design."

"Girls!" Vivian sighs. "Stop. I'm sure Barrett will figure out what's right for *them.*"

Sienna rolls her eyes and then looks at me. "Just tell Lincoln when he goes to buy yours to call me. Not Camilla. You don't want some old thing with a loose gem."

My cheeks flush and I ignore Lincoln's gaze from the side. He rubs his hand beneath the back of my shirt, caressing me. I lean into it, but still can't look at him.

"You're going to be the death of me," Vivian says, one hand on her hip. "I'm sorry, Danielle."

I just laugh. "It's fine. And for the record, I'm not big on jewelry."

"So you *are* talking about getting engaged?" Sienna chirps.

"No," I say quickly as Lincoln says, "Maybe."

I look at him and he smirks. "I think it's a fair topic," Lincoln shrugs. "Wanna marry me?" he asks, the corner of his lip twitching. "I'm sure my mom and sisters can put something together by the time we leave."

"Oh my God!" Camilla squeals. "Yes! Let us!"

"No," I giggle, putting my hands in front of me. "We just met not that long ago. Let's get to know each other and all that before you go marrying us off."

Harris clears his throat. "I knew I liked you," he says, taking one finger off his tumbler and pointing at me. "Level head. Smart. Keep this one, Lincoln."

"Yeah, not like that one with the fishnets—" Sienna clamps her hand around her mouth.

Lincoln throws his head back and everyone in the room laughs. Even me because his reaction *is* funny. Whoever fishnet girl was, it's clear she's not here and was a joke when she was.

"Sorry," Sienna cringes.

My hand is tugged as Lincoln stands. "On that note, we are going to bed. I'll be down later if I can't sleep. Otherwise, we'll see you at Christmas."

We exchange quick hugs and goodbyes with the room. I keep it as fast as possible because it's obvious Lincoln wants to get out of here, and by the look in his eye, I do too.

Nearly dragging me up the stairs and into our room, I'm thrusted against the wall before I know what hit me. His gaze sears into mine, heat rolling off his body.

"I need you. Now." It's not a question, not a suggestion. It's an order, one I'm all too happy to oblige.

THIRTY-THREE

DANIELLE

IT FEELS LIKE WE'VE TRAVELED forever when, in reality, it's not been an entire day. We left Savannah first thing this morning, before the sun was up. Troy drove us back to the airport and we nearly missed our connecting flight in Atlanta because of fog. By the time we landed in Memphis, we were both completely wiped out.

I flop on my sofa and it's not two seconds before Lincoln collapses beside me. His head crooks to the side and he grins. "Been a long day, huh?"

"Yeah," I whine. "And it's not even two in the afternoon yet." I rub my stomach. "I think I'm still full from yesterday."

"So, what did you think?" Lincoln asks, his hand resting on my knee.

I smile. "I loved the Farm, Landry. Thank you for taking me for Thanksgiving."

"My family is pretty awesome, huh?"

"Yeah," I laugh. "I can't imagine growing up with all of them. Was it as chaotic as I imagine?"

"Absolutely. There was always something happening, someone

into something they shouldn't be. It was a great way to grow up." He stretches his neck before resting it against the sofa.

"I hope to have a family like yours someday."

"Me too." He draws a pattern on my knee that I can't decipher. Over and over and over something is traced onto my skin. "What did you think about my sisters?"

"They were sweet. Sienna reminds me of you and Camilla needs a friend that isn't a Landry."

"I would recommend you, but she did suggest you be added as a Landry." His gaze holds mine as I digest his insinuation.

"She's crazy," I whisper, feeling the weight of his words sitting on top of my heart.

"Is she, Dani? We've been exclusive since I walked off the elevator. You just didn't know it."

"You think so?"

"Oh, I know so," he grins. "It's been me and you from the start and that's the way I want it to be. I want you to start staying at my house."

I begin to object, to give him an opening to reassess. The pad of his finger touches my lips, effectively silencing me. "Dani, I mean it. I want you with me."

"I want to be with you too."

"I hear it. But what?"

"But I want to be careful we don't rush this, Landry."

"We aren't rushing anything," he insists. "We're adults." He takes my hand and presses a kiss to my knuckles. "We love each other, right?"

"Right," I whisper.

I've never said something as truthful as that. I love him. I love Lincoln Landry. It scares me, both from the power of the feeling and from who he is. I don't know what the future is going to hold. I just know that it's him and me. Together. And we can write our own truth far away from the poison that tainted me.

"I don't want to think about coming home and not having you

there. I'm not saying move in," he says as I try to object again, "but I do want to think you like being with me and want to be there. A lot."

"So don't bring my bed, just my lingerie?" I joke.

"Bring the fucking bed if it'll keep you there," he laughs. "Bring what you want. That's the thing: I want you to feel comfortable at my house. I want to blend more of our lives together. I've realized the more we do that—getting your favorite things at my place, seeing you wear my shirts, sleeping in my bed, having you meet my family—the happier I am and the happier you seem."

He's right. I don't have to say it because he obviously knows, but he is absolutely correct. There's not a part of me that feels unchanged from the me before Lincoln Landry waltzed off the elevator onto the wrong floor. I can't remember what I did after work or what I thought about then as I went to sleep. I surely don't remember my face hurting from smiling so much.

"I love you," I say.

Kissing the top of my head and then unfolding himself from the sofa, he stretches his arms overhead. "I need to go. I have a meeting with the Arrows in a few hours and I need to unpack and grab a shower and shit."

I stand too. "How do you feel about it?"

"My shoulder feels better. But the thing is, I don't know what they're going to say about it. Once you've had this happen, it tends to reinjure and that means games on the bench."

My stomach twists as the game that ruined my life comes back into play. I've put off thinking about this meeting, not asking too many questions and not pressing for details. Lincoln has seemed fine with that. But now, knowing it's looming over his head, I can't help the series of questions firing through my mind.

"Do you want to stay in Memphis?" I ask, biting my bottom lip. "I mean, if you have the choice, is that what you want?"

"Of course." He takes a step to me and brushes the back of his hand down the side of my face. "Really, I'd be happy anywhere if you were there with me."

"I live here," I point out, my voice wobbling.

"And, right now, so do I. Most likely I will when I get back later today too." He bends forward and takes in what I'm sure is anxiety written all over my face. "Hey. Relax. It's just a meeting."

"It's just a meeting," I repeat, although that's not true and I hate that he's comforting me. "I know that. Now go, get it over with so we know what we're facing."

"Exactly." He kisses my forehead. "It's what we're facing because we'll figure it out together, all right?"

"All right."

He gives me one final, reassuring look and then leaves. As soon as the door closes, the walls cave in. The hum of the ice maker in the kitchen dances through the air and it only makes the quiet more obvious. No one is laughing, no one arguing. A television isn't on in another room and cell phones aren't chirping from some far corner of the house.

It's just me.

And I hate it.

I drag my luggage to my room and empty the clothes into the laundry bin. Sorting my toiletries in the bathroom, I try to hum, sing, talk to myself out loud just to break the stillness. It seems that is something that can't be fixed by my antics alone. It's something deeper that yearns to be filled.

Pulling my phone from my pocket, I type a quick text to Lincoln.

Me: Good luck today.

Landry: I don't need luck. I have you.

Me: Charmer. Call me when you get home.

Landry: Just be there waiting on me. Key is under the front mat.

Me: Gasp! That's the most obvious place to put it.

Landry: Good point. Use the one I put on your keychain then. ;)

I bounce to my purse in the living room and dig until I find my keychain. There's an extra key with a purple rubber band around the top dangling in between my car key and my house key.

Me: Sneaky!

Landry: I should be home around eight. I'd love for you to be there.

Me: I might be able to pull that off.

Landry: If you need a moving truck to help you . . .

Me: What happened to one day at a time?

Landry: That idea sucks. I've moved on. Note: You have too. ;) Jumping in shower. See you soon.

Me: xo

***

Danielle

I'VE DONE THREE LOADS OF laundry, folded them, and put them away. I've reorganized my bathroom cabinets and purged about twenty bottles of crusty fingernail polish that outlived their expiration date by a few years. Then I sorted my lingerie into two piles—pretty and Aunt Flow. Looking at the clock, I still have a few hours before Lincoln is done.

There would be no issue with me going over there early. I have a freaking key. While that seems like a winning idea, and one that will make me less likely to end up in the looney bin this afternoon, I don't want to do it. It's too presumptuous.

I've jumped into a lot over the past few weeks, much of which I promised myself I never would. But I trust him. I want him. I even love him, which is enough to make me want to absolutely freak out if I think about it too long. So I don't let myself go there.

Rushing into my bedroom and opening my suitcase that still sits on my bed, I toss in a few days' worth of clothes and cosmetics and latch it shut. Grabbing a phone charger from the wall in the kitchen, as well as my keys, I head out the front door and lock it behind me. Within a few minutes, I'm in my car and heading across town towards the Smitten Kitten.

When I arrive, the eatery is bursting with aromas unusual for a

Saturday afternoon. My brows are pulled together as I make my way to the counter.

"What's that smell?" I ask. "What are you doing?"

Pepper is covered in flour. It dusts her nose, cheekbones, front of her apron and both arms. She blows out a breath and little white particles go floating. "The mixer had a mishap."

"You or the electric one?" I laugh. "You look like a ghost!"

"I'm trying to make this soup I found online from China. I spent a fortune, a literal fortune, Danielle, on ingredients and it turned out to be the worst thing I've ever made."

"Maybe it's not," I suggest. "Maybe it's just not what you're expecting."

"I don't want to talk about it. I'm grieving."

Laughing at her dramatics, I order a chocolate croissant and a cappuccino and then burrow down in my spot in the corner. Pulling out a notepad, I plan on making notes for work next week but instead finding myself sketching the tree line from the Farm.

"What's that?" Pepper asks, sitting my items in front of me. "And why are you here now?"

"I'm waiting on Lincoln to get done at a meeting," I tell her. "We had the best time in Savannah."

"What was it like?"

"Perfect," I gush. "His family is incredible, the property was breathtaking. Now I can't stand to be home alone. It's just too mundane compared to the Landry's."

"Don't go comparing stuff," Pepper warns. "That's a dangerous game."

"I know." I lift my cappuccino and watch the foam swirl. "I need you to make me feel better about this."

"About what?"

"About this thing with Landry." Taking a hesitant sip, I feel a sting as the drink trickles down my throat. "Tell me this will end okay. Tell me I'm not foolish to try this. Tell me this isn't Einstein's definition of insanity."

"Well, it is," she laughs, "but . . ." She slides into the booth across from me. "Did you know I owned two eateries before the Smitten Kitten?"

"No."

"I did. I had a little place in Nashville that was tucked next to a deli. Cute as hell, but terrible location. Then I had a little café here in Memphis that I couldn't get off the ground."

"I had no idea," I say, taking another sip of my drink. "How did you get here?"

She smiles, picking a chunk of my croissant off and popping it in her mouth. "I'd closed shop three years before. I was working as a paralegal and had an appointment on this side of town when I saw this building up for sale. I was so drawn to it. I could see myself in here, baking and decorating and cooking my life away. I was terrified to tell my husband."

"Why?"

Pepper looks at me like I'm crazy. "Because I'd failed at this game twice! How could I expect him to want to take the chance on me a third time? It was insane, even to me," she sighs. "It was all I could think about. All I dreamed about. I could see the menus in my head and smell the coffee roasting. Eventually my husband got to the bottom of my little daydreams and told me to go for it."

My jaw drops. "Just like that?"

"Just like that," she smiles. "Well, not *just* like that. He told me to learn from my past experiences and to go into this one smarter. And I had to give him an epic blowjob. Look at me now!" Her hands extend from her sides, motioning to the café. After a few long minutes, she drops them. "That's what you need to do, Danielle. Learn from your past experiences and go into this one smarter. Maybe Lincoln Landry will be your Smitten Kitten. Or maybe you'll be his," she giggles. "Either way."

"How'd you get so smart?" I can't deny her words do soothe me, make me feel a little less frantic about this new situation.

"It's genetic. Now I need to go make another batch of cupcakes for a party this evening I'm catering."

"I need to go too," I say, gathering my things. "I think I'm going to head to Lincoln's."

The words make me giddy, the thought of seeing him makes me happier than I could imagine I could be.

"Have fun," Pepper winks before scurrying into the kitchen.

Oh, I fully intend to.

THIRTY-FOUR

LINCOLN

I IMAGINE THIS IS WHAT Graham feels like. Tucked in a shirt that buttons up the front and threatens to choke you, uptight as hell as you walk into a meeting. Only difference is that my brother likes this shit. I hate it.

Give me a bat and a ball and I don't care who watches or who I have to talk to about it. I can dissect numbers and stats all day. Need someone to study a batting stance and give you a dissertation? I'm your man. Hell, I'll even wear a suit and tie and charm voters or patrons of a charity and I'll make you a ton of money. But make me *talk* about money? I'd rather play basketball.

Coming off the best couple of days of my personal life, I'm swinging open the doors of the Arrows building with a whole lot of nerves. I think it's worse because I've been so relaxed lately.

Just like that, I'm grinning.

Now this, this must be what Barrett feels like. Happy. Content.

Excited about the future.

Greeting the receptionist and ignoring the eyes she makes at me, I hit the button on the elevator. Even this reminds me of Dani. As if on cue, my phone rings and I see her name lit up on the screen.

Dani: If you didn't mean for me to use the key, too late. I'm sitting on your sofa with a pink mug of coffee and hazelnut creamer. ;) Can't wait to see you. Go get 'em, tiger.

Me: Tiger, huh?

Dani: I like when you growl.

Me: I like when you scream my name. And when you whisper it. And when you think it.

Dani: I hope to do all three within a few hours this evening. Hurry your ass up, Landry.

Me: Going in. Phone off. Talk soon.

Flipping my device off and shoving it in my pocket, I take a deep breath and push open the door to the General Management office. The secretary sends me through.

The carpet silences my steps as I take forty-six to the back conference room. Billy Marshall and my agent, Frank Zele, face me. They stand as I enter and shake my hand.

"How are you, Lincoln?" Billy asks "Good. How are you?"

"Doing good, thanks."

Frank and I greet each other and we all take a seat. "How was your holiday?" Billy asks.

I grin. "Excellent. Went home to Savannah."

Billy doesn't look at me or acknowledge my response and that concerns me. Greatly. He's always so talkative—the guy could talk for two hours about a bright, sunny day. Now he won't look at me? My shoulders stiffen as I clasp my hands in front of me and await the verdict. Frank gives me a look, one that further chills my hopes.

"So," Billy says finally. "I'm just going to get down to business, if that's okay with you?" He looks at me and his features are hardened. This isn't the guy that threw a Fourth of July party last year on Tybee Island and let me take out his brand new fishing boat. This is Billy Marshall, General Manager. I'm just not sure what I am today and that scares the ever-loving fuck out of me. Glancing at Frank, he's poring over a stack of papers in front of him.

Billy clears his throat. "We've been going over next year's forecast and roster. We really believe we have a shot at a title."

"I agree. We were the best team in the league this year," I say with enthusiasm. "I really believe we'll nab it next year if we can just stay healthy."

"That's the thing—staying healthy." He pushes a paper towards me. My name is at the top, followed by a list of items and numbers and dollar signs and percentages. "This," he says, indicating the first column, "is our win percentage with you in play. It's great. But this one is the percentage with you out."

I look at the numbers and feel a ball tightening in my gut. "I'll be ready," I promise him.

"Lincoln," he says, blowing out a breath. He rests back in his seat and takes his glasses off. "While we don't have a salary cap, as you know, we do pay a luxury tax. The higher our payroll is, the more we pay. This year, the organization paid the highest tax in the league."

"Let's talk numbers," Frank says, as I swallow a searing breath. "Let's see if we can get to a place where we are all happy."

Billy watches me for a long moment before sitting up, his hands folded in front of him. "You are the highest paid player, by far, on the team. You're worth it, I'm not saying that," he says. "But when we calculate how many games you missed this season along with the report on your shoulder, you just aren't worth it to this team."

"What?" The room could explode into a fiery inferno at this exact moment and I wouldn't be able to move. I'm frozen in my seat, trying to convince myself I misheard him. "Say that again."

"I'm sorry, Lincoln. You know I love having you on staff and I think you have a lot of baseball left in you. But that specific injury coupled with the pressure I'm getting from the top to get our payroll down and manageable . . ."

"What's this mean?" I utter, looking between the two men in front of me. My hand shakes as I place it on my lap and look at the Arrows logo on the paper in front of me. It's my team. My brand. A part of me. But is it? Now? *Oh God . . .*

"It means we can offer you less, significantly less. Let's face it—even if we get you back one hundred percent, the odds of re-injury sometime in the next five years is pretty much a guarantee. That means I'm looking at this win percentage," he says, tapping that fucking paper again, "and I can't swing that. It doesn't work, Lincoln."

"How much money we talking?" Frank asks.

"Less than you should or would agree to," Billy sighs heavily. "We also have negotiated a trade with you to the San Diego Sails. Their payroll is one of the smallest in the league—"

"As is their winning percentage," I scoff.

Billy shoots me a look. "You can stay here. This is the number you're looking at." The page flips and I see a salary I can't believe is real.

"This? Are you serious?"

"Yes. Or you can agree to San Diego and look at it as rebuilding, restructuring, extending your fan base," he says, trying to make it sound appetizing, "and take this one."

"You know that's unacceptable," Frank insists.

The number Billy shows me on another sheet is much better. But still. "Billy," I say, laughing in disbelief, "you're really letting me go?"

"This is business. You know that. It just happens to be a business where we play baseball for a living. Think about that. You're still playing a damn ballgame for a paycheck. That's a good thing whether it's here or in San Diego."

My head hangs, my heart skimming the floor. Never did I dream they would trade me. Is this even happening right now?

"Take some time," Billy says. He stands and puts his hand on my shoulder. "Go home and think about it. Discuss this with Frank. Figure out what you want to do. You know I'm happy to pay you to stay here. I just know it's probably not feasible."

My entire body feels the weight of the world and my brain is a freeway full of racing thoughts and colliding ideas. It makes me want to vomit . . . which I do once I'm out the door and find the nearest bush.

**

The drive home took three times longer than it should've. I spent a good hour sitting outside of Arrows Stadium, trying to get my head wrapped around the situation before going home. To Dani.

I grip the steering wheel as I wait for the gate in my subdivision to lift. Every muscle in my body is sore. My jaw hurts from clenching it. My knuckle aches from slamming it into my steering wheel.

I might be coming out of shock. I don't know. Things are starting to fill the void that seemed too deep to get across until now. I can only make sense of some of it if I block out what the media is going to say and the articles that will be put out as soon as this comes to fruition, one way or the other.

Swallowing this is so bitter I can barely manage to deal. How did this happen to me? I was king of the world only a few months ago. How did I fall so far so fast?

Taking the money the Arrows offered would be a joke. It would make *me* a joke. I think I make more money than that off of Graham's investments every year. A player like me can't play for that; I wouldn't be taken seriously. No one would hire me as a spokesman. My jerseys would stop selling. It would be one, big disaster. They know that, which makes it even more humiliating that they even bothered to offer it.

San Diego is the only answer. Not one I like and not one I want to make, but I don't have another choice. The money is generous and maybe they can build something around me. I grin, thinking about how awesome that would be—to win a championship with another team. One that didn't really exist before me.

Pulling into the driveway and jumping out and locking the door, I'm in the foyer before I know it. "You here?" I call out.

She comes around the corner of the kitchen in a pair of yoga pants and a red t-shirt. "How'd it go?" she asks cheerfully. Her smile drops.

"You okay?"

"I've been better." My keys drop into a little dish on the table. I take her hand and pull her into the living room and onto my lap as I sit on the sofa. She returns my embrace and I take a deep breath, letting her settle over me and calm the turmoil within.

"What's wrong?" she asks.

"I got traded."

She stiffens in my arms, but doesn't pull away. I go over the numbers, and still, she doesn't respond.

"How do you feel about San Diego?" I ask.

She pulls away. Then stands, straightening her shirt. "Why do you ask?"

Her voice is eerily calm with just a hint at the end of something vulnerable. It's the Danielle I met in the hallway: a tough front with a sweet interior she works hard to protect. But why now?

With a dose of unease, I say, "Because that's where we're going."

Her back turns to me, her head bowed. "I'm not going with you."

"What?"

"I'm not going."

Scrambling off the couch, my brows pulled together as my heart misfires, I stand behind her. "I . . . But. . . . Dani?"

"Don't go, Landry."

The way she says my name, like a plea that she has no faith behind, hits me like the third strike. It wallops me. Breaks me. Leaves me looking and wishing I could do something different, but I can't because that pitch has been thrown.

"I told you," I say carefully. "I have to. San Diego is where it's at right now." When she doesn't respond, I feel panic setting in. "I have to go where the work is. I'm not a carpenter or something with ten jobs to choose from and another forty years to work. I have maybe five years, Dani. Five years to do what I do. Baseball is what I do. You have to understand that."

My trembling hand cups her shoulder, and with the care I'd give a wild grounder, I turn her to face me.

To my surprise, there are no tears in her eyes. Just a steely resolution that feels like a bucket of ice water.

"I do understand," she says evenly. "I understand better than you'll ever know."

"Good," I sigh, relieved. "Then come with me. Let's do this together. Let's pick out a house, on the beach if you want. Let's—"

"Landry . . ."

"What?" Irritation nudges ahead in the battle of my emotions. Why is she making this so hard? It's not like I want this, so why is she acting like I have a choice? Taking a deep breath, I try again. "Let's start over. New city. New relationship. Think about it." I reach for her, but she takes a step back. My hand hangs in the air.

The tears I expected earlier fill her eyes as she takes another step back. "I have thought about it. I've thought about it before I even met you," she sniffles.

"What are you talking about?"

"This," she laughs through the tears trickling down her face. "Your passion for the game is what makes you so incredible, both on the field and off. You're right, Landry. You have a handful of years left and you should play. Absolutely. And if that's in San Diego, then it is."

"You know I'd rather be here, right? I love Memphis. And it would be so much easier on you to just stay here. I hate even fucking asking you to leave, baby, but there's no other way. I have to play. It's who I am."

She nods, wiping the tears off her face. "You're right," she chokes out. "It's time for new beginnings. Go to San Diego, Landry."

"Where are you going?"

"Home."

She turns her back and covers the distance to the front door faster than I can process it. The cool, wintery air is gushing in the house when I reach it and Dani is almost to her car.

My heart in my throat, my blood soaring through my body, I race through the open garage door and make it to the side of her car as she slides in the driver's seat.

"Dani!" I call, wedging myself between the door and the frame. "What are you doing?"

Her face is soaked, her lips trembling. "I'm going home."

"Why? I don't understand."

"Let me ask you one question." She looks at me, taking a deep breath, steadying herself. "Are you going to San Diego no matter what?"

"I have to," I whisper.

She nods and seems more confident in her decision, which terrifies the fuck out of me.

"My father is the General Manager of the San Diego Sails."

My world is twisted on its head and spun a hundred miles an hour.

Nearly dizzy, I grab the doorframe. "What?"

"Yeah," she smiles through the tears. "My dad, the one and only Bryan Kipling, is your new boss."

As I try to process that, she continues talking.

"It's why I knew this was coming. I've seen baseball take over his life. Take over my mother's. It's their love for the game that trumps any love for me, Landry. If it can be that way for a parent, there's no way it won't be that for a boyfriend. I knew this before I met you, so I can't blame you."

She tries to shut the door, but I don't budge.

"Why didn't you tell me this?" I ask, still in disbelief. "That motherfucker is the GM? Of San Diego?"

"What do you want me to say? Everyone loves him. He's on television, smiling and playing Mr. America. Of course it'll look to you like I'm some kind of weirdo . . . unable to even win my parents' love."

My heart cracks, breaking in two jagged pieces. I reach for her. She swats my hands, but eventually relents and lets me pull her into me as I kneel by the side of the car.

Her body racks with tears as her life comes full circle again. Tears lick at my lashes too because, without a doubt, this is nonnegotiable for her. She won't go with me. This will be the end of us.

As if she reads my mind, she pulls away and gives me a soft smile. "Go, Landry. Go play ball."

I plead with her without words. I can't ask her to go near her parents, not to the people that hurt her so badly. I can't even figure out how I'm going to do that, but I also can't think about going without her.

"Lincoln," she says, the ring of my first name, the one she never uses, pierces the air. "This was always going to be the way this ended. I knew it before it started." She wipes away a tear. "I'll always be thankful for the time we did have together, and I'll always root for you."

"This doesn't have to be the end."

"No, it does. You live a life I can't," she says, a hint of a laugh in her voice. "If you're ever in town . . ."

"Dani, don't leave," I say as she shuts the door. The car lurches backwards as she puts it in reverse. I pound frantically on the window because when she's gone, she's gone. My throat tightens and I fight myself from screaming in the middle of the fucking driveway. "Roll down your window. Please, give me that."

She looks away, like it pains her to look at me before she concedes.

Her eyes flicker to mine, and we both smile at the same time.

"I need to say something," I say, a break in my voice. "I don't know what it is, but I need to figure out how to rewind the last few hours and stop this from happening."

Her hand falls over mine on the ledge of the window, her thumb stroking the side of my hand. "If you think of it," she says, "mail me the pink mug you bought me. I'd like to keep it as a reminder of you."

"I can bring it to you. I won't leave for a week or so."

Her head swishes side to side. "I can't see you again. It'll make it worse."

She's right. This isn't a girl I can be friends with. It's a girl I want to fucking crawl inside and never leave. It's all or nothing with this one, a grand slam or a strike out, and right now, I'm watching the ball hit the catcher's mitt.

"Goodbye," she whispers, her eyes filling again as the car rolls backwards.

Panicked, I jog alongside it. "I love you, Dani. Okay?"

"Okay, Landry," she chokes out. Her chin bowed, she hits the road and drives right out of my life.

THIRTY-FIVE

LINCOLN

THEY JUST TALK. I DON'T even think they know what they're talking about. Their mouths move and shit spills out.

"Let's be fucking real," I say to the television hosts, lifting a bottle to my lips. "None of y'all played ball. Of any kind."

This beer tastes as bland as the first ones. Plural. Lots of plural. Well, it tastes way more bland after the seventh inning stretch of whiskey I added to the mix. I'll feel this tomorrow.

Tomorrow. The chorus from some play my mom took Ford and the girls and I to one summer rings through my memory banks and I find myself humming the tune. How do I even remember this?

My laptop glows in front of me with housing options in San Diego. I hate them all. I even try to convince myself that the beach-front bungalow is everything I've ever wanted. That it probably comes with beachfront bunnies. That the beach equals no clothes and lots of girls.

I fail.

Every house I find, I think about stupid shit. Like Dani. And how she won't be there. And how much that fucking burns right now. Blisters my heart. Poisons my soul. Then I drink more. Maybe eventually it will drown out. Or I'll pass out. I'm good with either option.

Something catches my attention but I can't focus on it. I'm in a lovely state of buzz, a muddy, fuzzy warmth that sort of bubble wraps everything. But it's there. Something is, anyway. When I reach over to put my drink on the table, my ass lifts off my phone and I hear it ringing.

"Aha!" I say, nearly falling off the couch. Stabilizing myself, I answer it. "Hello?"

"Hey, Linc," Graham says.

"Hey, G! What's happening, man?"

"Well," he says slowly, "I called to see how your meeting went and to ask you a question. But after hearing you, I have a brand new set of questions," he chuckles.

"Did you say you needed to ask me something? You need advice? I didn't drink that much, did I?"

"No advice. I'm not that fucked," he laughs. "I wanted to know if you knew Mallory Sims. But that can wait."

I try to remember the name. "Mallory Sims. Should I? Because I really don't associate anything with that name."

"She's a friend of Sienna's."

"She must not be hot because I got nothing."

Graham laughs, clearly amused. "Okay, moving on. What the fuck is wrong with you tonight?"

"With me?" I ask, swaying a little.

"You drinking tonight."

"Fuck yeah."

"Why?"

"Because . . ." I say, my eyes sinking closed. "Oh! Because I got traded to San Diego."

"Really? Wow. How do you feel about that?"

"Drunk. I feel drunk, G."

"When do you guys move?"

My ass tumbles off the sofa and I land on the ground with a thud. For some reason, I find it hysterical and nearly drop the phone as I laugh.

"What the hell is wrong with you?" Graham asks.

"I fell off the couch," I say, catching my breath.

"Shit, Linc. Take it easy."

"There's nothing fucking easy about this." I hate the way my voice wavers and sounds weak. I'm not weak. I'm Lincoln Fucking Landry.

So why do I feel like crying?

"You don't like the trade?"

"I don't give a flying fuck about the trade," I say, more coherent than I anticipated. "Less money. New city. Opportunities. It'll be fine. But Dani won't go."

The line stills. I give Graham a second to really feel that . . . and myself a second to get back on the couch again. This time, I lie down and secure the phone against my ear with a pillow.

"Why isn't she going?" Graham asks.

"She hates fucking baseball. I told you that a long time ago. Remember?"

"But that's not enough of a reason."

"And her dad is the fucking GM."

The sound of understanding slips by his lips and he sighs. I sigh too because I can. Because I don't know what else to do. Because it's not crying and is acceptable.

"I'm sorry, Linc."

"Me fucking too."

"There's no way to make this work? Did the Arrows offer you anything?"

"Basically, no. I mean chicken scratch. Just a little more than average. How can I take that much of a cut, G? My entire stock, my brand, goes down if I accept that."

"True."

"I just . . . you know . . . ugh."

Graham takes a long minute. "The real problem—is it the trade? Or Danielle?"

"She won't go," I say, sadly.

"And you have to go."

I'm not sure if that's a question or a statement. So I don't respond.

"You can have a job and a girl, Lincoln," he says. "But sometimes you can't have *the* job and *the* girl."

"But I want both. I need both," I insist. "Baseball is who I am. It flows through my veins. It's how I define my life. But she makes me feel so alive, so much more than a ballplayer," I say, struggling to find the words through the haze of the alcohol. "I love her, Graham. I fucking love her."

"Then you might have to let the job go."

"Ah!" I yell through the room. The only light comes from the television and the blabbering idiots on the screen. It's late. How late, I don't know. It doesn't matter. Nothing matters right now except the pain stinging every aspect of my life.

"Why don't you sleep off whatever you've been drinking and see how you feel in the morning?" he suggests.

"I'm going to feel like shit," I sigh. "I need to go back to Arrows headquarters tomorrow and let them know which way I'm leaning. If I'm going to San Diego, they need to get the paperwork going."

"You okay tonight?"

"Do I have a choice?"

"We always have choices, Linc."

"Take that philosophy minor and shove it up your ass," I laugh.

Graham chuckles and releases a heavy breath. "Call me if you need anything. Or if you just want to talk."

I scratch my head. "You wanted to ask me something?"

"Don't worry about it. We'll talk tomorrow."

"Tomorrow," I yawn, stretching out on the sofa. My eyes get heavy, the voices on the television mute. "Talk to you tomorrow."

My phone tumbles to the floor as I fall in a deep, nightmare-filled sleep.

**

Danielle

THE BLINDS ARE OPEN. I know this without opening my eyes. I'm hesitant to do that because I can already feel that they're swollen. My back aches from sleeping on the sofa in a wine-induced decision.

How much wine did I even drink?

My stomach sloshes and my head pounds in what can only be a red wine staccato. It's enough to be labeled as a verifiable hangover, one reason why I never drink too much. I hate this. Yet, it's nothing, not a scrape, against the pain in my heart.

Forcing a swallow to hopefully somehow make the tickle in the back of my throat go away, the tickle that comes right before the burn between your eyes that lets you know the tear maker is firing up. That one little movement, the bobbing of my throat, sets off a riot inside me and suddenly I'm alive and feeling every ounce of horror I expected and then some.

As if someone set a weight on my lungs, I can't breathe. Struggling to sit upright and not puke or press the headache into a full fledged migraine, I battle to drag air into my body. It shouldn't be a problem. I feel hollow.

"Damn it," I cry, battling the agony that is swelling up and overwhelming me. I touch my eyes. They're swollen and so are my lips. This is an ugly cry. This is what it feels like to lose, what I'm sure, is the love of my life so he can have his.

Still dressed in the clothes from the night before, the wine still heavy on my tongue because I apparently didn't brush my teeth, I sit on my sofa and watch the sun come up through the bay window. There's no beauty in it. The colors are lifeless, dull. Peace doesn't come with the new day either and I wonder how long it will take to not wake up and think about him.

The clock tells me it's too early to find Pepper and I'd feel like a jerk if I woke up Macie. It's just me. Alone. And damn it if it doesn't feel unbearable.

I miss his arms around me and the way he tugged me closer to him. The way his eyes looked when he woke up and his sleepy, sweet smile. The smell of him. The feel of his breath on my cheek. The way his laugh made me feel like the world was splashed with a rainbow.

The tears come, dripping off my chin. With each drop comes a new flurry of despair and I feel myself starting to fall off a cliff. My phone is on the table in front of me and I pick it up and call Macie.

It rings five times and I'm ready to hit "end call" when it picks up.

"Hello?" The voice is sleepy, rough, and very much not Macie.

"Will?"

"There better not be another guy answering this phone," he says, a little more awake now.

I wipe the snot off my face. "I'm sorry," my voice cracks and I mentally berate myself for behaving this way.

"Hey, who is this?" Sheets rustle in the background. "Danielle?"

"Yes," I whisper.

"What's wrong?"

"I need to talk to Macie."

"Are you okay? I mean, I'm up looking for her now, but you're gonna have to tell me you're all right."

"I'm fine," I sniffle. "No, I'm not Will. My heart is so broken."

I don't know why I'm telling him of all people this, a man I only talk to when he answers her phone or if he butts into a conversation we have while they're together. Still, he's the only one around to listen.

"I'm sorry. He's an idiot, fact as fuck."

"You don't even know him."

"I don't have to know him. I know you."

"No, you don't," I laugh through the tears as I hear him telling Macie I'm on the phone.

"Macie knows you and loves you. Therefore, you're family. Whether you're right or wrong, he's an idiot. That's how this works over here."

"Thanks, Will."

"You need to get away, you're welcome here. Our door is open. Well, proverbially. I'd stay away from the bedroom one unless you—"

"Give me the phone, you fucker!" Macie says. I hear the phone go between them. I can't help but laugh. They always make me laugh. Their relationship is not perfect by any means—Macie wants to kill him half the time. But she loves him. Respects him. And he wants to be with her over anything else. I cry harder.

"You okay?" she asks as I hear a door shut in the background.

"No," I sob. "Why did I do this to myself?"

"Oh my God. What happened?"

I go through everything with her, listening to her gasp when I tell her where he was traded.

"To your father? He's going to play for San Diego?"

"Yes," I breathe, heading into the kitchen for a cold towel. "I can't go with him."

"No, you can't."

Wrapping a few ice cubes in a dish cloth, I return to the sofa and put it on my eyes. "Macie, I knew better than any of this. I knew I couldn't resist him and I knew I'd be in this exact position sooner or later."

"I know, I know. But you followed your heart."

"Fuck my heart."

She laughs, but it's not at me. "So that's it between you?"

"Doesn't it have to be?" The ice clinks in the cloth. "I don't want to be my mother and I can't be near them. They destroy me. It's just . . . not healthy. Even my therapist suggested I break off all contact. That's why I use my mom's maiden name of Ashley and not Kipling. To distance myself. They're so toxic to me and I can't imagine what they'd do if they knew Lincoln was involved with me."

"I really don't know what to say. This breaks my heart."

"Your heart? I don't think I have one anymore. It's completely shattered," I whisper. "I lost Lincoln not just to baseball, but to my father."

We sit in silence, her looking for words to make me feel better and me trying to figure out if I could drink enough wine to pass back out without puking. There has to be a ratio. I would know it if I'd lived a little more wildly.

"I don't even hate him," I say finally, breaking the quiet. "I can't, and trust me, I want to. He's leaving me, choosing to be traded. But this is just how he's built. This was inevitable and he's right—this is the choice he has to make for his life. I can't fault him for that."

"You're a bigger person than me," she laughs.

I sigh. "I just sit here and think, 'How am I supposed to just go on?' How do you move on from something like this when everything reminds me of him? I feel like I'm going to be stuck walking by that damn elevator every day, coming home to an empty house, having a phone that doesn't get a selfie of his abs at least once daily," I laugh through the sadness. "It's going to be purgatory."

"Come here."

"What?"

"Julia said she'd hire you. She needs help. Her foundation is picking up and she needs a hand she can trust. These people, the Gentry's, are huge on loyalty, Danielle."

Her idea sounds better than I'd like it to. Moving across the country, or half of it, isn't something you just pick up and do. But the other option of living in a post-Landry world doesn't seem like something I can just do either.

"I'm being serious," Macie insists. "Money isn't really a thing for you. Just pick up and come and rent something until you find what you want to do. Think about it. We can shop and go to movies and concerts and . . ." The phone muffles as I hear her say, "Stop that,

Will. Just give me a few minutes. Oh, my God. Don't stop that though."

Rolling my eyes, but laughing too, I get the picture. "I'll think about it, but right now you need to go apparently."

She sucks in a breath. "Think about it and call me later."

I look around the living room and make a decision. "I don't have to call you later. I'll be there in two weeks."

THIRTY-SIX

LINCOLN

THE ONLY SOUND COMES FROM the water dripping in the bathroom sink. I let it drip, even though I could reach over and turn the handle. It makes me feel less alone and keeps me half distracted, which is a godsend.

"You might have to let the job go." Graham's words from last night sweep through me again, and just like they do every time, strike me hard. They needle my brain, sear my heart, gnaw at my soul. Letting this go is the hardest thing I've ever done.

I button my shirt, and before I get to the top, grip the edge of the sink and bow my head. This isn't normal. Even the two other times in my life I've thought maybe I was in love, it didn't hurt like this. It didn't feel like my entire soul had been yanked out of my body.

I don't think I'll ever be the same. Not without her. Yeah, I'll smile again at some point and I'll laugh at stupid jokes. I'll even regain my status as the best centerfielder in baseball, but even that seems so unimportant. Who will be home after the game? Who is going to ask about my shoulder and not about my statistics? Who will be my friend?

That's the thing: I've lost my friend before anything else.

Everything falls. My spirits. My heart. My shoulders. I'm falling into some dark abyss, and I can't find a ladder to pull myself up. I'm going into the biggest slump of my life and it's the post season. The one that really matters.

If I take this trade, I show up in San Diego in just a few days. I'm property of the Sails as soon as the ink dries and I'm expected to pack a bag and head out. It's what we do as athletes. We go where the money is. Where our careers lead us. Where we can work for as long as we can. The idea started floating around my brain last night. What if I don't want to go where the money is? What if I'm tired of chasing a batting title? What if living half the year in a hotel doesn't seem like a good time?

What if I break her father in half?

My jaw clenches, my teeth grinding together as I realize I haven't figured out how to deal with this little issue. I'll see him every day in a work capacity. I'll get to know him. He'll control my future. All the while, I will know who he truly is. Can I do that?

"I have to do that," I mutter, putting on my shoes. Reaching over I turn off the water and the silence suffocates me right away. I miss her smile. Her giggle. The way she calls me Landry.

I grab a jacket and my keys. Sliding my phone in my pocket, it immediately buzzes with a text. I pull it out and stand in the middle of the room staring at the screen.

Good luck in San Diego. I'll be rooting for you. Xo, Dani

THIRTY-SEVEN

DANIELLE

THE BOXES PEPPER HAPPENED TO have in her store room are spread around me. I sit in the middle of the living room, a haphazard collection of figurines on my left and a box of donuts on my right, bubble wrap in front of me.

I managed to get dressed, wash my face, and brush my teeth. I made it to the Smitten Kitten and took all of the boxes, two cappuccinos, and the pastries and made it home without crying. It's a victory. Small, but a victory anyway.

Macie called and made sure I wasn't talking out my ass and was really coming. I told her I am. I have to. I can't stay here. There's nothing for me here and everything I loved before Lincoln is tainted by my love for him.

My love for him. I'm so damn stupid. If I would've listened to my brain from the start, I would've been going through life like normal. Work. Smitten Kitten and cappuccinos. Baths and books. I was happy like that for so long and I went and screwed it up.

A twist in my stomach catches me off guard and I know I'm lying to myself. I wasn't happy then. Maybe I thought I was, but it wasn't until Lincoln that I realized what happy could mean. At least, in the midst of this heartache, I know what it feels like to love someone.

With a sigh, I grab a donut and shovel half of it in my mouth. The chocolate glaze coats my lips and the roof of my mouth and I can barely chew, or breathe, but it'll be a delicious way to go out. "Death by donut" somehow seems to read better on my tombstone than death from a broken heart.

I wrap my little teacup in bubble wrap but can't find the tape. Standing, I wipe a bit of chocolate off my lips with the back of my hand and head into the kitchen where the bag from the store sits. As I pass the foyer, the doorbell rings.

Pulling it open, I say, "Pepper, you didn't have to come. I can pack . . ."

My mouth drops and my hand falls from the door. I immediately glance in the mirror and feel the panic bubble set in. There's chocolate icing on my lips and smearing to my right cheek. My hair is in a messy bun. My clothes are clean but wrinkly and definitely not to my usual standards.

Oh. Fuck.

"Hi, Dad. Mom," I say, gulping. "I didn't know you were in town."

"Maybe we should've called," Mom says, taking me in from head-to-toe with a look of disgust.

Stifling an eye roll, I paste on the best smile I can.

I don't invite my father inside, but he doesn't wait on an invitation either. He clamps my shoulder as he walks by. "I'm not sure this place is safe," he says, looking around. "Do you have a security system, Ryan?"

"I've lived here for three years. It's safe."

My mother enters too and I shut the door behind them. My gut, already twisted from everything with Lincoln, is pulled tighter. So tight, in fact, that I think I might pass out or vomit.

"What are the boxes for?" my mother asks, taking off a pair of gloves that extend to her elbow. It's not that cold out, but they make a statement.

I consider not telling them anything. I usually don't. I'm not even sure how they got my address. But with them in front of me, face- to-face for the first time in maybe two or three years, I can't just not say anything. "I'm moving," I tell them, smoothing out my shirt. "To Boston. I got a great job there with a nonprofit that works with inner city kids."

"Ryan, when are you going to do something real with your life?" My father turns and faces me. He's aged, the lines in his forehead harsher than I remember. Or maybe it's just that I'm used to looking at the picture taken almost ten years ago. Either way, he almost seems like a stranger to me.

"Something real with my life?" I balk. "Excuse me?"

"Yes, something real," he huffs. "Kids your age have no idea what it's like in the real world. You've been pampered and coddled your whole damn lives and don't even take something good when it's offered to you."

"And what's been offered to me that I haven't taken?"

Instead of answering my question, he shakes his head. "You go from one dead end job to another, wasting your potential. It's such a shame that you have no interest in being anything."

I open my mouth, but nothing comes out. We just stand in the foyer, between the front door and the living room, and look at each other. A group of people tied together by blood, but divided by a poison that infects every strand of our relationship.

His words hurt. Sting. My wounds are already there, gaping from losing Lincoln, and he pours salt in with no consideration.

When I was eight years old, my parents told me they wouldn't be home for my birthday. I cried. Instead of comforting me, they laughed. They said it was silly to think I wouldn't get a cake or gifts; they'd arranged that. My tears weren't for teddy bears and chocolate icing. My cries were because it was apparent that day that I didn't matter.

I haven't cried in front of them since then. That is, until today.

If it were any other day, I would've held strong. But my heart too broken, the waterworks already started, and I don't bother to fight them. They trickle down my cheeks, across the smears of donut, and onto the floor. I consider how ridiculous I must look, like the calamity they think I am and I don't even care.

"Will you stop?" my mother breathes, tugging at her necklace. "I told you this was a bad idea, Bryan."

"With all the resources you have, why you live like this is beyond me," my father says. "It's absurd. You need to clean yourself up and get yourself together, Ryan."

"It's Danielle," I say, but I don't think he hears me over the knock at the door. Relieved at Pepper's perfect timing, I tug the door open.

It's not Pepper.

He looks so handsome standing in my doorway, the afternoon light shining around him. His eyes are wide, filled with the sorrow I feel. He doesn't move to me, doesn't try to reach for me, and he doesn't smile the way he always does when he sees me. This is us. The new us. And I hate it.

"Dani."

The one word, my nickname, the one I hate but now somehow love hearing from his lips, breaks the seal. The tears trickle down faster. "I brought your mug," he says and I want to laugh, but I can't. It hurts too much. His eyes land over my shoulder and then flip immediately back to mine again. "Are you okay?" The question is a whisper.

"No," I say back.

All of a sudden, he's taking me in differently. His pupils narrow, his green eyes darken and he steps to me. He pulls me into him and kisses the top of my head. I turn as he steps inside the house, keeping his arm wrapped tightly around my waist.

"Mr. Kipling," Lincoln says. I've never heard his voice this way. It's not playful or sexy or even engaging. It's professional. Hard. Maybe even cold. It takes me aback. "Mrs. Kipling."

"What is this? Some kind of joke?" My father's eyes are wide as he takes in his new centerfielder with his arm around me. I imagine he's worried I'll interfere in their life now if I'm somehow dating Lincoln and he's playing for the Sails. The fury in his eyes dampens a piece of my soul.

"What is it you'd like explained?" Lincoln asked.

He clutches me tightly and I'm so thankful he's here. Glancing at my mother, I see her dipping her chin, looking at me down her perfect, plastic-surgeon-created nose.

"Did she put you up to this?" my father snarls. Looking at me, his repugnance of me is palpable. "This was your doing, wasn't it? Why, Ryan? Why do you have to act like such a spoiled brat? Is it attention you need? Is that what's wrong?"

"This has nothing to do with her," Lincoln fires back.

I look between the two of them, my head spinning. "What are you talking about?"

My father chuckles, his gaze on Lincoln. "You know you won't get another offer like the one I gave you. We were ready to build around you, Lincoln. There were good things happening, and instead, you listened to a little girl that doesn't know anything."

"What are you talking about?" I ask again, drying my face with the sleeve of my shirt, much to my mother's dismay. "Lincoln?"

He looks at me and smiles. Using the pad of his thumb, he wipes away the icing on my cheek and laughs. "You're a mess, Dani."

"It's your fault," I sniffle, wrapping my hand around his wrist and holding it so he doesn't pull it away from my face.

"I'll make it up to you." He winks and I drop his hand and he turns back to my parents. "Your offer was generous, Mr. Kipling. You definitely know how to make people see how serious you are about baseball."

"And if you were serious, we could've made something happen."

"Landry?" I ask, looking up at him. I can't fight the little blossom in my stomach that maybe something happened. But I don't want to get my hopes up.

"I am serious, Mr. Kipling. Serious about things that matter."

My father laughs, an angry vibe in his tone. "Don't even tell me . . ."

"All I've ever wanted to do is play baseball," Lincoln tells my parents. "I wanted to see my name on the back of shirts and to sign my name to pictures being held by little kids. I wanted to be the guy that hit the game winning run in the World Series and make my dad proud of me." He pulls me close. "I did that. All of it."

"And you can do it all again. A number of times," my father insists.

"I could. Yeah, you're right. But I've learned there are more important things in life than contracts and batting titles."

My heart slams in my chest and I feel tears build up in the corners of my eyes. I don't say a word, just listen, and hope, even if I'm wrong, that he's going to say what I think he is.

"There are seasons in life," Lincoln continues. "I spent my entire life up to now focused on baseball. It's been a great run. Fantastic, actually. I've done things and seen things most people can never dream of. But what do I have besides all that?"

"I have no idea where this is going," my mother answers. "Or why you are here with our daughter. Or why we are even here, to be honest."

I start to respond, but Lincoln's squeeze stops me. Instead, he chuckles.

"No one is keeping you here." He looks at my mother and then at my father. When they don't move, he laughs. "I'm here with Dani because I'm in a new season of my life. Today is opening day."

My eyes blur again and I lean my head against him. I breathe him in, all expensive cologne and male testosterone, and feel safe in the midst of my parents for the first time. For once, I don't have to battle them. Their ferocity isn't aimed at me. He's protecting me and it feels better than I even imagined it would.

"The trophies in the guest bedroom don't talk back. They don't keep me company or warm at night. They don't play catch and they don't drink coffee with me in the morning."

He looks down at me and chuckles at the smile on my face. "A mess," he whispers, swiping at my tears. "A total mess." I giggle as he kisses my forehead and looks back to my parents.

"You're just like Ryan," my father blows. "A kid born with a silver spoon in your mouth. You have no drive. No—"

"Say what you want about me," Lincoln booms over top my dad, "but don't talk about her. You know less about her than you know about me."

"She's our daughter. What in the hell are you talking about?"

"You can rattle off my statistics, my contract terms, my health report. What do you know about Dani?"

They look at Lincoln like he's just asked them the equation for world peace. Their silence is so loud, the lack of response deafening.

"If I'm like her," Lincoln says, "then my mom will be proud. In my family, love isn't predicated on wins and losses, fame or persona. It's about who we are as people. What we are all about when all that shit is stripped away."

"You know nothing about Ryan." My mother eyes me like I'm an inconvenience. "You need to focus on what matters, Lincoln."

"I am."

My father eyes me with the hollowness I've come to expect. There's no love in his gaze, no adoration. No humor or pride like I've seen in the Landry family. No empathy like I see in Lincoln's eyes. "I hope you're happy, Ryan. You've just fucked up this man's life beyond repair." He jerks my mother along as they stride towards the front door, anger seeping off of him as his hand hits the knob.

"She will be happy. I'll see to it." Lincoln's voice is loud and clear in the foyer as we step to the side and let them pass. "You can help that out too by not coming around again."

"You will not tell me what I'm going to do, with my own child at that!" My dad turns on his heel and faces Lincoln, his face red.

"I'm not a child!" I shake off Lincoln's grip, and for the first time in my life, face my father head on. "I'm a grown woman, one that has nothing in common with you but some DNA."

"Listen to you," Dad seethes. "We haven't seen you in God knows when and you talk to us like this!"

Lincoln's hand finds me and he gently, yet forcefully, moves me back. He steps between my father and I. "You need to leave. Now."

"We—"

"Now," Lincoln repeats, a vein in his temple starting to pulse. "You will not stand in front of me and talk to her like that."

"And what are you going to do about it, you little punk?"

"There's nothing more tempting right now than slamming my fist in your face. But I won't do that . . . because of her. She'll just have to deal with it, and you've given her a lifetime of shit to work through, you fucking assholes."

My mother gasps. My father shakes from the wrath radiating off him. Lincoln stands calm and cool.

It's a scene from a movie, one that makes me swoon when I watch it on the big screen. I'm too caught up in the moment to do much but watch with an open mouth.

"Leave," Lincoln tells them, flicking the door handle. It swings open, the early afternoon air rustling through the house. "Now. And don't come back. Whatever obligations you feel towards Dani, consider them taken over by me. She doesn't need you. Now go."

My father steps to Lincoln and they square off, their noses nearly touching. Lincoln doesn't flinch. My father shakes harder until my mother wraps her hands around his bicep and guides him out the door, but not before giving me one final disapproving look.

The door shuts. My shoulders fall with a release of years of stress evaporating. I collapse into Lincoln's arms.

There are no tears, just an overwhelming sense of relief—that they're gone. That I don't feel picked apart. And that he's here.

"Thank you," I say into his shirt.

"Stop thanking me," he chuckles, his body rumbling. "God, this feels good."

"I hope you mean that you're in my arms . . ."

"That," I giggle, pulling away to look at him, "but also that they're gone. I've never stood up to them. And I guess I didn't this time either, but you did. For me."

"For you." His eyes are so kind, brimming with emotion that it makes my knees feel weak. "I have something to show you." When I do, I see he's extending a set of papers towards me. "My contract."

"Congratulations," I utter. It pains me to say that. I'd hoped he had walked away from it all, but seeing the sheets in his hand, it's obvious he re-signed with the Arrows. I want to take the crisp white pages and burn them and then take the ashes and dilute them in water and flush them down the toilet. Those fucking papers are destroying my life.

"Thanks." He peers into the living room. "What's up with all the boxes?"

Stepping away, I tuck a strand of hair behind my ear. "I can't stay here. I'm putting my notice in on Monday."

"Where you going?"

"Boston. My friend Macie lives there and has a job lined up for me."

"Boston? It's too fucking cold in Boston."

I pull away and head to the kitchen, needing some kind of buffer between me and him. At least in there, I can separate us with the table so I can think straight.

"I was thinking something the other direction," he says, following me. "How about Savannah? I could get you a job there, if that's what you want."

Sighing, I walk around the table and look at him over the top of it. "I don't need you to get me a job."

"I know you don't. I'm trying to sell you on an idea here, Ryan."

"I don't know where this leaves us now that you're staying in Memphis. I mean, on one hand, you're still here so that makes it easier. But on the other, you're still you and I'm still . . . me. Aren't we going to be in this same position sooner or later?" I shrug sadly. "I can't walk this line, knowing what's coming, Landry. It has to be all or nothing with you."

Those beautiful green eyes of his sparkle as his hands find the back of a chair in front of him. He leans his weight on it and smiles. "I pick all." It's a simple answer, one that throws me. He slides a stack of papers across the table. "Which is why I was thinking Savannah. But if you have another suggestion, I'm all ears. Just nowhere north of here. I don't do winter."

"What?"

He motions towards the papers. "Look at those."

Everything inside me stills. "Landry . . ."

"Damn it, Dani. Don't be so fucking hard headed," he laughs. "Look at the papers."

They rattle in my hand as I pick them up. The first page is an agreement for trade. It's a standard contract that I've seen in my dad's office a few times. I flip through until I find a little yellow arrow flag. There's no signature above his name.

I don't trust my voice and, instead, look up at him. He grins. Going back to the papers, white noise filling my ears as more hope than I can handle if this turns bad rushes over me, I find another paper clip. It's a notice of retirement.

I drop the papers. They flutter across the tabletop.

"What did you do?" I say, my words muffled with the emotion I'm trying desperately to hold back.

"I'm retiring."

"You can't," I say, shaking my head. "You're not thinking. You can't retire."

"I can do whatever the hell I want."

His long strides make it around the table and to me in about three steps. We stand inches apart, our breathing heavy as we look at each other. He's as nervous as I am. I can tell by the rigidity of his shoulders and the way his lips are pressed together. My fingers itch to touch him, my body desperate to hold his, but I don't. I need to hear what he has to say.

"I'm retiring," he says. There's no question in his tone, no uncertainty. He could be telling me it's fifty degrees outside with a thirty percent chance of rain.

"Why? And don't say because of me or that I won't go with you because I can't have that on my conscience."

He smiles faintly. "It has nothing, yet everything, to do with you."

"Landry . . ."

"I've told you that a baseball player is who I am. It's my niche. I'm the guy that the rest of the team depends on and the one fans come out to see. It's exhilarating, Dani. There's nothing like it."

"Which is why—"

"Seriously," he laughs. "Just. Let. Me. Talk. You'll get your chance. I promise." He shakes his head before continuing. "I only have a few years left of this."

"Which is why you have to play!"

"Cut me off again and I'll figure out a way to occupy your mouth," he promises, his eyes shining. I try to glare at him, but can't, and end up laughing. Even still, my knees are a little weak and I pull out a chair and sit down. He does the same. "As I was saying," he emphasizes, "I only have a few years, but what do those years consist of ? Traveling? Hotels? Maybe a championship and maybe a few batting titles, but I have both of those already. When I think about that, the trade-off, what it takes to get there, it's just doesn't have the appeal it used to."

He reaches across the table and takes my hand in his. "My dad told me he got out of politics, which was his passion, because my mom had enough of living as a politician's wife. He told me she'd never have asked him to quit, but he knew in his gut she wasn't happy and he'd rather have her and his family than another term. When you told me last night to go, it made me remember that."

"I—" I begin, but he squeezes my hand and I stop.

"My career came to a halt last year because of an injury. It could end this year if I re-injure. Hell, I could die in a fucking plane crash on the way there."

"Don't say that!"

"I could. And you know what I think about when I think about either of those things?"

I shake my head.

"Not a missed title or game or locker room. I think about you. Dani, I love baseball. I love it. But me playing was a pursuit of happiness. It's what made me feel whole. Important. Needed."

My vision is blurred as I listen to his words because I know what's coming and I'm not prepared. I squeeze his hand and try not to anticipate what's next because if I'm wrong, I'm done.

"It's like meeting you started a new season of my life, Dani. It's a new field with new rules and new challenges, and that appeals to me so much more than another nine innings on the field. My happiness is now with you. I think yours is with me too."

I'm in his arms before I realize I've even moved, my head buried in the crook of his neck.

"I ran this by Graham this morning," he laughs, "because if anyone can tell you you're fucking stupid with no reservation, it's him. He gave it his stamp of approval."

It's like every piece of the puzzle has been snapped back into place. I'm crying, but out of a mixture of disbelief and elation instead of fear and sadness. The one-eighty has my head spinning and I half expect to wake up and find out this is a dream.

His hands lock around my waist. "I really hope you're okay with this because, if not, I just gave up my spot on the roster," he laughs nervously.

I cup his cheeks, his skin smooth under my touch. "Are you sure? Absolutely one hundred and fifty million percent sure? Because I can't live thinking you gave up your dream because of me. What if this doesn't work out?"

"If it doesn't work out, I'll regret this one hundred and . . . how much? Fifty million?" he laughs. "Times less than I would regret playing baseball and wondering if we could've worked out. And," he says, moving his head side to side as he smirks, "G would've been pissed when he had to bail me out of jail for beating the shit out of your dad."

Laughing, I kiss his lips. "Are you sure? Like, completely sure."

He tongue darts across his bottom lip. "I'm completely sure you've been eating chocolate donuts," he chuckles.

I gasp. "I look like a mess." I try to get up and already mentally have the shower on when he jerks me back.

"You are a mess. Which is why I know that we're going to be fine." "How's that?"

"Because you look exactly how I feel. Like when we aren't together, the world is ending. Because if we aren't together, maybe it has." His features alight with mischief.

Leaning back on him again, I sigh. "I love you, Landry." "I love you, Ryan."

THIRTY-EIGHT

LINCOLN

SHE'S STANDING IN THE KITCHEN, her back to me. Her dark hair is a wild mess from last night, her ass only half-covered by my Arrows t-shirt. She has a mug of coffee in one hand, the phone to her ear with the other as she stirs scrambled eggs on the stove.

I stand in the doorway and watch her. This is what I've been looking for, the missing piece of my life that was only visible when everything else was stripped away. I never dreamed I'd be so thankful for my shoulder injury, but I am. God, I am.

There's not a play I could make, a hit I could take, a game I could win that would give me the feeling of being with her. The peace in my soul. The happiness in my heart. The feeling of doing something that makes a difference.

In baseball, I was another player. Number eight. A payroll check, a device to sell tickets until I couldn't play anymore. To her, I'm everything and can be that for the rest of my life. We can build our own empire together, our own team to take over the world.

"I called Gretchen this morning," she says. "I gave my two week's notice, but she let me leave immediately. I'm going without my vacation pay and all that, but I don't care." She sighs happily and then giggles. "I am," she responds to whatever the person on the line said. "I am so happy. I don't know what will happen, Macie, but I'm where I should be."

I can't take it anymore. I'm to her, my arms wrapped around her waist in two seconds. She nuzzles her head against me and I kiss the top of her head.

"No, the program will still go on thanks to an anonymous donor by the name of Lincoln Landry," she laughs, elbowing me.

"I didn't say it was me," I whisper.

She rolls her eyes. "Macie, I need to go. I'm burning the eggs."

I leave her to say goodbye and pour my own cup of coffee. Once she's finished, she looks at me. "Gretchen is still talking about that donation."

"Did you tell her it was me?"

Dani's eyes light up at my admission, but I don't care. She knows I did it. Or had Graham do it for me. Either way, same difference.

"I can't thank you enough," she says. "That program is so important to those kids."

"What if Rockster gets sick again?" I ask. "I have to take care of my man."

Danielle laughs and plates our breakfast. We sit at the table, her feet in my lap. "Do we even know what we're doing?" she asks. "I feel like this all happened so fast."

Taking a bite of the eggs, I shrug. "It did happen fast. At least this last part of it. And you know what?"

"What's that?"

"I woke up this morning happier than I did when I was drafted. I feel like the bat is in my hands now—not the Arrows' or my father's or in limbo. I have it. And it feels good to swing."

Her soft smile hits me squarely in the chest. Looking at her without the hesitation she used to have, without the fear, is everything to me. I wouldn't trade it for the world . . . or fifteen million dollars.

"Is it odd I don't feel nervous at all that I don't have a job or a plan?"

Laughing, I squeeze her feet on my lap. "No. I'll take care of you. Graham's made me a lot of money."

She giggles and sits upright. "I have my own money, thank you. But that's not what I meant. I mean, what are we doing?" she shrugs. "Are we staying here? Going somewhere else? We're like gypsies right now."

"I was thinking we could start someplace new. Together," I tell her. "It doesn't matter where to me. I'll coach at a college or do some personal baseball training. And hopefully, start practicing for those ten kids you want."

Her eyes go wide. "One step at a time, Landry." I hold up my hands and laugh. "Okay, okay."

She sets her fork on the plate and looks at me soberly. "What would you think about going to Savannah?"

I force a swallow and sit my fork down too. "Really? You'd want to go there?"

She nods. "I love it there. It's beautiful and your family is there and I . . . I think it would be nice."

"I would love that. Absolutely love that," I tell her.

Smiling, she goes back to her coffee. "I would really like to go soon," she says, her lips still a little swollen from our kisses this morning. "I can call and let everyone know we'll be at the Farm in the morning."

"Sounds perfect to me."

EPILOGUE

Six weeks later

Danielle

"SHIT!"

GRAHAM DASHES AROUND THE corner and only throws me more off balance. I grab the top of the ladder as it sways to the side and brace for impact. I'm saved as he levels it back out right before it hits the point of no return. "Get down," he orders in a way only Graham can.

"I'm just seeing if this picture will look good here."

"Where the hell is Linc?"

"Right here," Linc bellows, coming down the hallway.

I look over my shoulder as I climb down and he takes my breath away. Bare-chested and in a pair of low hanging jeans with rips in both knees. He's spattered with white paint and is holding a screwdriver in one hand and a bottle of squirt cheese in the other.

"What are you doing?" he asks, taking in the situation. "You didn't climb that ladder, did you?"

"Will you two stop it?" I laugh. "I'm just seeing if this is the right place for this."

"Didn't I tell you to wait on me?"

"I'm excited, all right?"

"I am too. I've never hung my own fucking pictures in my house before, but that doesn't mean you can be stupid." He gives me a warning glance. The same one I see Graham giving me from the side.

I throw my hands in the air, sitting the picture on the floor, and head to my drink in my pink mug sitting by the stairs. Sitting on the bottom step, I watch the two brothers talk.

We've been in Savannah for two weeks. Our little house is bright and airy and overlooks a big field that quiets my soul. It's so different from anywhere I've ever lived. It's perfect. It feels like home. It's loud and messy and the Landry's are in and out. It's amazing.

"Mallory starts tomorrow?" Lincoln asks Graham.

"Yeah." He sticks one hand in a pocket of his jeans and looks at me. "I don't know why you just won't work for me. You're unemployed and all."

"She's not working for you," Lincoln barks, making Graham and I laugh.

"Who's Mallory?" I ask.

"A girl Sienna went to school with. The fact I'm trusting Sienna's judgement is not lost on me, but I really am at my wit's end. I've gone through three temps. One couldn't handle the workload, so they sent another to help, and she was worse than the first. The second came in, gave me a lecture that I need to switch to decaf at noon, and I sent her home." He rubs his hands down his face. "The applications are horrible. Awful. Is there anyone out there that has a brain?"

I shrug. "Maybe this will work."

He shrugs too. "I need it to. I'm getting behind, working twenty-hour days. I need help."

"Want me to come in?" Lincoln asks with a wink. "I don't need to fix any more of your fuck-ups."

Standing, I take a spot next to Lincoln. Resting my head on his shoulder, I smile at Graham. "Thank you for helping us get relocated."

"It was just a few calls. And I didn't even call about the coaching job. When the college heard Lincoln was retiring, they called me. It really happened on its own. No big deal."

"It is to me," I say. "Your family has been incredible about this whole thing—Lincoln's retirement, our moving here, starting the children's charity. I still can't believe it."

"It's the way it's supposed to be," Lincoln says. "When things go the way they're meant to, they just line up. This is where we're meant to be. It's obvious."

Graham watches us both and tries to hide a laugh. I still haven't figured him out all the way, but I like him. I just don't know what makes him tick.

"I'll leave you two alone. You coming to the Farm for Sunday dinner?" he asks as he opens the door.

"We'll be there," Lincoln tells him.

They whisper back and forth, and I'm curious, but don't push. It's something I'm still learning, the dynamics between siblings.

"I'll see you later," Graham says with a little wave and then disappears.

Lincoln stalks across the floor to me, stopping right in front of me. "Want to come inspect my work?"

"I'd like to inspect you," I tease.

He takes my hand and leads me down the hall and into our bedroom. Boxes are still stacked everywhere and our bed is a mess because we can't stay out of it. It's perfect.

He sets the screwdriver on the floor and stands, looking at me wickedly. He holds up a can of squirt cheese.

"What are you doing?" I laugh. "You like this stuff?"

"No. It's fake cheese, Landry."

"I never knew this existed until yesterday when Huxley threw it in the cart at the store." He squirts some into his mouth and grins. "See? It's great."

"Your abs are great," I say, running my finger down the bumps lining his stomach. They tighten as I stroke them.

"Want to lick cheese off them?"

"No," I laugh.

"Come on. You know you want to. It's okay."

"Cheese isn't sexy, Landry."

"This isn't technically cheese. It's fake cheese."

"Same thing."

He backs me up until my knees hit the back of the bed and I collapse on the mattress. "Fine," he says, reaching down and pulling his Wrecked tour t-shirt up. "But I like it and can eat all I want now that I'm not training for baseball."

"Don't get anything on this," I gasp. "Stone Lockhart touched this. Breathed on it. Maybe his sweat touched it."

"I've washed it a thousand times, Dani. Don't get all sentimental."

"Let's not risk it. He's so gorgeous. I might just live in this t-shirt forever."

"First, you're going to grow out of it soon. Second, what about my Arrows jerseys? Don't you want to get all sentimental about those?"

I sigh and flutter my eyelashes. "When I saw him live in Nashville, I swear to you Stone looked right at me. Right at me, Landry."

"You and your damned rock stars."

Before I know it, I'm in a fit of giggles as he sprays a line of fake cheese down my stomach. He bends down and his tongue strokes my skin from just under my swollen breasts to right above my navel. He pauses, looking at me and I at him. We exchange a sweet smile and he presses a kiss to my belly.

"One down. Nine to go," he whispers.

"Let's get through the first one before we go counting more," I giggle.

"You're the one that wanted ten kids. I'm just giving you what you want. And," he says, his fingers working against the button of my jeans, "I can't keep my fucking hands off you."

I lift my hips so he can slide them down. Once they're on the floor, he hovers over me.

"Whatcha doing, Landry?"

"Gearing up to hit a homerun."

And he does.

The End

Switch, Graham Landry's story, is up next. Keep reading for the first chapter.

CHAPTER ONE: SWITCH

Graham

I'M NOT USED TO THIS. Hell, I'm really not even *okay* with this.

The stillness before the sun comes up is *my time*. I get more accomplished in that precious window than I do all day long. Why? No one else is up and around to bother me.

That is until my brother Ford came back to town.

Glancing across my desk, he's leaned against the wall with a paper cup in his hand. His sandy, military-cut hair has started to grow over the last couple of weeks since he was released from the Marines with more medals than an Olympian. He knows his morning visits annoy me, but like our other siblings, a part of him finds frustrating me amusing. Assholes. Still, as he meanders his way towards my desk, I can't *really* be mad. At my oldest brother Barrett? Possible. At my youngest brother Lincoln? Often. But Ford? It's hard to do.

"Do you show up here *just* to throw off my day?" I try, and fail, to hide my grin.

"What can I say?" he laughs. "The military doesn't approve of staying in bed. After all those years in the service, old habits are hard to break." He takes a sip from his cup and sits in the black leather chair across from me. "I need to find a new routine. I've had one imposed on me for so many years, it's a little odd not having someone threatening to have my ass before dawn."

"I can assure you I'll be tossing you out on your ass if you keep showing up here before the day starts. It throws me off schedule." Glancing at my watch, I scowl. "And so does being late."

Ford raises his brows. "Your new secretary starts today, doesn't she?"

"She's supposed to. Mallory Sims. Remember her?"

"Sort of. Did I go to high school with her?" He scratches his head. "Damn, that feels like a long time ago."

"Because it was," I laugh. "She's a friend of Sienna's."

At the mention of one of our twin sisters, the youngest of us all, Ford looks worried. I get it. It also worries the fuck out of me to know I've stooped this low. And low it is. But I didn't have a choice.

My former Executive Assistant, Linda, up and quit on me a few weeks ago. She was everything you could want—efficient, orderly, experienced. She worked for my father before I took over for him and knew this business inside and out. When she left, I realized she was irreplaceable.

I've gone through so many temps in her vacancy, hired people from ads placed in newspapers, and even tried promoting one woman from another department and none of them worked. Not one of them meshed with my style or filled the role as I needed them to.

One weekend night, after missing a family lunch because you couldn't see the top of my desk for papers, contracts, and files, Sienna called. She'd run into a girl we used to know. In the midst of conversation, my sister realized she had experience as an administrative assistant, needed a job, and grabbed her resume for me.

It looked good. Her references checked out. She had experience as not just a secretary, but as an Executive Assistant. I also remembered her from before and was fairly certain she wasn't a psychopath.

So I forwent the standard interview and just hired her. What did I really stand to lose?

"Can I just ask what on Earth made you think that was a good idea?" Ford asks. "I mean, I love Sienna and Camilla, but their friends aren't exactly . . . employable."

"Desperation is the name of the game."

My brother stands. Although he's a couple of years younger than me, he's a few inches taller. "It must be."

"Tell me about it," I groan. "But there is a method to the madness."

"Let's hope. If not, I'm calling Dad and letting him know you've lost your mind and we need to vote you off the board."

"I vaguely remember Mallory. She must've been a freshman or sophomore my senior year. I had Latin Club with her," I say, picking up a pen.

"You and Latin Club. I just . . . I can't."

"Fuck you," I say, throwing the pen at his head. Because Ford has reflexes similar to Lincoln's, it misses and clinks against the wall. "You better be glad one of us takes things seriously. Can you imagine our family being reliant on Barrett? Or, worse, Lincoln? We'd be investing in baseball and Skittles."

Ford picks up the projectile. "Speaking of Lincoln, how weird is it to see him so pussy-whipped?"

"It's one of the oddest things I've ever seen happen with my own eyes. He went from total man whore to monogamy at the flip of a switch."

"Danielle must have some good pussy," Ford chuckles.

"That or a magic wand."

"Yeah, but I get it. I think he made the right decision. Seeing some of the shit I've seen overseas really puts things in perspective for you. Often the things we think are important aren't." Ford's gaze hits the floor. "But," he recovers, pasting on a smile, "Lincoln doesn't have to worry about money. We have you."

"If only I had an assistant."

"What time was she supposed to be here?"

Glancing at the clock, my irritation grows. "Six minutes ago. She's supposed to start at eight."

"That's what you get for choosing employees out of Sienna's circle."

My hand flies through my hair as every worst case scenario plays out before my eyes.

Looking at Ford, I know his main concern: Landry Security. I can't blame him. This is his dream, much like managing Landry Holdings is mine, and he can't get to work until I do mine. I get it, that's why it drives me insane that Mallory isn't here and I'm not working at full capacity.

Sighing, I shrug. "Her resume was infallible. The references she listed all checked out—sang her praises to be exact. They all said she has unlimited potential and would be an asset, even knowing it's Landry Holdings we're talking about. I can't believe she's late. Who does that? On their first day, no less?"

My brother tosses the pen on my desk. "If you need help with Landry Security, let me know." I can tell he's antsy and is trying to play it cool and that frustrates me. He shouldn't be worrying about this. He should have faith in me, and my lack of a fucking assistant is shaking that.

"I'll be fine," I reassure him. "I have a plan. Even though things here have been a little more unsettled than I'd like with Linda's departure, I have been moving forward. Landry Security is happening."

Ford's hand rests on the doorknob and he looks at me. His brow is furrowed, reminiscent of our mother's when she's trying to decide how to broach a subject with us.

There's no way he knows how much this has affected me. Losing sleep. Popping antacids like a motherfucker. All because I. Don't. Fail.

"I'll help you however," he reiterates carefully.

"I know. And I do appreciate that—"

"But you're too fucking anal retentive to let anyone else get involved at this stage," he grins.

"I prefer the term 'professional.'"

"I bet you do," he laughs. "I know you have control issues and all, but consider trusting someone else to help out. You don't have to do it all yourself."

"This is my legacy. You have your hero medals. Barrett has his public service. Lincoln has batting titles and Golden Gloves. I have *this*."

"No one wants to usurp you," he insists. "We just want to help." When I just look at him with no response, he sighs. "Fine. But cut the new girl some slack. If you look at her like that when she walks in, she'll probably march right back out."

"What? I don't give off the empathetic boss look?"

"Uh, no. You give off the asshole dictator look."

"Good. At least she'll know what she's in for," I wink. "Now get out of here so I can figure out what to do when I fire Mallory Sims on her first day at the office."

He chuckles. "I'll call this afternoon and see if anyone has sent you to the psychiatric ward."

"Make sure the walls have extra padding. If it's an added expense, charge it to Barrett."

"Will do." With a shake of his head, he disappears out the door. The silence I love so much descends around me, the only sound coming from the coffee maker in the corner. The city below the third-story windows encompassing two walls of my office is just beginning to awaken. I love to watch everything sort of turn on for the day. Being awake and working before that happens makes me feel like I'm a step ahead of the game. That no one got anything over on me while I was sleeping.

Sleeping, like my new employee probably is when she should be here.

I fire off an email to Human Resources, letting them know I plan on not hiring Ms. Sims after all, and print out their response to hand to the almost-employee if she ever shows up.

Slipping off my suit jacket, I hang it on the hook behind the door. Rolling my sleeves up to my forearms, I'm mentally going over the list of applicants to replace Mallory when a loud clamor booms from the entryway into the suite.

As I round the corner and peer into the reception area, I spy a woman bent down. The floor is spattered with miscellaneous items. Bobby pins, sheets of paper, a water bottle, and a paperback are being scooped up and shoved into a large bag.

Irritated at another disruption to my day, I lean against the door-frame. A million thoughts roll through my mind, most of them along the lines that as CEO of Landry Holdings, I should not be dealing with this hassle. As my temples begin to throb, I fold my arms over my chest.

She stuffs the last sheet of paper into the bag and stands. Her eyes flick to mine and she stills. I think I do too.

Her skin is pale and creamy, a soft framework for the deep chestnut hair hanging to her waist. A dress the color of moss in the summer showcases toned arms and a long, lean line from her shoulders to her calves. A thin rope belt cinches her trim waist, one that I can imagine digging my fingers into.

I clear my throat. "Can I help you?"

With something besides getting out of that dress?

"I think you probably can," she says, then blushes a pretty shade of pink. "I'm sorry, I didn't mean it like that. What I mean is . . ."

She's flustered. It's adorable and sexy at the same time. I should say something, interject, help her out, but I don't. I like this entirely too much.

"I'll stop talking now." She flashes me a pretty smile, one that catches my attention in ways it shouldn't at eight sixteen a.m. Taking a step towards me, the toe of her shoe catches on the water bottle she didn't pick up and she comes barreling my way.

Before I know what's happening, I reach out and catch her under a spray of loose leaf paper.

"Oomph!" she heaves as she lands in my arms and I'm surrounded by a sweet, floral scent.

I should let her go. I should back away, direct her to the front desk to get directions to wherever she's going, and retreat to my office. Regardless of how sexy her breasts feel pressed against me or the way her ass pops as my fingers lace together at the dip at the bottom of her spine, I have things to do today. Important things. Lots of them. Even if I can't pinpoint one at the moment.

Large, nearly golden eyes peer up at me. They're crystal clear, almost like I can see all the way to the depths of her soul. They're incredible tones of the purest gold and I can't look away.

The feel of her body against mine sparks something inside me—a carnal, visceral reaction that's led by feeling rather than intellect. "Are you okay?" I ask, trying desperately to use the brainpower I'm known for in most circles and not the cock I'm known for in others.

"I think so." She pulls her gaze away from mine. A connection is actually snapped between us and I'm almost certain she feels it too because her features fall. "I'm just running late . . ."

Hell. Fucking. No.

I'm afraid to ask the next question. If the answer is what I think it is, I'm going to kill my little sister.

ACKNOWLEDGMENTS

THANK YOU TO THE CREATOR, first and foremost, for giving me the courage, tools, and faith to continue this journey.

To my family, Mr. Locke, the Littles, Mama, and Peggy and Rob: Thank you for your incredible support. You see the best and worst of me and still stand behind me one-hundred percent. I thank God every day I landed up in this amazing group of people. Love you all. So much.

To my team, Kari (Kari March Designs), Lisa (Adept Edits), Kylie (Give Me Books): We did it again! I'm honored each and every time you all hit me with a "Yes!" when I ask if there's room for me on your calendars. You are simply the best in the business. Thank you for working with me again.

To my beta team, Jen C, Susan, Jen F, Carleen, Candace, Joy, Ashley, Michele: There aren't enough thank-you's in the world for what you do for me. Your time, attention, eyes, love—you give it all in abundance. I hope you know how much it, and you, mean to me.

To my admins, Jen C, Jade, Tiffany, and Stephanie: Every day, you make me laugh. Keep me focused. Shower me with GIFS. (Take videos at concerts—ha!). Keep my groups running. Fix my

Goodreads. Without you, I'm a mess. Without you, this train stops chugging. Without you, my heart would be sad. Thank you for being my friend.

To Mandi: You are so many things to me. My easy friend, my Pres, my voice of reason (sometimes, sometimes not). Thank you for always believing in me, making me laugh, letting me vent, and keeping me entertained. #ELC

To Lisa, Jade, and Alexis: You are such a part of my Life . . . Ish. (See what I did there?) I can count on you for all things at any moment. Jokes, laughs, graphics, tea. ;) Thank you girls. MUAH!

To the real Danielle: Here's to another summer of baseball and sweat and travels and laughs. Xo

To Mary Ruth: Your love of Lincoln Landry was there from the start! Thank you for your support, excitement, and friendship. And the awesome Arrows logo.

To bloggers: Your passion is what makes this possible. Your love of the written word drives my stories into the hands of readers. It's incredible what you do. Thank you for taking a chance on me, for giving my words a spot on your blogs and in your heart. I appreciate it more than you'll ever know.

Books by Adriana Locke and All Locked Up: My happy places! You put a smile on my face, a laugh in my voice, and a fire in my rear. Thank you for so many things, but for each of your friendships before anything else.

ABOUT THE AUTHOR

USA Today Bestselling author Adriana Locke lives and breathes books. After years of slightly obsessive relationships with the flawed bad boys created by other authors, Adriana created her own.

She resides in the Midwest with her husband, sons, two dogs, two cats, and a bird. She spends a large amount of time playing with her kids, drinking coffee, and cooking. You can find her outside if the weather's nice and there's always a piece of candy in her pocket.

Besides cinnamon gummy bears, boxing, and random quotes, her next favorite thing is chatting with readers. She'd love to hear from you!

www.adrianalocke.com

Subscribe to the exclusive Locke List.

Made in the USA
Las Vegas, NV
08 March 2021